I0658643

The Night Rider's Call
A Tale of the Times of William Tyndale

by
Albert Lee

# The Night Rider's Call
## A Tale of the Times of William Tyndale

by

Albert Lee

A Harbinger House Book

Apprehending Truth Publishers
*Brookfield, Missouri*

Published by Apprehending Truth Publishers
P O Box 249 - Brookfield, MO - 64628 - USA
www.atpublishers.com

Cover Design by Pure Light Graphics

ISBN13:  978-0692585511
ISBN10:  0692585516

AT  10 9 8 7 6 5 4 3 2 1
151101

# Harbinger House Titles

Martyr of the Catacombs
Tip Lewis and His Lamp
The Night Rider's Call
The Adventures of Sir Constant


Harbinger House titles
are also available in audiobook
from Open Vision Media.

# CONTENTS

# The Night Rider's Call
A Tale of the Times of William Tyndale

# THE MAN IN THE MEADOW

As she walked across the meadow, carrying a basket in one hand and swinging a dainty blue hood in the other, Margaret Byrckmann made a picture that was pleasing to behold. She looked up as she moved along, but her eyes went down again before the dazzling sun which was setting in a blaze of red splendor, silhouetting the battlemented walls of the city.

She gave this evening beauty scanty attention, for her dark eyes were watching the meadow. Then a cry of pleasure broke from her lips, and she hastened forward; but before she had gone far, her face filled with disappointment, and she stopped abruptly.

"I thought it was Herman!" she exclaimed.

She watched a man who was walking wearily. He looked dusty and way worn, and the movement on the beaten path seemed to be toilsome and painful. She thought he must have travelled far, for he carried a heavy-looking wallet on his back, and the staff in his hand was used as though it was real labor to go forward.

"He is tired to death, poor man!" she muttered, her sympathy getting the better of her disappointment, and she crossed the meadow to intercept him.

Until he halted, in sheer weariness, to look around for some spot – a tree, or a bush – anything that would screen him from the glare of the sun – the man in the meadow did not see her; but the moment he spoke, Margaret knew that he was not one of her countrymen.

"Mistress, how far is it to the city?" he asked, in a foreign accent.

"That is it," she answered softly and full of concern, for the stranger's limbs trembled, and his hand shook when he raised it to set his cap straight. With the other he gripped his staff tightly lest he should fall.

"Yonder?" he exclaimed, gazing beneath his hand. "I did not see it in the blaze of the sunset. It seems a long way off."

"More than two miles," said Margaret.

"Two miles!" was the dismayed response. "So far as that?"

"Yes, sir. But how will you think to enter the city, since 'tis but a few minutes to Sundown? They close the gates the moment the sunset bell has stopped."

"Is it so?" came the discouraged response. "I forgot that it is not here as it is in England, where our walled cities are so few Then I must lie in the meadow till sunrise."

"You could enter if you had a pass," said Margaret, who was concerned for the stranger; for, in spite of his wallet and the travel stains, she saw that he was no common wanderer.

"But I have no pass."

The stranger and the girl, standing in silence, while the slanting sunlight was sending long shadows over the grass, looked around for some place — a hut, or a barn, or anything where a man who was tired could lie down and sleep; but there was nothing of that sort in view, no village, far or near.

"There is no place that I can see," said Margaret, who had never noticed how empty the fields were of houses until now when they were so badly needed.

'Ah, well! I may not complain," the stranger muttered. "Why should I? Even the dear Lord saw many a sun go down and had nowhere to lay His head."

He spoke more to himself, as if forgetful that the girl was near, until she moved.

"I will sit down under the chestnut tree, and take my chance, unless your home is anywhere outside the city walls."

"I live in the city sir, but they know me, and I have a permit to get in after the gates are shut," said Margaret. 'And yet I am so sorry for you," she went on softly.

"If I only knew where I might find some food I would not care," the stranger said, gazing around him, his hand above his eyes.

A low call came while he was speaking, like the sweet note of the last evening bird. It travelled over the meadow from the river, and Margaret looked up quickly. Her dark eyes flashed, and her lips parted with pleasure; then she sent back an answering cry, full of soft, rich music. The stranger, watching her pale face, saw the flush of color darken it, and, worn-out though he was, he marveled at her beauty and smiled to himself.

"Pardon me for a moment, sir," she exclaimed, when her answer ended. "I will come back again."

While she spoke she moved away with hurried steps to meet a young man who had appeared on the bank of the broad river. He had been bending low to fasten his boat to the root of one of the willows, but when he saw her coming, he came to meet her.

"There's a stranger yonder, Herman!" she exclaimed.

"Where is this stranger? I can't see anyone."

Margaret turned and pointed toward the man she had left standing near the chestnut tree.

"He's gone!" she exclaimed, in real surprise, and ran to the spot where she and the stranger had been standing.

3

Then a cry of dismay broke from her lips. The man lay in a heap in the hollow, and, leaping into it, she dropped on her knees and gazed at him with startled eyes.

"Is he dead?" cried Herman, who had come at her heels and now was in the hollow by her side.

"God forbid!" the girl exclaimed, beginning to chafe the unconscious man's hands.

"He came here while I was waiting for you, Herman. He wanted to know how far it was to the city, and he seemed so distressed when I told him the gates would soon be shut – long before he could reach them. We cannot leave him here, poor man!"

She broke off almost abruptly at a thought that came.

"I might have known! He asked if there was any place where he could buy some food, but when your call came I left him to go to you. It was so thoughtless of me!" she added reproachfully.

"You couldn't come to anyone better," said Herman with a laugh, but only in jest, for he fully appreciated her regret.

"He must be hungry" the girl exclaimed. "He shall have some of this to help him on till he can get a good meal."

She drew her basket closer and opening a jar that was there, handed it to Herman. He placed his arms around the shoulders of the helpless one, who was crouching in a bundled heap, and sat him up. Herman gently poured some of the remedy between the stranger's lips.

The man swallowed it slowly, and presently his eyes opened.

'Ah, I remember," he exclaimed weakly "I have travelled far today, and, not being well, the heat and hunger have been too much for me."

"Drink more of this," urged Margaret, and when the jar was once more to the parched lips, the stranger drank the cool draught almost eagerly

"Now eat this," said Margaret with a pleasing peremptoriness, when, with one of her hands, she drew a parcel from her basket and deftly unfolded the spotless cloth which wrapped round something. It was food, and she placed it so that he might help himself as Herman held him steady. He seemed too weak otherwise to sit up.

The sun was now gone down, and the heavens were glowing with many-colored splendor. Away to the west lay the emerald river, whose silver-crested waves rolled against the sapphire shores, while purple islands dotted the waters and rested there in stately stillness and the snow-clad mountains on the mainland caught the changing glory. Some of that last beauty of the summer's evening entered the little hollow where these three were grouped together, one helpless in his weariness, the others wondering what they should do with him.

"I am another man," said the stranger presently, sitting up, while Margaret sat back on her heels, watching his face keenly. "Whoever you may be, may the Lord reward you both for dealing so kindly towards me."

He attempted to rise but failed completely. Not until Herman lifted him in his strong arms could he feel his feet, and even then he swayed and flung his arm about the young man's shoulder.

"That does not look like walking two miles," said Herman seriously. "Do you know anyone in the city with whom you thought to stay?"

The stranger shook his head. "No, I started on my way this morning. And, from what they told me, I expected to arrive in good time to look for a lodging; but the heat was so overpowering that I was forced to go slowly and here I am, outside, and the city gates are closed."

Herman, still with the man's weight on his shoulder, wondered what he could do for this helpless one, whose face had won his confidence. Presently his perplexity passed.

"I have it!" he exclaimed. "I was to bring in that man whom the Burgomaster sent me to meet, and my permit was to admit both him and me by the water-gate. 'Tis the very thing, since Manton has proved a laggard, and word has come that he won't be here for a week or more. I will take you to my mother's house, master," he exclaimed. "Margaret, unstrap the wallet and carry it, while I take him to the boat."

The girl's fingers moved about the buckles, and in a little while they were on the move, Herman giving the worn-out man the help of his strong arm. He stopped before they had gone far.

"We can't go on like this," he said decisively. And, taking the stranger in his arms bodily, he went forward with strong, swift strides, but as gently as he knew how, toward the river. The boat was there, and, laying his burden in the stern and bidding Margaret sit beside him, Herman pulled the little craft down the darkening stream, not pausing till he reached the water-gate.

He answered the challenge. What he said satisfied the sergeant of the gate, and, mounting the green-stained steps, now once more with the stranger in his arms, and Margaret following anxiously lest his feet should slip, he stood on the topmost step of all and waited for her. Passing along the dark and narrow streets, they paused at last at the door of Herman's home.

Margaret threw the door open and waited for him to pass in.

"Mother," he cried, when, at the end of the passage, he stood in an open doorway "I have brought you a lodger!"

6

The woman who sat at the table looked up, her needle half drawn through the cloth, and her blue eyes opened so wide that Herman laughed at his mother's surprise.

Mistress Bengel started to her feet in wonder at seeing her son so burdened.

"Who is it?" she exclaimed. "Is he ill?" she asked, before there was time to answer her first question.

"Nay not ill, but worn-out. I will take him upstairs to the empty chamber."

He turned as he spoke, and mounted the stairs. At the top, before he thrust the door open with his foot, he called down to the others:

"Mother, you will find that I have brought home an angel unawares."

He laughed again. Yet he felt that it was no jest. He had watched the stranger, and something told him he was above the common run of men.

When the stranger lay quiet on the bed, sighing contentedly to find himself at rest, and clasping his hands for silent prayer before he slept, Herman turned away and crept down the stairs softly.

"Mother," he said, in little more than a whisper, when he entered the living room and closed the door behind him noiselessly "do you guess who that man is?"

The woman watched her son's face and marveled at the kindling of his eyes.

"No, my boy, I cannot. I did not so much as see his face."

Herman gazed around the room before he spoke again. His eyes turned to the window as if he thought someone might be peering in. He went to the passage and looked along it. He did more than that, for he went to the street door and, opening it, looked into the dark street, but it was silent, and he saw no one. There was not so much as a footstep to be heard anywhere.

"Margaret," he asked, when he came back to the two wondering women, "did anyone, think you, see us enter the house?"

"No, Herman," the girl responded, in a whisper, awed by this mystery Herman had brought downstairs with him. "I looked about, but I cannot tell you why and I saw no one. It was so dark. But what of it?" The question came eagerly.

"What of it?"

Herman's voice sank to a scarcely audible whisper. "Mother, that man upstairs! He is the Englishman for whom such tireless search is being made, and his name is William Tyndale! What would the Familiars of the Holy House say if they knew that he is here?"

# THE MAN ON THE STAIRS

Margaret stood at the door of her home in the Merdenstrasse and looked in all directions anxiously before she stepped into the street and closed the door behind her. Her face, lit up dimly by the lantern which hung over the shallow portico, would have shown anyone who saw it that the errand on which her father had sent her was distasteful; for it was dark, and the rain was coming down in an uncomfortable drizzle.

It was not any unwillingness which made her hesitate. It was this going at night, when all that was of ill repute came out of hiding – the scum, one might call it, of the city-and made the streets dangerous.

The Merdenstrasse was empty, but there were sounds which made the delicately nurtured girl shrink. Among them was the clash of steel somewhere, which meant a savage onslaught on a wayfarer who had drawn his sword and was fighting desperately in self-defense. The scream of a woman was heard. The ribald jests and foul songs sung by men who were leaving the taverns where they had spent hours in heavy drinking and gambling came on the night air. At times she heard the tramp of horses' hoofs and the clink of chain and armor, reminding her that the mounted watch were on their rounds, to make some sort of show of maintaining law and order. But largely it was mere pretense, and it brought no assurance to Margaret.

Whenever she heard the approach of some drunken roisterers, hooting and shouting out their songs, she drew into the shadow of a portico to hide herself, and once or twice, when the sounds were more than usually startling, she ventured in at some stable door and waited in the darkness till the way was clear again.

Constantly in that night journey through the drizzle, she thought of the stranger whom she and Herman had brought into the city some time before. She did not know how he spent his days, closeted in his room in Herman's home, where he sat from early morning until sundown. What his task was, neither she nor Herman nor his mother knew. Yet they felt that what he did was of the first importance in the man's estimation, and secret. There was no doubt as to the secrecy for whenever he left his chamber for meals or, after darkness had set in, went into the streets for air and exercise, he locked his papers in a strong oaken chest that was in the room. He had asked for the use of it when he saw it there, and never left the place without turning the key and bringing it away with him.

What was that work which so absorbed him? There was never any trace of it when Mistress Bengel tidied his room in his occasional absence for the night walk in the streets; nothing on the table but an odd scrap or two of paper without a mark to indicate what he had been doing, and the pens with which he wrote.

Surely there was nothing wrong in this task in which he was engaged! Such a man, a friend of the reformers, would not stoop to what was ignoble and unworthy!

Margaret had the feeling whenever she thought of him, and more this night than usual, that Master Tyndale's deep thoughts were at work, and that he was bent on holy purposes.

Something had made Herman and his mother, as well as Margaret, lock up in their hearts the secret fact, that such a man was in the house; for, while he never asked them to be silent, they had the idea that trouble would come, disaster, indeed, if it were whispered abroad that William Tyndale was inside the walls of the city.

She was thinking of this, forgetful of the drizzling rain, when she was startled by a laughing question. Her alarm was gone in an instant, and her soft laughter burst out on the night air.

"And why are you out alone?" asked Herman seriously, for it was never safe for a woman to be alone in the dark streets at so late an hour.

"My father asked me to carry a message to his foreman," Margaret answered, as they went on together. "He had no help for it but to send me to Gropper."

Talking quietly, they came to a house in the Wendenstrasse, behind the cathedral. Leaving Herman in the street, Margaret opened the door, moved along the dark passage, and finding the stairs, groped her way up them, counting the doors until she came to the room she was seeking.

She gave her message and turned to go.

"I'll see you to the door, and partway home, Mistress Margaret," said the man, standing and reaching for his cap.

"There is no need, John. Herman Bengel is outside waiting for me," the girl said.

"To the door, then, for the stairs are awkward," said Gropper with a smile, for he had known the girl from her babyhood, and they moved down the stairs together.

They had not gone more than a few steps when they halted, for a man was ascending, carrying a candle which he shielded with his hand, and the light falling on his face showed it plainly. A moment later he had passed into a room

11

on the landing below Margaret heard Gropper gasp, and it sounded so much like a suppressed cry of dismay that she turned involuntarily, but could not see the man's face at all, not even his form in the darkness.

"What does that man want here?" Gropper muttered.

"Who is he?" she asked, in a startled whisper, for something was surely wrong, or a strong minded man like Gropper would not be so put out.

"Who is he?" the answer followed, and the words were whispered in her ear, in trembling tones. "He is that Argus-eyed heresy hunter who goes by the name of Cochlaeus. Surely mistress, you have heard of him? He is a deacon of the Church of the Blessed Virgin in Frankfurt, and when he ever comes to our city there is trouble for some poor soul who has dared to have anything to do with the Reformation doctrines."

Margaret had not lost a word, and she shivered, for the man's reputation was wide and thrilled so many with a sense of dread.

They moved on almost unwillingly, going down the stairs with stealth, afraid lest they should attract the attention of this man who had disappeared into the room below. They had to pass the door, and to their alarm it stood slightly ajar.

Neither of them had any wish to play the part of eavesdropper, and were passing on, but as they moved they caught sight of a man who sat at a table in the room, as well as of the other who was in the act of blowing out the candle. But what they heard held them both spellbound.

Cochlaeus either did not notice that the door was partly open, or he was careless as to whether his words were overheard.

"Buchsel," he exclaimed, in a jubilant tone, "I have made a discovery-a wonderful one!"

"Ha!" was the response of the man who was gazing at Cochlaeus questioningly but in a tone of perplexity. It was plain that he was wondering why the deacon of the Blessed Virgin was in the city and coming to his room of all others.

"Yes. I have made a discovery! That accursed English heretic – that limb of Satan! – William Tyndale – is here, within the city walls, and I can give a broad guess as to what he is doing. You remember how he started the translation of the Bible in England?"

He paused, but Buchsel's only response was a nod, for he was waiting for Cochlaeus to tell his story which he did, not knowing of those two who were standing outside and heard every word with growing dismay.

"He must be here at his old work – that devil's work, I call it! – translating the Scriptures, meaning to scatter his pestilential stuff far and wide, seducing the people who read it to heresy."

The man at the table stared at Cochlaeus incredulously.

"William Tyndale, that arch-heretic, here, in this city, did you say?" he asked, in an amazed tone.

"Yes, I said here. Where could that mean but in this city?"

Margaret's heart beat so wildly that she held her hands to her bosom as if to still it; but she waited eagerly for what would follow. There was no thought about eavesdropping now, much as she abhorred it, for she was asking herself what this would mean for the man who was lodging in Herman's home.

"Where does he lodge?" asked Buchsel, standing up so suddenly that the chair fell to the floor noisily. He was staring hard at the heresy hunter.

Margaret felt faint with fear of what the answer might be.

13

"Where? I've got to find out. He is here in the city. I know that much. But he shall be found, and then – ah, me! – I will hand him over to the tormentors. He shall be lodged in the dungeon of the Holy House, and the Familiars shall deal with him!"

He paused, and there was silence for a few moments – silence so intense to Margaret that she could hear her heartbeats and the quick breathing of the startled man at her side.

Cochlaeus broke the silence.

"Only today I heard it, not an hour since, in fact. I was passing the Gurzenich, where two men were talking in whispers, but my sharp ears – Buchsel, " he broke off, "if ever you go on the hunt for heretics, be sure to thank God if He has given you a quick ear! He has given me that, and I praise Him! My sharp ears caught the words, for I was going softly, my noiseless shoes giving no token of my passing in the dense darkness, so I halted, scarcely daring to breathe lest I should betray my presence."

'And the man – what did he say?" interposed the other, for Cochlaeus went so slowly with his story lingering over it as though he enjoyed it.

'Ah, yes! He said that William Tyndale was inside the walls, somewhere, that he had spoken with him and had been told that he was prospering with his translation here, because England had become too hot to hold him. And that was not all. He was on the lookout for a printer who would put his vile sheets through the press! This accursed printing!" Cochlaeus burst forth, in savage anger. "It will be the ruin of the Church! It will render the whole world Protestant. We must find the fellow and crush him!"

Silence followed again, and those who stood on the landing could not move on. They seemed compelled to take the risk of discovery rather than miss what was to follow.

"What do you propose to do?" asked Buchsel, presently.

"Burn the printing press, and the printer, if I can induce the authorities of the city to display sufficient spirit. And if I can lay my hand on that fellow, Tyndale, he too shall burn, and all the papers he has shall go to the flames with him. God help me and give me the joy of doing it!"

Suddenly the speaker crossed the floor and slammed the door, leaving Margaret and her companion in the darkness.

# THE PICTURE IN THE FIRE

When Margaret stepped into the street, she was trembling with anxiety Herman, who was waiting for her, saw by the light of one of the swinging oil lamps that her face was white, and he marked the startled look in her eyes, as well as her trembling hands.

"What's wrong?" he asked in some concern.

"I dare not tell you here in the street," she answered in a frightened whisper. "Oh, the very stones of the city have ears. Let us talk of something else until we get to your home. Then I will tell you all."

She shivered as she spoke, and looked behind her, for she seemed to feel the approach of that man Cochlaeus, or, still worse, the coming of one of the cloaked and hooded Familiars of the Inquisition. She shuddered. Scarcely a word passed between them until they reached his home.

When they stepped into the dark passage, and Herman closed the door, Margaret turned and thrust the bolt into its socket.

"What's that for?" asked Herman, surprised at the movement.

"It will keep out all intruders," she exclaimed, and moved on to the door of the room in which Mistress Bengel was busy with her sewing at the table.

The woman looked up with a smile, but when she saw the girl's face the smile vanished.

17

"Has anything frightened you, my child?" she asked, dropping her work from her hands and looking at Margaret with great concern.

"Yes," the girl answered, going forward, but halting partway to look behind her. "I bolted the street door, Herman, so I suppose none can hear what I am going to say?"

"It's safe, Margaret, and no one can come in," said Herman, wondering still more, for he had never known her like this before.

They sat before the fire, but Margaret would only sit where she could see the door. Then the story of the man upon the stairs was told, and what she and Gropper had heard as they listened.

The faces of her listeners blenched, for the penal- ties of heresy were many and fearful.

"They talk in that manner of that godly man who is under our roof!" exclaimed the elder woman in tremulous tones. "Herman, do you realize Master Tyndale's danger?"

"I do, Mother, but we must contrive to save him," Herman answered, wiping his face, which had gone damp with the horror of these possibilities. "That man, Cochlaeus, must not find him!"

"He must not!" cried the mother, in suppressed emotion. "No, he must not! They shall not take him! And yet," she added, with a shudder, "what can we do? What has anyone ever done, when those wolfhounds of the Inquisition were on the trail? Oh, why did the poor man come here, into the very jaws of danger?"

She buried her face in her hands, and sobbed, for her memory was busy in those moments, and she had in mind the penalty that had been levied on one who was so dear to her, and who would never come home again.

The others watched her, their own eyes blurred with tears, for they guessed what her sorrow was, and what her

18

memory was telling her. They sat in silence, speechless, because they saw that words would be of no avail. They thought, as well, while Herman's mother rested her elbows on the table and wept in silence, of the great danger, if William Tyndale were to be found in this home of theirs. The only way to escape punishment was by betrayal, but that could never be; and Herman clenched his hands and closed his teeth tightly in keeping with his resolution.

"Mother," he said, breaking the stillness, "we shall not betray Master Tyndale?"

"Betray him?" his mother cried, looking up, her face, tear-wet though it was, almost indignant at the bare suggestion. "God helping us, never, my son! God sent him here for some wise purpose, and we must do our solemn best, my boy to save him. He's doing God's work. Yesterday, when I expostulated with him about working so strenuously, he said, 'Wist ye not, mistress, that I must be about my Father's business? I must-I can do no other!-I must work the work of Him that sent me!' I can't forget that, Herman."

"Then you will never give him up? Oh, I am so glad!" exclaimed Margaret, leaning forward and laying her own soft hand on the other woman's.

"Give him up? God do so to me, and more, if I betray the saintly man!" the widow said, in tones that left no doubt. -

It was growing late, and Margaret got up to go, knowing that they would be anxious at home. Herman stood up to go with her, and they went into the pas- sage. When they walked softly past the door of the front room where Master Tyndale worked, it was slightly ajar and a streak of light fell across the floor of the passage and on the wall. They saw him seated at the table, the candlelight shining on his face, and his elbows on the table, and nearby a pile of manuscripts. His hands were clasped, and his eyes closed. He was speaking, and the low-spoken words came to them plainly

"Dear Lord, did I not solemnly vow, long years ago, that if my life were long enough, I would cause the boy who driveth the plough to know the Scriptures?"

There was a pause in the prayer, and they watched his face, which for a moment he covered with his hands; but he lifted it again, since the prayer was not yet ended. There was more to hear, and this time the words came even more earnestly

"O God, the task set for me is great. The burden is almost too heavy for me! And I am compassed about with dangers. I tremble lest something should come to bring ruin to my endeavors. Yet, Lord, it is not the thought of threatening death that troubles me. My fear is lest my enemies should compass my destruction before I have done my work and placed the Word of God within the reach of the people at home. Spare me until I have fulfilled my task, and then I will say 'Lord, now lettest thou thy servant depart in peace.'"

They watched him. They were unable to tear themselves away. It was something to hear this holy man pleading with God, asking for nothing for himself, but only for time to complete his work, and ready after that to live or die, as God would say it should be.

Tyndale unclasped his hands and, taking up his pen, began to write as a man would whose time for work was limited, and whose salvation depended on the completion of the task set for him.

Herman and Margaret went along the passage in silence, almost in stealth, and, closing the street door after them softly, they hurried toward the girl's home in haste. When they stopped at her father's door, Margaret gasped.

20

"Look, Herman," she whispered. She did not point with her finger, but he saw in what direction Margaret was gazing. On the other side of the street were two men, both looking at her father's house, and Margaret gasped when the lantern, swinging in the night breeze, cast a light on their faces. One was Cochlaeus, but Herman did not know him, nor had he ever seen the other; but the girl knew him for the man she had seen at the table while she and John Gropper listened on the stairs.

"The man on the right," she whispered, shuddering, "is Cochlaeus. The other is the man he was talking to in Gropper's house. Why should they be watching our home?"

The answer seemed to come in natural sequence with the question, for her memory recalled what Cochlaeus had said concerning the fate of the printer who should be so daring as to print Tyndale's translation of the Bible.

Surely oh, surely, her father had nothing to do with that work?

The men passed on. It was a relief to see them going; a greater relief still when they had gone out of sight.

"Herman, they have come back."

The young man looked up and saw them. The men were at the corner of the street, just visible in the lantern light, and it seemed to him and Margaret, as they watched, that they were gazing at the house once more.

But what could he do?

He was asking that question when the men again passed out of sight.

"Good night, Herman," said Margaret. A fear had come that something tragic and terrible might happen before they met again – if ever they did meet. That presentiment of coming trouble made her tremble as she entered her father's house.

"You are late, my child, and I was growing anxious," said her father when she had lifted the latch and entered the room where he was sitting before an open book which contained the account of his sales in the printing shop.

"I have been hindered, but I will tell you all," the girl exclaimed, going to his side to give him the answer from John Gropper.

"Father," she went on, when he had made a note of her message in the book that was in front of him, "do you know Master William Tyndale?"

The printer's face paled at the unexpected question, and the pen dropped from his fingers onto the open page. The impulse came to prevaricate, but after some hesitation the answer came slowly.

"Yes, my child. I know him."

"Do you know a man named Cochlaeus, Father?" she asked when that answer came, and almost before she had ended her question, Byrckmann sprang to his feet with a cry.

"God be our helper! Why do you mention that man's name?"

His face betrayed the intensity of his fear.

"Sit down, Father, and I will tell you," said Margaret, dropping on a stool at the hearth, where, when he should sit, she could see his face.

The printer sank into his chair, when he had turned it to face the fire, looking down at his daughter with eyes that were filled with terror. She saw that his body trembled as an aspen leaf shivers on its tree, when she told him what she had seen and heard in Gropper's house. When her story ended, he rested his elbows on his knees and buried his face in his hands, and for some time not a word was spoken. Margaret, sitting in silence, wondering, yet almost afraid to speak, gazed into the fire, save when for a brief moment now and again she watched her father furtively.

Horror gathered about her in those waiting moments, for her imagination revealed some terrible pictures in the fire. She saw a dungeon there, and in it were some dark-robed Familiars. Around were all the instruments of torture, and a red fire glowed in which were thrust the implements that were to do some deadly work. And presently into the chamber came two men, their hands chained, and about them were four Familiars. But it was these two chained ones to whom she looked, for she knew them. One was William Tyndale-the other was her father!

Her father's voice helped her to smother her cry of anguish at a picture which seemed so real.

"My child, if Cochlaeus were to 'come to this house, it would mean ruin for us all and death for me."

Her lips parted, but she was speechless. It flashed upon her that the printer of Tyndale's sheets was her own father, and if Cochlaeus came he would find them in the house, somewhere, she could not think where; but in that case the terrible picture in the fire was not imagination, but something too real-too fearful-and the day might not be far away when her father and William Tyndale would actually walk into the dungeon to face the tormentors.

"Come with me, my child," said Byrckmann, standing up and staring before him with a face so full of pain that she was alarmed more than she already had been.

He said no more, but went out of the room, carrying the lamp with him. She followed him into the workshop where the printing presses were; then going to a room beyond, he walked to a corner where piles of paper stood. Giving her the lamp to hold, he cleared a space on the floor, and to her surprise she saw him go on his knees. Had trouble so overwhelmed him that he meant to pray?

But it was not that. He drew a key from his pocket and inserted it in a hole from which he carefully scraped the dust. Standing up, he bade her move back to the doorway and bending low, raised a portion of the floor, making it lean back against large stacks of paper. What she saw brought a cry of surprise to her lips, for she was gazing into a dark cellar. A printing press stood in the center of the stone floor below, and close by it was a great pile of paper.

Following her father down the ladder, carrying the lantern with her, she looked around. Thrust up against the walls were other piles, and, going to one of them, she saw that they were printed folios. She picked up the top sheet and read it and trembled, for it was a printed sheet of a part of the New Testament in English, which she was able to read; and now she understood why her father spoke of ruin being possible. She was realizing the far-reaching consequences when she recalled what Cochlaeus had said.

She almost whispered her words when she had looked around to be assured that they were alone.

"Father, is it not perilous for these to be here?"

She pointed to the pile on which she replaced the sheet she had been reading. "I only ask because of what that heretic hunter said, and especially after I have seen him and that other man in the street gazing at our home."

There was silence. No sound came until a few moments later the cathedral bell boomed out the hour with slow and heavy strokes.

"Can we not destroy all this, Father?" Margaret asked, when the last sound of the bell came; and she crossed the floor to where her father stood in dumb perplexity She looked into his face with glistening eyes.

"Destroy God's Word, my child?" he asked. "That would be cowardice. It would be like a man throwing down his cross because the crowd was threatening. The Word of God is far too precious; but if you are ready to help, we can make these papers fit for removal, so that if Cochlaeus came he would not find them."

"If I am ready, Father?" she asked reproachfully. "How could you question it? I am more than ready. Tell me what to do."

She set the lamp down on the printing press, and waited to be told.

For long hours, on through the dark night, she toiled with him, putting the precious sheets in bundles and covering them with strong paper, that none might see their contents. The great bell of the cathedral boomed out twelve slow and heavy strokes at midnight, and the task had barely begun. They never thought of time, and scarcely heard the strokes, for here was a matter of life and death-an endeavor to hide these folios from the hunters of heresy and, as Margaret felt while she toiled on feverishly, to save her father from the torments of the Inquisition.

The bell boomed out a solitary note, and the work was not yet done. Again and again Margaret paused to listen. She thought she heard footsteps-the rattle of steel, the sharp word of command, and then a noise on the street door; but it was her fancy, and her father assured her so when she spoke about it.

Again the strokes boomed on the night air-two. They came an hour later-three. But not until the fourth stroke sounded and the city settled again into silence was the work ended.

"What next, Father?" Margaret asked, sitting down on one of the bundles, too weary to stand after the long night of strain.

"That, my child, the Lord must decide. Let us make sure of His guidance, for everything touching on our safety lies with Him."

The printer went on his knees, and Margaret knelt beside him on the stones, her hands clasped and her eyes closed, while her father prayed that the work of sending forth the Truth for the enlightenment of men might not be hindered. Margaret listened in wonder, for there was not one word in the prayer for his own escape. He was centering his thought on the safety of these precious sheets on which he had been working night after night for many weeks, and as well on the safeguarding of the man of God who dwelt in Herman's home.

The day was breaking when they rose from their knees. Climbing out of this unsuspected cellar and lowering the floor into its place again, they piled great bundles of paper round the shop on that side, leaving everything as it had been before.

# THE COMING OF THE GUARD

The long day passed, and every hour was filled with intolerable anxiety for Margaret. She went about the household duties in her home with a heart that was heavy with dread. Every unusual sound had menace in it for her. Had anyone been there to notice her they would have wondered why, again and again, she glanced around with startled eyes, while her parted lips went far to betray her distress.

Her mother was ill at the time, and again and again Margaret had to go into her room to see to her com- fort; but when the girl's hand was on the latch, she was careful to throw aside all traces of anxiety, and she went in with a loving smile and a happy face, not wishing to add to her mother's care or to set her thinking that something was wrong. It was a hard task, but her eyes glanced about the room merrily, and she stood at the bedside and chatted pleasantly of things that made for laughter.

But God knew how the poor girl's heart and mind were strained, and how, when she heard some measured footsteps in the street, she listened with an anxiety that almost amounted to agony, lest it should be some of the City Guard coming to the house to search in her father's printing shop for what some esteemed tenfold worse than treachery.

Once, while her mother was asking a question as to some petty household matter, she heard the sound for which she had been listening ever since she had gotten out of bed in the early morning. She gave an answer which made her mother wonder what she was thinking of, and then hurried to the window and looked into the street below.

She clasped her hands in dread, and almost cried out in her terror, for the thing had come that might well mean ruin. Below were half a score of soldiers of the City Guard with their halberds gleaming in the watery sun, and the soldiers' eyes were carelessly scanning the houses around them as they stood at ease, or were nodding to some acquaintance who went by. Margaret had seen the men do this many a time and thought nothing of it; but now she gazed into the street with frightened eyes, and her clasped hands resting on her bosom to still the beating of her heart.

"Father!" she murmured noiselessly, for she thought of that picture she had seen in the fire.

The officer of the Guard was carelessly looking at some papers in his hand, turning one over the other, as if searching for one in particular. Never had she gazed as she was gazing now, her breath coming and going in gasps.

"Why are you breathing in that way my dear?" the sick woman asked, looking at the girl at the window.

"Was I breathing differently than usual, Mother?" Margaret asked, turning for a moment, careful to hide the look of dread and with a forced smile for her mother's sake. "Perhaps I was!" she added lightly "Ha! There's Targon, the butcher. I must go down and give him an order for tomorrow's dinner."

She moved to the bedside, and, bending over to give her mother a kiss, she hurried down the stairs.

What did it mean? For when the Captain of the Guard had found the paper he wanted and had thrust the others back into his belt, he moved straight to her father's door, as if to enter the shop. As she descended the steps of the staircase at a dangerous speed, her mind was as quick as her feet. Startling visions of possibilities rose before her. It was that horrible picture again which she had seen in the fire.  There was more in it now than before. There was the stake, with its flames fanned by the breeze, and her father chained in the midst of them all.  There was that wheel of torture on which he was to be broken.  There was the dark cell, with its slime, and horrors, and blackness, all made more intolerable because there would be no more glimpse of the daylight for him, if they did not decide to burn him. Or there might be no death, but the galley to which her father would be chained, with his back bared to the sun and wind, while the whip of the galley captain would come down on his flesh and leave its streaks of blood.

She stood in the doorway of the parlor, in the shadows from whence she could see what was passing in the shop.

The Captain of the Guard was there, and the paper was in his hand.

"Master Byrckmann," she heard the soldier say, with a disconcerting lack of cordiality, "the Burgomaster bade me bring you this."

Almost rudely he tossed the paper on the counter among the printed sheets and other things that lay there.

"See to that without fail," he added curtly.

Without another word he stamped his way to the door, and, with a rattle of steel as his armor moved on his body strode into the street, and let the shop door to slam after him. The noise of the slamming sounded very much like a death knell to Margaret.

"What is it, Father?" she cried, hurrying to the printer's side behind the counter when a customer was served and was gone, and they were alone together.

29

She glanced into his face, and, although he had appeared unperturbed while the soldier and the customer were in the shop, it was white now; and when her father's fingers were put forward to take up the paper, they trembled so that he could scarcely close them on it.

"Something from the Burgomaster, my dear," Byrckmann answered, trying to appear at ease, but completely failing.

He broke the city seal, smoothing out the paper on the counter. They read it with their heads close together. It was written in the ill-formed characters which were so noticeable in everything which came from the Chief Magistrate's hand.

It told its own story Word had reached him that a notable and troublesome heretic had come from England whose name was William Tyndale. How it had happened no one knew but this fellow, so it was said, had contrived to get into the city Possibly he had come in disguise, a man with a godless heart, and a mind bent on spreading his scandalous heresy. He was hiding somewhere, but no one knew where, and was supposed to be translating the Scriptures into English. It was suspected, as well, that, if he had not already done so, he would be trying to induce one of the printers to run his wicked sheets through the printing press.

"I charge you, Master Byrckmann, as I am charging all the printers within my jurisdiction-" the paper ran-"to abstain from having anything to do with this scandalous fellow who, like Martin Luther, is working out the devil's wicked will, and seeking to wean away the people from his holiness the pope and Mother Church.

"For bethink you, Master Byrckmann, what can happen more calamitous to the credit of our famous city than that this man, Tyndale, should be sheltering in a house inside our walls, and daring, in his insolence, to interpret divine law, the statutes of our Fathers, and those decrees which have received the consent of so many ages, in a manner totally at variance with the opinion of the learned priests of the Church! Yet this fellow has dared to do this thing! He has done what Luther dared! And now, like him, he is tampering so wickedly with the Word of God.

"I demand of you, Master Byrckmann, that if you come across him you shall take his work with a subtle readiness. Pretend to applaud his endeavors. Make him all sorts of promises. Make him believe that it is a joy to you to be of service in his cause; but when he is gone, send me instant word as soon as you have traced him to the house wherein he is lodging."

"Father," said Margaret.

He looked at her and saw the color coming back to her face, and her lips were now relaxed to their usual softness after this intolerable strain.

"What is it, my dear?" Byrckmann asked.

"The Captain of the Guard had other papers in his belt, so he must be going the round of the printers. Do you not think so?"

"That must be it, my child. I thank God," he murmured, clasping his hands like one in prayer as they rested on the counter. "None knows but God, and Master Tyndale and you and I-"

"And Herman, Father, and his mother," said Margaret softly. "They know."

'Ah, yes! I had forgotten. Now may God send the good man safe deliverance."

He unclasped his hands, stood upright, and gazed out of the window with eyes that gleamed with tears which blurred the forms of those who walked along the street. None of the passers-by suspected what nearness to tragedy there had been in the printer's shop. He had always loved his daughter, but here was an even closer bond; something that was linking them to other things- things that were sacred and beyond the matters that came in the common round of daily life.

Margaret went back to her mother, singing softly as she went from place to place in the bedroom, putting things right and making the chamber look more cozy. When she moved it was with a tender grace. When she spoke it was with a gladness and a smile that were restful to the sick mother on the bed.

Who could wonder? That string of visions was passed at all events for the present. Her father, so far, was safe. But at odd times, when she moved about the house, she stopped to say a prayer, pleading that the dear Lord would keep the secret from the ignoble Cochlaeus and all others who were scenting heresy and striving to find Master Tyndale and all who had dealings with him. Their success meant so much. Ruin for her father! Ah!-and she went pale at the thought-ruin for Herman!

As the day went on, the relief gave place to anxiety. Her heart grew more and more heavy. For after the first revulsion from that deadly fear, her memory served her with a cruelty that was hard to bear. It brought back all that happened the night before. The coming of the man on the stairs of Gropper's home; the enforced but unintentioned eavesdropping outside the door on the landing, and hearing what Cochlaeus knew; and, later still, the watchers in the street just opposite her father's house. It was terrible to contemplate the possibilities, for who could tell whether that paper from the Burgomaster was a blind--something to throw her father off his guard? She shivered at the thought; then she went so hot that she drew forth her dainty kerchief to wipe the dampness from her face.

A change came over her father which greatly puzzled her. She could not understand how he could move among the workmen, and be so cheerful, and smile so comfortably at the customers who bought things over the counter of the shop. Not one among them would have suspected that he had been faced with death, and even now might see the Captain of the Guard enter, and take him away.

She did what under other circumstances she would have despised herself for, but she could not help it now. She felt she must do it, or she would die of anxiety. She stood where she could hear what was said when all the workmen had gone save Gropper, who closed the street door so that no one should enter the shop and break in on their conversation without it being known.

"What say you, Gropper, now that you know as much as I do?" her father asked when the foreman stood before him at the counter.

"Get Master Tyndale and everything belonging to him out of the way" came the answer, in decisive tones.

"Out of the way?" the printer interrupted. "What do you mean by that?"

"I mean, get him out of the city; but where, I cannot say for the moment. We'll pray over it, and God will show us which way the path lies," the man said quietly.

He was going to say more, but a customer came in noisily, and the foreman stood back, and waited until the man was served and went away.

Margaret crossed the shop, and, going to the door, called to the customer, who was their butcher, and gave him an order for the next morning. Her face was aflame with having played that mean part of listener, but so much was at stake. It was a matter of life or death. And Herman was involved; for if Cochlaeus or the Burgomaster found him harboring that arch-heretic, there was no other end but death. .

In her confusion she gave Targon an order which made the butcher stare at her in surprise.

"Haven't you made a mistake, Mistress Margaret?" the man asked, wondering at the paleness; which flooded over her face.

"What did I say?" she asked, and when he repeated the order her face crimsoned. "It must be this thunder in the air," she answered, by way of exculpation, and with an effort she told Targon what she really required.

She wanted to get away, to see Herman and tell him all she knew. If she could talk the matter over with him, he might suggest something, and she could tell her father of the plan. But she was hindered. Her father went back to the workshop with Gropper, and left her to look after the customers, who came in one after another, some for the merest trifles, and some on matters of importance.

Two or three stopped to talk of what was being said in the city. First and foremost Cochlaeus was there, and that suggested heresy. Then a special body of the Guard had been out most of the day, halting at every printer's shop to leave a letter which, of course, was from the Burgomaster. But what was of more importance still was this-that it was declared that William Tyndale was somewhere in the city, and that tomorrow a great reward was to be offered as the price upon his head, and a price, also, on the head of any who harbored him.

Margaret thought she would choke when they talked on in that strain, little knowing what she knew, and what it meant to her beloved if the reward were to be claimed. Her Herman! the man who was all the world to her! Once again, while the customers were standing at the counter, talking on in that strain, she did not see them, for she was gazing afresh at that picture in the fire, and she shuddered because it seemed so real that her father and Herman alike were being broken on the wheel.

One by one the customers dropped off, and then none came at all, and the shop was empty when her father came in with a sealed letter in his hand, which trembled as he held it out to her.

"Take this to Master Tyndale," he whispered. "Put it so that none may see it, and wait to hear what he says concerning it. Go warily. But there! None will suspect, because Herman and you are shortly to be wedded."

She went to her room for her cloak and hood; and standing at the window, she gazed into the street, which was shadowing into dark twilight earlier than usual because it was raining, and black clouds were sweeping up from the river and spreading over the city. Preparing for bad weather, she went out into the street, after first concealing the letter as her father had told her.

The rain was coming down steadily, but presently it came pelting, and the wind rushing along between the houses of the narrow streets blew into her face. But she scarcely noticed it. She was absorbed with the thought that she was going to see Herman, to whom she would tell all she knew. Perhaps he would propose that William Tyndale should get away at once, lest tomorrow should be too late.

The rain came down so heavily that the streets were almost empty, although it was not late. It was one of those storms which no one would face if it could be avoided.

At the corner of the street in which Herman lived, she paused, not for the wind, although it was sweeping along with the force of a tempest now, but because of what was happening. Out of a narrow passage, where some wayfarers sheltered, there swung out, two by two, some of the City

Guard, and at their head the Captain who had left the Burgomaster's letter with her father.

If they had turned her way, she would have been relieved, and the fear would have passed which shook her terribly; but they went the other way. Was it possible that they were going to Herman's home?

# THE MAN IN THE ARCHWAY

MARGARET hurried into the archway, where others were sheltering, and a man who was standing near shifted to make room for her. As she stepped in the raindrops came down so heavily that they leapt up from the stones. The water ran from the edge of her hood in little streams which trickled down her face; but it was relief rather than otherwise, for the coolness revived her.

Heavily as the rain was pouring, she bent forward to see whether the Guard were going to Herman's house, but the man's voice drew her back. They were alone now, for the other people, believing that the rain had set in for the night, hurried away.

"The water is falling down on you, mistress," he said, civilly enough; and he pointed to the gargoyle over the archway, where the water came as from a pipe, and spread out like a fan.

"I was anxious to see where the Guard were going in all this rain," she explained, looking round at him; and the man, catching a glimpse of her face by the light of a lamp which a stableman had just hung up in the arch, saw the look of dread upon it.

"Stand here, then, and you will not get that shower bath," said the stranger, almost roughly, motioning her forward, although he had no thought of rudeness. He wondered whether this dainty little damsel, whose pretty face looked so startled, had any reason to dread the City Guard.

Margaret gazed from her new standing-place unrestrainedly, and with her eyes glued on that moving company of men, she noted every step they took. It appeared to her, in her anxiety, that their movements were relentless. They were even cruel, she thought. They passed the greater buildings, looking neither to right nor left, each man resting his chin tightly down on his muffling collar, so that the water which streamed from his helmet should not find its way down his neck.

Even that indifference to what was on either side of the soldiers of the Guard seemed sinister to Margaret. It left everything in such uncertainty. The shock would be so much greater if, after all, the Captain called a halt at Herman's door.

She wished she could see the officer who showed the way, but she could only obtain an occasional glance at the streaming helmet whenever he passed a swinging lantern. She thought that if she could see him she might judge his purpose by his bearing, whether he meant to pass on or slow down to a pace which would enable him to find the house.

The man in the archway became infected with her eagerness, for he, too, stared down the street despite the pouring of the water from the ugly gargoyle's mouth. But she was scarcely aware of his presence. At another time she would have stood out in the drenching rain, in the midst of it, where it poured its heaviest, rather than trust herself in the gloomy archway with an unknown stranger whose presence might well be intolerable to a defenseless girl. But her mind was altogether on Herman, and all other considerations receded. The man nearby was an incident in her night's experiences, while the absorbing thought was the disastrous consequences if the Guard went to Herman's house and found Master William Tyndale there!

The Guard moved on and on, going more and more slowly, she thought. Were they doing it deliberately so that the Captain might not miss Herman's home? The thought made her feel sick at heart, and for a moment she reeled.

"Dear heart!" he muttered. "I know it all. They stopped at my door one night — just such a night as this!"

The words came unexpectedly, and Margaret turned quickly, looking into his face inquiringly, for she could not miss the pain that was in that almost whispered exclamation.

"'Tis all right, little one," the man said tremulously. "The memory came like a flood upon me, of a night like this, when a City Guard came to my door and took away my darling, just such a girl as yourself."

He held his hands to his face for a few moments, and his body shook with sobs, as it can only do with a strong man in his agony.

Margaret gazed at him. He spoke with a foreign accent, and something reminded her of Master Tyndale.

Brushing his hands across his face, and without another word, the man stepped to and fro in the narrow archway, and then went into the storm and walked away with bent head, while the pelting rain beat on him. Margaret marked how his hands clenched while he passed along in a direction opposite to that which the armed Guard had taken.

His going after those unexpected words made her heart palpitate the more, for if the Guard took that man's daughter, would they hesitate to take a man?

"No! They would not!"

The words were cried out on the night, but the wind beat them down, and perhaps no one heard them.

The thought that obsessed Margaret was that the Guard were going for Herman. They must have discovered that it was Tyndale whom he had carried up the steps at the Water-Gate. It must be so! Five hundred golden pieces were to be the reward of the man or men who found him who harbored William Tyndale. Five hundred! It meant wealth. Who would care for rain, or pity, when so much gold was to be had?

Lower down the street, which was a very long one, there was a bend, and from the archway Margaret could not see Herman's house. She must see for herself whether the Guard passed it by, in spite of the pelting rain and the boisterous wind.

She left the archway and ran along the causeway with a light, swift tread, careless as to the beating of her sodden dress against her knees. Herman's home lay beyond the bend, but not very far, and they must be very near to it by this time.

She was soon close up to the Guard, but was careful to keep well out of sight, walking as near to the doors of the houses as the projecting steps would allow. Not far away was Herman's home. She saw it, and wondered what would happen, whether the soldiers would halt there.

Her heart almost stood still, and she sank on a doorstep nearby, for the Guard had halted opposite Herman's door. The thought of the inevitable discovery, now, was overwhelming. There was no hiding place there, for Herman had never spoken of one. And William Tyndale was in that house!

Her eyes were riveted on the men whose halting spelt ruin to her own hopes, to Herman's destiny, and to William Tyndale's splendid endeavors to set the Truth before the world. Ruin! Yes, nothing less than that!

She saw the men turn half-way round so that they formed a double line in the middle of the road, the ends of their halberds resting on the ground, and the steel end of each gleaming in the lantern rays.

The Captain of the Guard went to the door which she prayed he might pass by — to Herman's! He mounted the steps — one, two, three! There could be no mistake. It was Herman's home, for, as she knew, and he had often boasted, no other house in that street had that number of steps. There were houses with four, with two, with one, with none, but only Herman's had three.

The soldier struck on the door with his sword handle, and the sounding blows reached her ears, loud, even in the swishing rain.

No answer came, and the summons was repeated.

The heavy shutter opened at one of the windows, and a head appeared, but it was too dark to see whose it was.

"What is your will?" came the question, and Margaret's heart leapt at the sound of Herman's voice.

"I must come in to search your house, Master Bengel."

"To search my house?" interrupted Herman, who did not betray any perturbation in his voice in spite of the sight of a double row of soldiers in the street. "For what? For whom?"

"For one named William Tyndale," answered the Captain, who was taken by surprise at this show of ease — the absence of confusion and fear.

Margaret could scarce believe her ears when a laugh came through the rain; a laugh she would have known if all the men in the city had been there.

"For one named William Tyndale?" Herman cried, after the laugh, and in such a tone of incredulity that Margaret was amazed at his courage, and his ease in carrying it, when he must have known that he was faced with the prospect of the wheel, or prison, or the stake, with torture pre-ceding it. Who told you such a mad thing that the Englishman should be here in my house, of all houses in the city?"

"Never mind that," was the impatient answer. "Open this door, and let me enter."

"I protest that you will find no William Tyndale here, if you mean the so-called Reformer who, they say, came over from England some time since," said Herman, as he leisurely pulled the shutter into its place.

It astonished Margaret that he should play this part; and yet she admired his effrontery, and was taken with his boldness in meeting the inevitable disaster. That inevitable thing was ruin. It was death! But her heart bounded with a certain pride at Herman's fortitude. Better die a bold man than a craven. And he was bound to die, because William Tyndale was in the house!

She heard the bolt being drawn. She heard the clinking of the falling chain. She caught the sound of the screaming key in the lock, and then the dull grumble of the opening door.

"Come in," she heard Herman say in an easy tone.

The Captain called to three men to step forward, and the four soldiers entered the house.

Margaret asked herself the question — what should she do? But what was it possible to do? Her presence or her absence could in no way serve Herman; and yet she wanted to be near him in his trouble, to comfort him ere they took him away to those horrible dungeons in the Holy House — the headquarters of the Inquisition — and whisper in his ear that whatever came she was his, for life or for death, just as God willed.

The thought decided her. She sprang up from the step on which she had been sitting in the shadow, around which, unknown to her, the water had gathered and soaked into her dress, and hurried across the road. Disregarding the soldiers lined up in the middle of the street, standing still in the pelting rain, she was moving up the steps, feeling the water squashing in her shoes as she went.

The soldiers inside the house were standing about; one in the front room with the Captain — in the very place where she had last spoken to William Tyndale — and two others near the foot of the staircase, and in such a position as to look up the stairs, or into the room where Herman's mother usually sat.

Margaret's lips parted in wonder, for Mistress Bengel, who was there, was perfectly self-possessed, her hands idle, it is true, and her usual sewing lying untouched on the table. Whether her ease was real or assumed it was difficult to say, but Margaret was puzzled.

When the girl entered the room, white faced and startled, she looked up and smiled.

"I have visitors, my dear," she said, in her pleasant way.

It was mysterious. Was William Tyndale gone away from the house, so that Herman and his mother could afford to be at ease even with the Captain of the Guard paying this unwelcome visit? Or — and the thought came over her with startling force — was the poor man dead, and, being so, was it of no consequence if the soldier should find his dead body lying in his bedroom?

But dead!

The bare thought of it was a troubling one; for a few hours before she had seen the dear man in the attitude of prayer, with his hands clasped, his face full of fervent entreaty, and she had heard him plead in an earnestness that was indescribable: "Spare me, O God, until my work is ended."

The prayer was surely heard; but had it been answered? Or was Tyndale dead after all, before his work was done? Was it to be as she had heard her father say, more than once, that God buries His workmen, but carries on His work?

From where she stood, undecided as to what she should do — whether to go into the room and stay with Mistress Bengel, or follow her son with her watchful eye, and perhaps be of some sort of service, if the opportunity came — she could hear Herman's voice. Shifting a little, she saw what was going on, since the door was partly open. Herman was holding a lighted lamp in one hand, and making a gesture with the other; but his face bore no trace of anxiety as to the issue of the search.

"The room is at your service, Captain Berndorf, but there is no William Tyndale in it. Nor is he anywhere in the house."

The soldier was looking round searchingly. Margaret marked his eager glances, and saw how he passed round the room. He opened a cupboard, and ran his hand round the sides; he shifted pieces of furniture, and pulled down some of the pictures if they suggested space sufficient for a man to go into hiding.

The search in that room was a vain one.

The Captain, with the soldier, came out of it, and not seeing Margaret he brushed against her. When he saw her he was not surprised at the startled look on her face, for such looks were usual in his experience, when he went hunting for rogues and rascals, and honest men and women whose crime was heresy. What was more, he knew her to be Herman Bengel's sweetheart, so that he merely asked her pardon for blundering up against her, and did not inquire why she should be in the house. It seemed to him the most natural thing in all the world that she should be there, and for a moment a sympathetic thought came that the poor girl should witness the arrest of the young man.

"I must go through the house," the Captain exclaimed, turning his back on Margaret, but he had more to say, which plainly showed that he had no sense of certainty as to this errand on which he had come.

"Why it should be suggested that a fellow of Tyndale's stamp should be lodging under your roof," he went on, "I cannot imagine. It was mentioned, probably, by someone who owed you a grudge. Still, here's my warrant to search for the man, and I may not leave you until I have thoroughly satisfied myself that he is not here."

He walked into the room where Herman's mother sat, and Margaret entered that one where the search had been just made. The lamp stood on the sconce, and she looked around. There was nothing on the table where Tyndale had so often sat to write. Nothing was in the place to suggest his presence; not a sheet of paper, no clothing, no traveler's wallet, nothing that could in any way be connected with the stranger whom she and Herman had brought within the city.

Would Master Tyndale be in hiding elsewhere in the house? There lay the question, the tarrying of the answer adding to her heart-beats and her despair. This inexplicable indifference on Her-man's and his mother's part would go dead against them when discovery came.

She went sick with dread. Her knees so trembled that she sank into a chair close by, regardless of the sodden clothes which clung to her. She could only bury her face in her hands, and hope, and pray. There was plenty of scope for prayer; so little for hope.

When she felt she could stand again and move about, feeble compared with the sound of loud beating in her heart, she heard the Captain's voice once more.

"He is not here ; but he may be upstairs. Men, see that none pass you to go into the street. I will go up and make sure for myself."

He began the tramp up the stairs while he was speaking, and other heavy footsteps followed his.

# THE SEARCH

MARGARET'S heart quailed when she hurried out of the room and followed the men up the stairs. Now, for a certainty, Herman's protégé would fall into the hands of his enemies, and escape seemed impossible. Her pulse beat high, and despair swept over her, to think how she was to witness the undoing of one who was striving for the triumph of the right.

To be caught in a trap like a rat! It was unbearable to think of.

The dulled sound of the footsteps on the carpeted boards of the stairs seemed to call up a vision of a scene which would ere long be real — the vision of a prisoner on his trial; condemned in effect by his judges before he had made his defense, just because he was William Tyndale. And then the attitude of the crowd that thronged the marketplace where the stake was standing and Tyndale chained to it. She could imagine it all, and she could almost hear the babble of execration against him.

To think of it! A man of such noble mien to be browbeaten and battered by the screaming mob, cursed, reviled, and mud-covered. She shuddered at the thought, and while the impulse came to follow the others up the stairs, she hid her face while doing so, and sobbed.

She stood at the top of the stairs and looked around. Here, on her right hand, was the room into which Herman carried the tired stranger that night they brought him into the city. On the left was Herman's chamber. Just beyond it, again, was his mother's. Master Tyndale must be in one of them.

Captain Berndorf went into Herman's room, followed by the others, and in a few moments Margaret heard the soldier say roughly:

"Are you here? Come out of it, if you are!" Resistance would be unavailing, for the Captain's sword was drawn and ready, gleaming in the lamp-light.

Margaret went into Tyndale's chamber. It was lighted by the lantern in the street, for the rays came through the rain-splashed window, and as she stepped in she almost expected to see him sitting somewhere, or lying on the bed, waiting for the inevitable. Yet, when she stood well within the place there was a sense of emptiness. William Tyndale was neither in the bed, nor at the table near the window.

Was he really gone?

While her keen eyes ranged around she saw a square of whiteness on the floor, by the table, and went to it quickly, with an instinctive feeling that it was something which would betray Tyndale, or Herman. When she bent down and caught it up she knew that it was a printed sheet. Under it lay another; under that, again, a third. By the dim light she saw that they were printed folios, and one glance was sufficient to show her that they were proofs of the New Testament, such as she had seen in her father's hidden cellar.

She glanced towards the door, wondering whether the soldiers were there, and had seen that she had some papers in her hand, but the doorway was clear. Bending her head a little, she saw that the passage was empty. The men were still in Herman's room.

She thought of the way out of this very real danger with her swift wit, and hastily pushed the sheets into the inner folds of her dress. It was nothing that they were

48

crumpled. What were three sheets of printed paper compared to the lives of two men?

She turned her face to the window, where the rain came against the glass in heavy gusts, just as the wind drove it. Below were the soldiers of the City Guard, as when she saw them last, two lines of silent, unmoving men, with their halberds gleaming.

The hope sprang in her heart that William Tyndale was really gone. He was not in Herman's room, or they would have found him. They were now going into Mistress Bengel's bedroom, and would they find him there? If not, he could not be in the house, for he was not in this chamber. Her woman mind showed her what a man might not have noticed. The bed was not made as if waiting for a sleeper. It was surprising. Herman's mother had taken away the sheets from the bed, and it looked as though the room had not been used for a long time past.

Margaret centered her attention on what might be taking place in that bedroom, and because the suspense was more than she could endure, she went to see what they were doing.

The men were there — the three; and it was a strange scene on which she gazed. Herman was standing aside, his back to the window, where he could see everything, and Margaret wondered at the expression on his face. It was something like injured innocence, and, painful though the tension was, she could not repress a smile when she saw him watching with the air of a person subjected to the ignominy of suspicion, and to have his home invaded for the search of a man who was not there.

The Captain had his sword drawn, and was walking round the room, looking into the cupboard, and under the bed, and behind the dresses which hung in a screened-off corner. In all reality serious, disastrous in its promise, it yet appeared ludicrous and undignified.

The man-at-arms was standing apart, and the look on his face when he glanced towards Herman intimated that he thought this a fool's errand, on which they had been sent by some mischief-loving fellow who wanted to hoax the City Guard. And on such a night! Of late they had been brought away from the comfortable guard-room for many a fruitless hunt for this fellow, Tyndale, and this was all of a piece with the past experience.

The search was fruitless, but the Captain was suspicious of a hiding-place. Going to the walls, and bidding the soldier do the same, he began to beat the handle of his sword against the walls. First resting his halberd in one corner of the room, the man drew a dagger from his belt and did as his Captain did. He banged on the wall until the dust began to fly, and the plaster began to drop in flakes upon the floor. William Tyndale was too big a prize to lose for the sake of a few bits of mortar. They were sounding for some hollow place where a man might hide.

"You need not spoil my home like that!" a woman's voice came unexpectedly, and Herman's mother pushed past Margaret into the room, speaking with some asperity. "I shall appeal to the Burgomaster, and require him to pay for the repair of this wanton damage."

She wrenched the dagger from the man's hand, and held it out for the Captain to see. Her eyes were on a picture through which the fellow had driven his weapon, a picture which had been her dead husband's handiwork in his hours of leisure.

"Is that how you come to an honest woman's house?" she cried, swinging round to face the astonished soldier, her eyes flashing, while she thought of this willful damage done, when a hand put out to remove the picture would have prevented its ruin. "I will go to the Burgomaster even now!" she exclaimed, taking down a heavy cloak from a nail in the corner, and throwing it about her shoulders, with the dagger still in her hand while she began to tie the cord at her throat.

The Captain had turned to look at her, the point of his sword held downwards. He saw the damage that was done, and realized the reasonableness of the woman's resentment.

"You were over-rough," he exclaimed, looking at the picture. "But, on the other hand, since we were told that Master Tyndale would be found here we must needs miss nothing in our attempt to discover his whereabouts."

"His whereabouts?" cried Herman's mother, usually so gentle, rarely other than placid, but now roused by the roughness shown towards what to her had such holy associations. "Find the man if he is here; but neither you nor that fellow there shall damage what is precious to me, since it was my dead husband's work, finished but three days before he died!"

She sat on the bed, and, burying her face in her hands, wept, and the two men could do no other than look on her in concern as her sobs shook her. Margaret stepped forward like Herman, and sought to comfort her, but the girl's face went hot when she heard the papers crinkle as she put her arms about the weeping woman.

The men stole away into the other room, carrying the lamp with them, leaving the others in the darkness.

"Is there any danger, Herman?" Margaret asked, drawing her face away from his mother's, which was wet with tears.

"Not unless they find Tyndale, and they won't do that," said Herman confidently.

Again they heard the sound of shifting furniture, the slam of a cupboard door, the tapping of walls, but less roughly; and, after a while, the soldiers stood in the doorway.

"It is as it has been frequently of late," said the Captain, almost angrily. "We are being fooled by someone, and could I but lay hands on the miscreant who sends us on such errands, I would wring his neck"

He turned to go away, but paused.

"I am sorry, mistress, the picture was damaged. Send it to Josef Amon, the picture dealer, and tell him to put it to rights at my charges."

He moved away, and tramped down the stairs. To make quite sure that they were not deceived, he and the man with him, and the soldiers who waited below with their feet in a pool of water which had dripped from their clothing, passed through the lower room to the yard, tapping wherever they went.

They were absolutely baffled, for they found nothing which betrayed the presence of the man they sought, and on whose head there was so big a price.

The Captain's voice travelled up the stairs.

"Goodnight, mistress.   Send the picture to Josef Amon."

The street door slammed.  A word of command was heard outside, made tremulous by the gusty wind, and a tramp of soldiers followed, sounded less and less, and before long was no more heard.

Herman had gone to the window which looked into the street, but when he returned the candle showed a laughing face. His eyes danced.

"To think how God has protected us!   He has delivered us all from certain ruin! Oh, to think of it!"

It was then that his mother saw how wet Margaret was, and she stood up, in concern, wiping her eyes quickly.

"My child, you are soaking. Herman, go down stairs, and I will put this poor girl into some dry clothes, else she will be chilled to the bone, and ill may come of it."

52

Herman went away, and in less than half an hour Margaret came down with such clothes as Mistress Bengel could find. Then she told her business.

"Where is Master Tyndale? Has he left the city?" she asked, "Is he gone out of the city?" she asked again, because her question had not been answered.

"Come with me, little woman," said Herman; and he led her into the front room.

Moving the table when he had made sure that the shutters were safely closed, and the window so heavily curtained that no one could look in from the street, Herman cleared the center of the floor, removed the carpet, and tossed it in a heap into one of the corners.

"Just a word, little one," he said, before he did more; and he sat down while he spoke. "I never told you, but years ago my father made a discovery when he was digging for a safe place in which to hide what bit of money he had, in case of war, and he came across something. You shall see it."

He went on his knees, smiling when he saw Margaret's wide-open eyes. Taking the knife from his belt, he drove the blade deeply into one of the boards, and using it as a handle moved the board aside. He moved the next with his hand, a third, and another also. Asking for a lamp, he held it over an open space, and looking into the blackness Margaret exclaimed in surprise.

At her feet were some rough, wooden steps, leading into what seemed to her a deep well, the bottom of which was not visible. Herman put a foot on the topmost step, and descended a little space, when he asked for the lamp.

"Come with me," he said, as she handed it to him, and Margaret followed without hesitation. Reaching the bottom step, she found herself in a chamber about ten feet long, six feet wide, or thereabouts, and rather more in height. At the farther corner was a spiral staircase, and when Herman went down with the lamp, and she followed, she came to another room.

Herman saw her bewildered looks, and explained.

"My father thought it was a stronghold for heretics when, a century ago, persecution was keener even than now. There were tokens of it in abundance; but never mind that at present. I'm going to let you into the secret of Master Tyndale's strange disappearance."

He cried, but not loudly, and to his call there was a hollow return of the sound.

"Master Tyndale!" he cried again.

"Who is it?" was the response.

"It is I. Herman Bengel."

# THE PASSAGE

MARGARET gazed into the darkened space, and listened, with increasing wonder.

"That was Master Tyndale's voice," she whispered, half frightened.

"It was. I put him down here because I chanced to hear that Cochlaeus had been suggesting that he was lodging with us. I told the good man what I had heard, and proposed that he should go into hiding, and he did not hesitate, for he guessed how big and terrible the net which had been cast for him was. When he had gathered in his arms all that was most precious to him, his Bible and his papers, he followed me to this dark place without any demur."

Herman drew the girl aside a little, and pointed into the darkness. From where she then stood she saw a light some distance away. Then she saw a man moving towards her and carrying a lamp in his hand. When he drew nearer she saw a face; and the nearer it came, the more plainly did she see it. It was so close at last that she recognized the man to whom she was desirous of giving her father's letter.

"Master Tyndale!" she exclaimed, with bated breath, going forward to meet him.

But something like revulsion came. Her heart had been crowded out with anxiety all that day, and during the night which preceded it she had slept but little, because of the many hours in which she and her father had been packing those incriminating sheets which meant so much. Then had come the journey through the rain-driven streets, and the anxious waiting in the archway, watching the passing of the City Guard. Her hopes had scarcely any being. Her fears were dominant. It was a wear on the mind, and to crown it all was the tension while the house was being searched.

It was more than she could bear. The man who approached her seemed to sway. She felt that the place where they were standing was closing in on her. The floor appeared to ascend, and the roof to sink upon her. Then all was blank.

Herman saw her swaying and caught her before she fell.

"Margaret!" he whispered. "What is wrong?" he asked, full of fear when he found that she took no notice of him.

"I will carry her to my mother," he exclaimed, taking her bodily into his arms, and turning back to the spiral staircase.

"Nay, bring her to my chamber, my son," said Tyndale, who took both lamps and led the way, while Herman followed with Margaret.

How long she lay on the rude bed she did not know, but when she opened her eyes, Herman's mother was kneeling by her side, doing what she could for her restoration.

"Now, dear heart, take it quietly," the motherly woman said tenderly. "We are safe here. Give your message, and Herman shall presently take you home."

The words were reassuring, and presently she sat on the edge of the bed.

"Master Tyndale," she said, one hand holding the woman's, and drawing out the crumpled papers with the other, "I found these in your room when Captain Berndorf was searching the house for you."

She held the sheets towards Tyndale, but a cry of dismay escaped not him alone, but the others. Their faces paled, and Tyndale, calm though he was, with deadly danger circumscribing him, trembled. For a few moments he was dumb, but at last he spoke tremulously.

"Ah! If these had fallen into the Captain's hands, of what avail my hiding in this dark place? And what of the danger to my friends?"

His hand shook while it rested on Herman's shoulder.

"I should never have forgiven myself," he muttered. "Never! To have brought sorrow to a home where I have received such unstinted kindness! But there," he added solemnly, "so much the greater reason for thanking God!"

Margaret drew out the sodden letter.

"My father sent me with this, Master Tyndale."

Tyndale took it from her, and sitting at the table, he broke the covering and smoothed out the damp sheet, laying it flat on the table. The others watched him while he read, and saw how, when he came to the end, his fingers closed over the written sheet convulsively.

"God's will be done," he exclaimed, with his head bowed low. The anguish of the tone betrayed the intensity of his suffering. He looked up presently, and saw the faces of his companions, and read in them how they anticipated the worst, if deliverance did not come soon.

"It will all come right in time, my friends," he said quietly, and his eyes and face glowed with confidence. "Are we not in the hands of God? We are always safe under His guidance. I wronged the Heavenly Father when I said that all things were against me. There is surely some blessing in our reverses."

He read the letter through again with greater deliberation; then, laying it on the table, he sat back in his chair, with his head bowed down and his thin hands folded.

"Your father bids me leave the city tonight," he exclaimed presently, looking at Margaret.

"Tonight?" she cried. Her eyes were fixed on him as on one who was set an impossible task. "Where would you go?"

"I will go and continue my work in the city of Worms."

He stood up and began to pack his papers, the precious sheets on which he had spent his fine scholarship with such unremitting patience and splendid zeal. Apparently he did not realize the futility of it, as the others round him did. How could he think to get away from the city now that Cochlaeus had set the hunters on the move? It seemed to Margaret and the others, while they watched in silence, that William Tyndale was like a rat in a trap; not safe behind the iron bars, but certain to be routed out and snapped at by the sharp teeth of the dog the moment he left the cage.

Their minds were active as to the possibilities. Suppose Tyndale ventured into the streets and made his way towards the quay, would he not meet someone who would challenge him, since it was posted up all through Cologne that a heavy price was on his head? Heavy if he were brought in dead; heavier still if alive, so that he should be dealt with by the tormentors. If he got as far as the ramparts would he be likely to find the sentry asleep? The shuffling gait of the scholar, so Margaret thought, would betray him. While he moved he would run the gauntlet of a dozen who would know him for a stranger, dark though it would be in the stormy night. Even on the quay, were he to get so far, who could suppose that he could slip on board any of the rivercraft unseen? Captain Berhdorf and his men had marched away from the house in that direction, and were possibly searching the ships.

"You cannot go tonight, Master Tyndale," said Herman presently. "Lie here in peace, and be content where you are safe, where no one could suspect your presence; and I will watch for an opportunity."

The younger man spoke with an assurance he did not feel. Already he looked on his protégé as a man within the toils — himself scarcely less so. But why display any doubt when a way, in God's mercy, might open?

Tyndale realized the reasonableness of Herman's words, and, desisting from his eager task, he sat at the table, drawing away from the others the printed sheets which Margaret had saved from the eyes of the soldiers. He read some portion of them aloud while the others sat and listened. Then came the kneeling moments, when he committed himself and his companions to the Almighty hands. Still more urgent was his entreaty that he might be spared to complete his task of making God's Word ready for the multitude to read.

When the prayer was ended and the little company stood again, Margaret wondered at Herman's face. His eyes were bright. His face expectant. Going to the table, he took the lamp, and was about to walk away; but he paused.

"Master Tyndale, while you were praying," he exclaimed, "something came to my mind, and now I feel sure that God will answer that petition of yours."

They looked at him in wonder.

"What do you mean, my son?" asked Tyndale.

"That God may show us a way out of the city, which will spell safety for you. Margaret, come with me. Mother, stay with Master Tyndale."

Margaret went after Herman, who scarcely waited for her, for he was on the move.

"What is in your mind, my dear?" she asked, while they moved on into the forbidding blackness beyond the room where they had been praying.

Their eyes met, and she saw how his sparkled with what seemed to her to be hope.

"I'm going to explore, little one. It came to my mind while we were on our knees that I had heard my father say that once the city nearly fell into the hands of an enemy because of a secret entrance into it from the meadows. May not this be it?"

Margaret's eyes grew round with astonishment, and instantly she was alive to the possibilities. If it were as Herman's father said, and this proved to be the passage which was in reality the city's vulnerable point, William Tyndale could get away without having to run the gauntlet, as it were, in the streets and on the quay. He would escape Cochlaeus, and possibly some of those black-robed Familiars of the Inquisition who infested the city. What fear and grief and humiliation it would save if such a way could be found! No danger would threaten her beloved. There would be a safe retreat for Tyndale, or at least the opportunity for finding securer quarters elsewhere; and Cochlaeus would waste some valuable time prosecuting his search.

They came to a door which opened when Herman pressed against it. It moved silently and heavily, and when they had passed through the opening, and turned to look at it from the outer side, they saw that it bore the same appearance as the rock in which it was set. When they closed it, it was impossible, in the dim light of the lamp, to detect any difference between it and the rock itself.

The two went on slowly.

Sometimes the path on which they found them-selves descended; but as they went, they saw that it was leading on to some definite spot. Surely it could not be a cul-de-sac? They could hardly fail to find an outlet, but the question was, where? Would it be as Herman's father had said — in the meadows? Or would it lead into some house, just as it had begun in one? In that latter case it would mean the realization of their worst fears, and Tyndale would either be compelled to make his venture through the streets, or if Herman should be taken prisoner by the City Guard on some suspicion, and Margaret as well, and Herman's mother, he would lie in that hidden chamber, in darkness and starvation, dying at last, rotting and forgotten.

Margaret shuddered at the thought.

"Art cold, little one?" Herman asked, aware of the shivering of the girl at his side.

It was nothing to wonder at that she did so; for here, where they were walking, their feet were in the mire. The dark walls were streaming with water which spread out on the floor, forming pools in places through which they splashed.

"I shivered at my thoughts," said Margaret quietly, gazing into the darkness, wondering whether she would see any sign of an ascending passage, which might mean a rising to some house cellar like Herman's. She felt more hopeful when the floor dipped again, and so suddenly that she slipped on the slimy earth, nearly falling.

"Your thoughts?" exclaimed Herman questioningly.

"I was thinking of what would happen if this path ended at someone's house," she said, looking carefully to her footing.

An exclamation escaped Herman's lips. He had hoped that a fear like that was only his, and not hers, for the same idea had come to him.

"Who would have thought of such a thing as that?" he said half laughingly, to hide his own anxiety, but the girl at his side was not deceived.

"I thought so, Herman, and so did you," Margaret said half reproachfully. The way in front grew blacker and more forbidding. But on they went, determined to know what the end of this under-ground path would be.

"I believe we are in a great cavern," said Herman presently, when they halted involuntarily. The floor on which they were treading was no longer soft earth, but gravel and hard rock. No walls were visible, nor could they see any roof.

Looking into denser blackness, they heard the splash of water, and the lantern light showed a gleaming drop falling.

Going forward, they came to a spot where the dropping water had made for itself a hollow basin, but, passing round it, they walked on. Before they had gone far they halted suddenly, and with an exclamation of dismay ; for, stretched full length against the wall, down which some water trickled freely, percolating through the rock overhead, lay the body of a man whose flesh had gone, and time had left nothing but the clothed skeleton — death in its grimmest and most forbidding form. By his side, and clinging to him, lay a woman to whom time had been just as unkind. The man's hand gripped a small book, and Herman, kneeling on the floor to look, saw that it was opened at a page where he read some words that were in startling contrast with the end which had come to these who lay so still.

"In my Father's house are many mansions."

It was easy to imagine the story of that tragedy. Years before, the Inquisitors had hounded these poor ones, and they had found a hiding-place which became a death-chamber to them. Not daring to venture forth for food or liberty, they had died in this cavern.

Margaret and Herman went on, the horror of this discovery, and the pitifulness of it, thrilling them. They had not gone far, tracing the cavern walls in the hope of finding an exit, before they came to an ascending passage, and they stood still again, wondering to what it would lead. Would it take them to a house, and therefore to almost certain danger? Or would it lead them to the open country outside the city?

The ground was damp and bare, and mildew was on the walls; but as they went forward slowly and cautiously, prepared to hurry back if danger threatened, the lantern showed them moss in little patches; then plants that were content with little light so long as there was air to play about them.

Because of the cool air they felt that they were coming near to some opening, and if they carried a light it might betray them.

"Suppose we leave the lamp here," Margaret suggested. "We can use it when we return."

Herman nodded and set it down, and again they moved on. Now there were bushes, and presently a sky was overhead, with scudding clouds, whose jagged edges were fringed with silver whiteness by the clear-shining moon. The storm that had swept the city had ended.

A few steps more, and they were confronted by a bush, high, broad, and almost impenetrable, but, finding a way through, they saw the meadow, skirted by the river that rolled on in a stately flow.

# THE PRINTER'S WORKSHOP

WHEN they had gone back to the house, and told of what they had seen, Herman took Margaret home, and then the story of the night's experiences was related to Byrckmann, whose eyes brightened.

"God is in this. Now I see daylight," he exclaimed, turning to his daughter with a smile, the first she had seen on his face, which was genuine, since he had heard that Cochlaeus was in the city. He had forced himself to look serene and unruffled when his customers came to the shop, and had spoken to the workmen as though care sat but lightly on him; but whenever Margaret watched him while he was alone she knew that he had covered his face with a mask to hide his fear of approaching disaster.

But things had undergone a change, and Byrckmann went to bed that night doing something that was unwonted — humming to himself as though he had no more dread. Her father's cheerfulness and obvious relief gave Margaret such a sense of safety that she, too, slept soundly.

It was early morning when she got out of bed, and, drawing back the curtain, she looked into the street to see what sort of day was promising. What she saw surprised her, for John Gropper was crossing the road to the shop.

"So early?" she muttered, for by the strokes of the cathedral bell it wanted two hours before the workmen would come for the day. But she asked no questions when it was her usual time for going downstairs.

During the day the horses came to the door, and the wagon was laden with bales; then moved away in the direction of the quay. She thought nothing of it, because it was such a usual thing. She saw at times how men came and went, talking with her father at the counter, or going with him into the workshop; but his care was so sensibly diminished that she was able to move about with-out that oppression at her heart. She laughed light-heartedly when Herman came, and told her that he had spoken to her father, and that the wedding could take place next week.

"Ha! You hold me lightly, as if I were goods and chattels to be disposed of as two men might arrange!" she cried, her face full of laughter, and her eyes dancing. "What if I decline?" she asked saucily.

"What if you decline, my pretty maid?" Herman asked. "When the morning comes I'll come and get you."

"And expose me to the ridicule of every passer-by," she exclaimed archly.

"That way, whatever the passer-by may think, my little maid, rather than not at all."

The day was ageing when a change came. She was telling her mother of things that had happened downstairs; the queer requests of some of the customers; the obstinacy of the new maid in the kitchen; the gloom on the face of one of the 'prentices because he had mistaken the day when his time expired, and he had two more weeks to serve; of an unusually large order that had come in—a dozen things like that; and the pale face of the suffering woman grew rosier, and the lips parted in smiles, and the mother chatted eagerly about her daughter's wedding.

The joy passed suddenly, like a thunder-clap, and the old care returned, and more fiercely because she had thought it gone entirely. The twilight was coming as she sat at the window, telling her mother what was going on in the street, the workmen straggling off in ones and twos because the day's work was ended. It was not that which made the rosy cheeks white, and drove the love-light from her eyes, and made her heart beat with anxiety. Not that commonplace thing.

Some men were moving along the street, and the sound came up to the open window, like the steady tramp of soldiers. Then she saw the City Guard.

She had already seen them go by twice that day, but the conditions of the coming had changed. Two men were walking with the Captain of the Guard: one of them Cochlaeus; the other the Dean of the Senate, who never accompanied the Guard unless the business was of the most serious import.

She hoped they would pass, but the soldiers ranged up in a double line before the door of her father's house, just as they had done in front of Herman's home; and then the Captain and the Dean followed Cochlaeus into the shop.

She was dismayed and confounded, for her thoughts went to the cellar where the bundles were hidden away. These men had but to go there, and the mere presence of the press would lend suspicion as to its use in that unusual place. They had but to strip away one of the strong wrappers and they would see those printed sheets!

"Mother, there is Mistress Amon passing!" she exclaimed, making that her excuse for leaving the room so abruptly. She was going down to face the trouble, for it must be that.

When she passed the doors on her way downstairs the rooms seemed silent, tragic almost in their suggestion of disaster. A hush had come over the place which boded ill, but there was the rush of sound in her ears, and the beating of her heart. A mirror was at the bend of the stairs, and she was startled to see her face; it looked so weary, and so drawn with fear.

She went on, wanting to learn the worst. It meant so much for the home; for her father, of whom she was so fond and proud; for her darling mother, from whom they kept all the rough winds of life because she had enough to bear in the way of bodily pain. Yes. And it meant so much for herself. For how could she think of marriage when she was known to the world as the daughter of a man who was to die at the stake, or, as an act of uncommon mercy, to end his days at the galleys?

At the foot of the dark stairs she stood unseen, either by her father, or the Dean, or Cochlaeus. The Dean was unusually serious, and it was easy to see that his errand was an unwelcome one; solely one of duty; whereas Cochlaeus betrayed his satisfaction at the prospect of seeing Byrckmann undone, and Tyndale's hope of getting his Bible printed vanish.

What struck her most was her father's bearing. He was faced, she knew, with ruin, and she did not see how he could escape discovery. Cochlaeus was reputed to be well versed in all the tricks of heretics to hide their guilt, and he was not easily baffled. Yet her father was quite at ease. He was grave enough, but he had not the bearing of a man who feared the outcome of this search. Margaret saw the Dean look at him askance.

They went to the workshop, followed by a couple of soldiers, who left their halberds in the shop as being too cumbersome to carry in the winding passages.

Margaret stole after them, but was careful to keep out of sight. The workmen were all gone home, and through the glass door she saw that the workshop was left as usual. Printed sheets lay about. The presses were there, empty, waiting for the morning. The written papers which were copy for the printing were in the usual places, and tools, and ink, and other things.

Her father contented himself with waving his hand, but she heard him say:

"This is my workshop. Search as you will."

The searchers moved in all directions, and Cochlaeus, more active than any, looked around for hidden places, and seemed to be calculating the thickness of the walls, suggestive of room for hiding; but there was nothing to bear out his suspicions in that matter.

Nothing was discovered in the workshop, although with his strong hand Cochlaeus tore open every package to see that nothing in them was likely to belong to Tyndale. Even the paper wanted for printing was dealt with in the same ruthless way, until Byrckmann's patience reached its limit, and he made a protest to the Dean.

"This priest, who has no official standing in the city, has chosen to suspect me, yet he is welcome to make his search. But prevent him from doing such wanton damage to my goods, or I will hold the Senate accountable for the charges."

Cochlaeus swung round and stared in amazement at the printer, but he caught the glint in his eyes, and saw that Byrckmann, far from being afraid, was almost defiant. He went about his work more carefully, and did no more preventable damage.

Nothing was found; nor in the inner shop, where special work was done. But what of that? Margaret's mind was on the cellar, where the real danger lay. She watched anxiously, lest any stray piece of paper might betray her father, but she wondered whether, with all his sharpness, Cochlaeus would think of the cellar.

"Master Byrckmann," cried Cochlaeus peremptorily, "remove the bundles from this side of the room, so that we may see the floor beneath."

"Nay; I do not make the search," came the sturdy answer. "'Tis not for me to give a hand in what you think will be my undoing."

The tone was decisive. The Dean looked askance at the printer, and muttered to himself that Byrckmann did not bear himself like a man who had anything to fear. He turned to the soldiers, and bade them remove the bales to the other side of the room. They responded sulkily, for this was not their work. As the last bale was dropped on top of the others, Cochlaeus stamped over the cleared space.

"Ha! This is hollow!"

Bending low, he scanned every part of the floor, and at last he went on his knees to feel about for any sign of an opening.

"Byrckmann, come and raise the floor!" he cried.

"Nay, 'tis your business, not mine," was the quiet retort. "'Tis your search, as I told you just now; not mine. You can lift it as readily as I."

The Dean looked round again and, ignoring the Captain of the Guard, who yielded to his superior, he nodded to a soldier. The man came forward and, looking carefully, thrust in the point of his sword at the spot where the floor seemed to be moveable, and, lifting it, threw it back with a noisy clatter and a prodigious dust.

"Now we shall see!" cried Cochlaeus triumphantly, and he hurried down the steps. The Deacon of the Church of the Blessed Virgin had discarded his dignity in his eagerness.

Every pulse in Margaret throbbed wildly. She felt like falling in a fainting heap, but she controlled herself, and watched, to mark the fatal ending of this quest. Yet she marveled to mark her father's ease.

As the last soldier moved down, and his head went out of sight, she was more amazed than ever to see him rub his hands, and his face broaden into a smile. She wondered whether he had suddenly gone mad with the strain of the last few days, and therefore he did not realize his danger.

Presently a soldier's head appeared, and his face, when it came in sight, had a whimsical look on it. So it was with the next, and he stamped his foot as his heavy boot touched the floor. He dropped his sword noisily into its scabbard, as if there would be no use for it.

The Dean came into view, impassive as before, unless one could interpret that peculiar look on his lean face as one of satisfaction because the quest had ended so. There was bewilderment in the Captain's face when he also emerged from the cellar.

Last of all came Cochlaeus, and his sinister face was red with wrath. As he stepped away from the ladder he swung round on Byrckmann, and spoke in a passionate tone.

"Why did you not say there was nothing here to connect you with that fellow Tyndale?"

"You put no question that I could so answer," was the quiet, but exasperating response. "You came to my shop, and without asking me anything, you said, 'We have come to search your premises.' You did not say for what, and since the Dean was here, a man whom I esteem, I offered no protest, although you have no authority in this city, and suffered you to have your way. You have had it."

While the soldiers left the house, Cochlaeus stamped to and fro, protesting against being made a laughing-stock.

"Nay," said the Dean quietly. "You came to the Senate House and lodged your information in such confident terms that Master Byrckmann was printing off this Bible for Tyndale, that we granted you the opportunity for the search. You cannot blame the printer because his hands are clean in this matter."

Cochlaeus scowled and walked away, while Margaret, still wondering how it came about that the cellar was clear, followed him through the shop, and gazed after him through the window when he stalked along in anger down the silent street.

# THE MAN BY THE RIVER

THERE was the sound of footsteps behind her, and, turning quickly, Margaret saw her father walking to the door, where he drove the bolt into the socket.

"What does it all mean?" she asked eagerly, looking at him across the counter. "Father, my heart was almost bursting with anxiety; for when I saw those men searching the workshop, and Cochlaeus asked for the floor to be raised, there was no way out of the dreadful pass that I could see. I thought to see them go into the cellar and find the printing press and those printed sheets. It was almost more than I could bear!"

She sank on the stool and buried her face in her hands, shuddering, and thus she stayed until her father bent over the counter to her, and gently comforted her.

"It was thoughtless of me, my dear," he said soothingly; "and I ought to have told you what I did. Gropper and I pulled the press to pieces and placed it in the storeroom. Then we spent another long night in covering William Tyndale's sheets with strong wrappers for a long journey, and they were taken in a wagon to a ship which is lying at the quay. There they are, stowed away in safety, where even Cochlaeus would scarcely find them."

"Then I saw them," she cried.

"They went this morning," the printer said light-heartedly; and for a while, as the shadows fell and twilight gave place to darkness, save for the light which came in through the window from the lantern in the street, they talked of this danger which had threatened them.

"If only Master Tyndale were well out of the city," Byrckmann muttered. "I would go to him, but it would be unwise. Someone would see me, perhaps, and Gropper must not."

"Let me go," said Margaret.

"'Tis dark."

"I have been in the streets far later than this, father. Don't you remember?"

Without waiting for more, Margaret went to her room for her cloak and hood.

"What is the message?" she asked, coming into the shop again, fastening a bow under her chin. She pulled the bow into shape and buttoned her cloak. "Give me the message and let me start."

"I will come part way with you, my dear," her father said;" but I will tell you before we leave the shop. The walls of the city seem to be all ears of late."

He took down his cap and having whispered the message, which he made her repeat, to know that it was thoroughly understood, he led the way into the street.

They parted at the archway where Margaret had sheltered from the storm, and she thought for a moment of the man who had been standing there. Byrckmann stood well in the shadow and watched his daughter, but when she came to the bend in the long street he hurried after her, to make sure that no harm came to her. From a dark doorway he watched, and saw her stop at Herman's door, and presently she passed into the house. After that he went to Gropper, but returned home, as he put it to himself, like a thief in the night, alert for every sound, and fearful lest he should meet the City

Guard. The experiences of the day had shaken his nerve, and the very air seemed full of danger.

Herman's mother answered Margaret's knock on the door, and when she saw the girl she drew her into the dark passage, and thrust in the bolt.

"Herman," she called.

"Yes, mother," was the answer from the top of the stairs.

"A young lady to see you, my son," was the laughing call.

"Tell her I'll be down in two minutes!" the young man cried, his strong, clear voice vibrating with pleasure.

"I was dressing to come round to see your father," he said, before long, gazing at her as she stood in the lantern's light, looking radiant in her young beauty.

"My father!" she exclaimed archly. "Would you dress like that to see him?"

"I am come on business, Herman," she said presently. "Father sent me with a message for Master Tyndale."

"He is in the cavern," returned Herman.

"Let me go to him at once," Margaret exclaimed, leading the way to the front room, and going into the darkness before Herman had brought the light; but ere long she was face to face with Tyndale.

"My father told me to say to you, ' Get you gone out of the city, for Cochlaeus is on your track.' He has been to our home to search for your printed sheets."

"And did he find them?" Tyndale asked anxiously.

"No. My father anticipated his coming, and the bundles are all on board a ship called the Marburg, now lying at the quay. She leaves tonight. He suggests that you should go through the cavern, of which I told him, and wait at the riverside, where you or Herman will send an owl's cry over the water as the vessel passes. He is gone to Gropper's house to bid him see the skipper, and ask him to leave at ten o'clock to-night. He is to listen for the owl's call, and take you on board."

There was no need for haste. Quietly and persistently Tyndale gathered up his few belongings. Some were most precious, but woe for him if Cochlaeus laid hands on them. He set them on the table at which he had been working when Margaret entered the lonely underground room, and he suffered her to look at them. One was a New Testament, the Latin version by Erasmus. The other was the Vulgate, and from these two books he was basing his translation into English for the people at home to read.

There was so much more than when he entered the city, a worn-out traveler, borne in Herman's arms. Then it was the heavy wallet, swung pilgrim-like on his shoulder, holding these precious volumes, and two or three necessaries, but no more. Now there were sheets on which he had labored incessantly, almost feverishly, page after page, making a heap of papers, each scored over and corrected before he placed it on the pile with the others.

These had to go with a few proofs which had come from Byrckmann's shop, smudged and rough from the printing press. They had to be wrapped about with something, and presently they were ready to be borne in the wallet like a soldier's knapsack.

"A dangerous burden," said Tyndale quietly, when it lay on the table, "but a precious one; and in God's mercy it may more than balance much of the wickedness and sorrow in the world," he added, with kindling enthusiasm.

It wanted nearly an hour until the Marburg would leave her moorings and move up the river. They divided the burdens among them, Margaret's share being the lantern, and with this she led the way. She shuddered when she passed the spot where those dead ones were lying, but she did not tarry, and she only spoke when she whispered back a warning where to stoop, and where the footing was treacherous.

When they came into the open the moon was low down on the horizon, peeping between the heavy foliage of some trees, but making the shadow dense in which they sheltered themselves. Overhead were the glinting stars, Venus riding a few inches higher in the heavens than Jupiter, and close at hand was the dark and slowly moving river which reflected the sparkling sky dots and the dense bushes on the opposite bank. The waters were almost soundless but for the gurgle as they played with the plants and flowers which bent and nodded as the current moved.

Waiting but alert, they saw a great mass moving in the middle of the stream.

"'Tis a raft," said Herman, when he had peered beneath his hand. There were lights on it, and, as they flared, the watchers saw people moving to and fro, and when the moon uncovered her face there were ragged tents, and women sitting near them with their little ones about them.

"So much the better for your journey, Master Tyndale," said Herman, as the moving mass went by. "The river will be clear for the next few days."

The huge floating mass disappeared at a bend in the stream, and again the eyes of the watchers scanned the waters for some sign of the Marburg.

"I would that William Roye had been less dilatory," Tyndale said presently. "He promised to meet me weeks ago, and said he would send word as to his coming."

"Perhaps he heard that there was danger and dared not come," Herman suggested, without taking his eyes away from the river.

"William Roye was ever afraid of his skin," said Tyndale half bitterly. "But he would have been useful to me as my amanuensis."

"Ha!" exclaimed Herman, starting. "What was that?"

A few yards away he saw a man crawl into view from the bank, and stand up at his full height. From the same spot a boat was pulling into the center of the stream as if to overtake the raft, which was no more in sight.

It might mean much. It might mean nothing. But whether friend or foe it was not desirable to have anyone so near when the ship they were awaiting might soon come into view. Yet nothing could be done.

"Stand well back in the shadows," Herman whispered. "The man may move away."

It was a difficulty for which they were not prepared. The bare idea of a little company, bent on furthering God's work in the world, resorting to violence was unthinkable; yet, to be cooped up like this, and suffer the ship to go by without her passenger, spelt disaster, for Cochlaeus was a veritable sleuth-hound, and might run Tyndale to earth.

The stranger appeared indifferent whether he was seen or heard, and time seemed to him of no importance, since he looked about him idly. The moon began to flood the meadows more freely, so that the fields and the dells, the woods and cornfields, the distant mountain slopes and their torrents became visible, but the man was the object from which those in hiding could not take their eyes.

The puzzle was to know what to do. The impulse came to Herman to walk along the bank as a casual wayfarer, and he would accost the man and lure him away, so that he would not see Tyndale join the ship. So much hung on the secret movements of him in whose wallet such precious things were hidden.

Before he had time to decide, the man was on the move. He walked at first apparently without an aim, but he swung round and approached the bushes where the others were hiding. As he drew nearer, the moonlight showed him plainly, a man of fine physique; and he, too, had a pilgrim's wallet on his back.

He paused to scan the stream again, attracted by the silver glint on the waters. The man coughed, and Margaret started. She had heard a sound like it somewhere, but where and when she could not tell. The man, drawing nearer to the bush, halted again, and spoke to himself in a grumbling tone.

"To think of missing my entrance into the city like this! Now I have to stay here the whole night through, and go in in the broad light of day, when God knows who may spot me, and what may chance."

Margaret remembered the voice. It was the form of the man to whom she had spoken when she sheltered in the archway from the pelting rain. It was certainly his voice.

"Herman," she whispered, "do you remember what I told you of the man in the archway the other night—the man who lamented for what the Inquisitors had done to his daughter?"

"Yes, what of it?" asked Herman, keeping a watchful eye on the intruder.

"That is the man."

"Are you sure?"

"Certain."

"I wonder whether I dare go to him and speak," said Herman, half to himself; but Tyndale suddenly sprang to his feet, and tramped past him, muttering as he went. Herman threw out his hand to catch at him, but was too late. Tyndale was stalking on towards the man.

"William Roye," exclaimed Tyndale.

The two men met, and clasped hands while they stood face to face.

# ROYE AND THE INQUISITORS

AFTER that hearty greeting, Tyndale and Roye walked to and fro on the river-bank, so absorbed in the pleasure of their meeting that they forgot the danger of moving about in the clear moonlight. Herman, growing anxious, called to them that they were running needless risks.

"I forgot!" exclaimed Tyndale. "It was such a joy to see William Roye that everything went."

"'Twas a dangerous absent-mindedness," said Herman, almost sharply, looking round while he spoke, to make sure that none were near enough to observe them. While he did so, Tyndale hurried to the bush, followed by his companion, and they hid themselves in the shadows, with the others.

"Now, my dear Roye, explain yourself," said Tyndale, almost peremptorily, sitting on the grass in a place so dark that one could scarcely see the other. "Why did you stay away so long? I have been working feverishly and unceasingly all these weeks, and the Lord's work has tarried because I have but this one poor pair of hands to do the work of two."

"Hush, master," the response came quietly. "In some degree I am to blame, but not so much as it would appear."

Tyndale answered half reproachfully, for now that the pleasure of meeting had given place to reflection, he felt that the man for whom he had sent so urgently had failed him, and hindered his task. So many weeks had gone.

"I cannot but blame you, whatever your excuse!" he exclaimed.

"Oh, master, do not say that. Let me explain. Your letter found me, and I read it by the light of a street lamp. Perhaps it was the act of a madman, but a lad gave it to me by night when I was out walking. He dogged my steps until we were in a quiet street, and he caught up to me and whispered:

"'Are you William Roye?'

"Yes, but why?' I asked, rather startled, for I thought I was an unknown man among strangers.

"'Then I have to give you this,' and he thrust your letter into my hand, and seemed to vanish in the darkness. I knew at once that it came from you, for I know your handwriting so well. I broke the seal and began to read, but by the time I got to the end and saw your name I was startled. I chanced to look up, and saw two black-robed figures coming towards me."

Roye stopped, and clasped his hands convulsively, as if the memory of it, even, was overwhelming.

"Were they Familiars?" asked Tyndale eagerly.

"Yes, master. Hear you me, Master Tyndale?" he exclaimed hoarsely, his voice little more than a whisper. "They were Familiars. You know what need I have to dread them," he went on, wringing his hands, his breath catching with a sob. "Did they not, or the City Guard for them, which was all the same—did they not come to my home and take my darling Gertrude from me to that dark dungeon of theirs?

"But these men came on me unexpectedly in the street; and they came with that horrible, weird tread, almost soundless, and so the more fearful. I stood where I was, beneath the street lamp, trans-fixed, holding the letter in my hand, and staring at them, open-mouthed.

"They must have seen that I was desperately frightened. Oh, fool that I was! I was betraying myself to those black-souled, black-robed night-hawks, and there was the letter trembling in my hand!

I knew not what to do.

"The Familiars were some distance away, standing beneath a swinging lamp to read the names, perhaps, on the sheet they held—the names of some poor creatures doomed to the torture chamber. I tore off my master's name, and, thrusting the piece of paper in my mouth, I ground it between my teeth and swallowed it. Then I tore out the address, and swallowed that as well. Even then I was afraid of the consequences. God alone could tell what they might have got from what was left, so I turned down an alley, and in the darkness swallowed it all."

Roye stopped. Margaret laughed low in sheer relief, for now no Familiars could be at Herman's street door. Herman chuckled, while Tyndale rubbed his hands with satisfaction.

"Still I do not understand your long absence, William," he said presently. "How does it account for the weeks that have gone by without your coming to my lodgings?"

"Why, master, of course," said Roye, who seemed to have forgotten the purpose for which he was telling the story of his adventures. "I ate the letter, but in my haste I had taken no note of the address. I wanted to know what you were writing to me. I only knew the name of the city, not the name of the street."

He heard the subdued laughter of the girl at his side, but was not much disconcerted.

"A natural thing, William," said Tyndale.

"It was, master. The great thing, first of all, was to prevent discovery. Then I was confronted with a real difficulty—the task of finding you. I came at once to the city, and all through the weary days since then I have gone through and through the streets, not daring to ask for you, but hoping as well as praying that I might find you."

"I saw you!" exclaimed Margaret.

"You saw me?" the man retorted incredulously.

"Yes. Do you remember the night when the rain poured down, and you sheltered in an archway? I came while you were standing there. Had I but known!" Margaret added earnestly.

"Was it you?" asked Roye, in surprise.

"Yes, and I was even then going to the house where Master Tyndale lodged."

"If I had but known!" the man exclaimed, repeating Margaret's words. "Then, master, I had proved my loyalty to you and your great work, and my honest wish to serve you."

Tyndale did not answer, for something came looming out of the darkness, when a heavy cloud had cast dark shadows on the river—the form of a slowly moving ship. She slid out into the moonlight, and as she took clear shape, Herman knew her by the peculiar figurehead at her bows.

"'Tis the Marburg!" he exclaimed.

Hurrying to the bank, and taking great risk while doing so, he sent a plaintive and monotonous owl note travelling through the air. He did it again and again until a man in the ship's bows held up his hand by way of answer to the call, and disappeared.

Before long a boat came noiselessly, the oars being muffled, and presently she struck her nose against the bank.

"Is Master Tyndale ready?"

The question came cautiously from a man in the boat's stern. Happily the clouds had again gathered, and none, had any been watching, could have seen Tyndale step from among the bushes and make his way to the bank.

"I am here. Are you not very late?"

"A bit," was the sturdy, but whispered answer. "It couldn't be helped. That fellow, Cochlaeus, has been prowling about the harbor for the last three hours, and, not content with asking who was on board any of the ships that meant to leave tonight, he went aboard every one of them, and rummaged about in the cabins and down the holds, tapping everywhere where there was a possible place for a man to hide in. The Marburg came in for special attention."

Tyndale stood on the bank and listened, and the moonlight, playing on his face, revealed the intensity of his anxiety.

"Did he find anything? Was he suspicious about those precious bundles?" he asked.

"No, master; his whole aim was to lay those long lean fingers of his on flesh and blood. And something laughable happened, although some of us sweated with anxiety at first. Cochlaeus got down into the hold, where there were some casks, and these he tapped with his staff, as he tapped every mortal thing there was. Some of them sounded hollow, and he turned them over, but when he came to one and turned that on its side, a man sprawled out.

"Cochlaeus caught at him.

"'Ha! Master Tyndale, I have you at last!' he cried jubilantly, but a moment later he screamed aloud. It was Heinrich, the simple lad in the city, who, for some freak, had stolen on board to have a free ride up the river, and hid himself thus, that none should know.

"He was frightened when he saw that it was Cochlaeus who had gripped him, and in his frenzy of fear he snapped at the hand of the heretic hunter, closing his teeth upon the long bony fingers, making him scream with pain. But Heinrich would not let go. Not he! He seemed to take a delight in making the Deacon of the Church of the Blessed Virgin dance about, and he bit the harder. Ah! how he bit! In part to repay the brute for the sorrow and pain he had caused to so many who had come into his power.

"When the Captain came, wondering what the laughter and the screams meant, he persuaded the boy to loosen his teeth; but not until he had clenched his teeth for a final bite.

"I'll bite harder if ever he lays hands on me again!' Heinrich cried, looking at the Churchman, and there was a mad light in his eyes."

The sailor dropped his laughter, and became serious.

"Poor lad," he muttered. "And yet I am glad he showed his teeth to that fierce tormentor, and made him think, perhaps, of the poor girls, and the mothers, and the men he has tormented in those ghastly cellars of the Holy Houses. But come, Master Tyndale. The ship is moving down the stream, and will not wait for us."

Tyndale stepped into the boat, dropping his wallet at his feet before he sank on the seat.

"Come, William," he said to Roye, whose foot was on the gunwale.

"Nay, William, if that is what they call you," said the sailor, holding up a refusing hand. "I only take Master Tyndale."

"But you must take him, friend!" exclaimed Tyndale, bending forward eagerly. "'Tis William Roye, my amanuensis, and if he does not come with me my work will be greatly hindered."

"Then in Christ's name, good man, come and be welcome. All who have a hand in spreading God's truth may have a place on board the Marburg, and I know the Captain will approve."

A few moments more and the boat shot away from the bank into the stream, and was lost in the darkness, which was providential when so many eyes might be prying into the doings of the night. For the clear shining moon had gone behind some dense clouds and shrouded the river and the meadows and the city nearby in blackness.

# ALONE IN THE CAVERN

ONLY once did the moon peep through a rift in the cloud to light up the waters and show the Marburg making her slow way against the stream. It was a fleeting glimpse which the watchers had as they stood on the bank before they turned to find their way back to the house by the cavern way. The shaft of silver, as it fell, revealed the dim form of the vessel which carried such a precious burden with it, and a life which meant so much for the world's weal.

Then darkness fell again.

Herman and Margaret stood, gazing into the blackness, hoping that the clouds would drift by, and the sky be cleared to show them the empty river, with the ship gone out of sight, and safely away from the jurisdiction of the authorities of the city. Instead, they came more and more heavily, and the darkness grew denser.

After a while they sat down and began to talk of their own concerns, and the married life they were going to lead within the week. Margaret, told him what her hopes were; but she spoke as well of her diffidence, lest he might be disappointed in his wife.

"Hush," whispered Herman. "'Twill be the finest bargain any man ever made; the best gift God ever gave to anyone. And when I think of it, 'tis hard to contain myself, that a week from this day you will be mine."

Margaret was going to answer, but a sound came, and she bent forward to gaze into the darkness towards the harbor from whence the Marburg had come.

"What's the matter?" Herman asked.

"Did you hear the sound of a man's feet? Can you not hear some voices?" she whispered.

The stillness of the night, while they listened, was broken by the sound of voices and the tread of feet. It was nothing of the imagination. At first there was but a distant murmuring, but now it was undeniable that men were coming, swiftly, persistently, and, judging from the tone of their voices, they were greatly incensed.

Before long, while Margaret and her companion sat shadowed from observation by the bush, they began to distinguish the words.

"To think that I should have been duped like that," cried one.

"'Tis Cochlaeus," Margaret whispered, but Herman made no answer. The man was saying more, and he would not miss a word.

"I went through the ship, and through it again, but found no trace of that accursed Englishman; not a sound nor a sign of his presence. Nothing came of my search but the discovery of that mad stowaway, who has left marks on my fingers that will stay for many a day."

The company halted close by, and Herman and Margaret, holding themselves in silence, neither moving hand nor foot, scarcely breathing lest they should betray their presence, peered into the darkness. Accustomed to it by this long night vigil, they saw the indistinct forms of six men, but who they were, or whether armed, it was impossible to tell. What they heard set their hearts palpitating with fear.

"What can you do?" one asked, who had gone closer to the bank, as if to gaze up the broad stream.

"I mean to overtake the Marburg, go on board, and search afresh for Tyndale," said Cochlaeus, almost viciously.

"And if you find him?" asked the other, speaking back over his shoulder, but not moving from the bank.

"Make an end both of him and his accursed practices," came the hot answer. "Canst see the ship?"

"No."

Margaret thought she knew the voice of the man on the lookout, and presently her suspicion became a certainty. The man who spoke to Cochlaeus on equal terms was the Dean, who had accompanied the search-party in her father's shop.

"Let us start, and we may overtake her!" cried the Deacon. "None will see us walking on the bank, so that for once the darkness is a blessing in disguise."

"And what then?" the Dean asked impatiently.

"What then?"

The response betrayed astonishment at such simplicity.

"What then? I will board her, of course, and search again. What else should I do? What less could I? That fellow on the wharf said that he saw one go on board who answered to Tyndale in every point, and I would give half of all I have to lay hands on him."

The Dean spoke curtly.

"Let us go if we must, since you seem so set on it. But I warn you that it will be a fool's errand."

Cochlaeus was on the move at once, and it seemed to those who were hiding in the bush that the company went forward in a straggling line, not one among them willingly, save the man who led.

It was alarming to Margaret and Herman to find that after all that had been done, when things appeared to be going so well, and when in fancy they saw Tyndale sitting in a quiet room somewhere in the city of Worms, absorbed in his holy task, this persistent sleuth-hound was on his track, and shortly, whereas he was imagining himself safe, he might be in the hands of his tormentors, and his dream of a great task completed broken in upon.

"Herman," Margaret whispered, afraid to move lest she might betray her presence, although the sound of the men's footsteps had grown indistinct as they fell on the meadow grass.

"Yes, little one?"

"They will find him, and they will kill him!" she exclaimed, her voice breaking.

Herman was recognized her sudden fear.

"I will take you home, my dear, and then go after them. I shall do my best to pass them, for I shall go fleetly, and give warning to those on board the Marburg."

"You will be too late!" Margaret protested. "It will take you an hour or more to go back with me, and then those men will have gone so far that you will not overtake them, much less pass them."

She buried her face in her hands, for the vision had come to her in those moments of dread, of a godly man in the hands of the tormentors, tortured, and then for a certainty bound to the stake for death. It was a terrible thought that this saintly man should be cut off in the midst of his splendid work, and be counted among the martyrs.

She lifted her face, and because at the moment the clouds drifted by, Herman saw that it was wet with tears.

"Go now, Herman," she cried, springing to her feet. "Go now!"

"And leave you to go through the cavern and home alone? I cannot. I will not!"

"You must, Herman. I can go alone. What is my loneliness compared with that good man's life? Would you have the world irremediably impoverished because a girl like me must needs have an escort? Go, Herman," she ended imploringly, as she looked up into his face.

He sought to persuade her, but she was resolute.

"Herman, go, and God go with you. Save the good man, for he will certainly die if Cochlaeus lays hands on him. And what of their plans then?"

Then she waited no more; turned away and hurried to the cavern's entrance. Before he quite knew what she meant to do she was on her way, and all that he could hear was the sound of light but hurried footsteps. He followed and called after her, but no answer came. He went to the entrance of the cavern and peered in, but saw nothing, nor did he now hear a sound, save the echo of his own voice when he mentioned her name.

He thought she had taken her courage in her hand, doing so in desperation, and knowing the place by this time, she must be making her way towards his home. Perhaps by this time she was close on the chamber where Tyndale had been hiding.

With this conviction he turned away, bent on overtaking and out-distancing the fiery-spirited Inquisitor.

He did not know that when Margaret had gone from him, her courage failed her as she thought of the place where those grim skeletons were lying. She was afraid to venture. She shivered at the thought; for, although she knew of the lantern, ready to be lit with the tinder-box at hand, she felt that she could not go through the cavern by herself. Rather than do that she would stay the long night near the river, taking whatever risks there were; for what men might threaten did not seem so terrible as the confrontation with that solemn silence which spoke so awesomely of a tragedy of bygone years.

At the entrance to the cavern her courage was still less, so that she crouched in the darkness of the bush and waited. She was wanting some sign that Herman was on his way, but instead she heard his feet thud on the grass not far away, as though he was following her. Then she heard his quick breathing, and marked how he halted. Although she could not see him, since, like herself, he was in the black shadows of the bush, she guessed what he was doing —that he was bending down to peer into the cavern.

His call came, but she remained still, scarcely breathing lest he should hear her. Then, when she found it so hard to be silent that she must betray herself, he went away.

She came from behind the bush, but could not see him. She could only hear his footsteps growing less and less distinct. He was going swiftly to make up for lost time, and she was relieved.

Standing farther out in the open, away from the entrance, she heard the faint thud of a man's feet on the sod, and fainter yet, and fainter still. Then silence, with only the sounds of the river, the sigh of the water among the rushes, the occasional hoot of an owl, the slight swish of the wind on the grass and among the trees, and the movement of some belated creature wandering from his lair in search of food.

The sense of loneliness disturbed her. To be here, in the meadow, with the black river on one hand, the stretch of dark country on the other, and, where the watchmen were on the city wall, some challenge coming, making the loneliness seem the greater.

The feeling sent her to her knees, crouching lower and lower; but another thought swept through her mind. A man of God was being hunted. The hunter of heretics was after him. Herman was on the path, seeking to save him. Could she not pray? Was not that the recourse for anyone in need?

She rose from the crouching posture until she was fairly on her knees, and with her hands clasped, she prayed for the hunted one. She thought it no shame to pray that the hunters might fall on some stumbling stone and be broken. She prayed that Herman might speed well on his errand of warning.

How long she prayed she did not know. There was no reckoning of time in those moments of pleading, for the thing that mattered was, that the prayer should be heard by Him who sat on the Mercy Seat.

She got up from her knees and moved slowly towards the entrance, for she must go home. But her courage failed, just as it had done before. She crept into the place in something like desperation, lit the lantern, and essayed to go forward.

She went haltingly, her heart beating wildly. She could hear the sound of its throbbing. Then, to her alarm, something came like a cry through the silence—a cry that must be from those still lips away to her left.

She held up her lantern high, so that the light should the better lessen the darkness, but it showed her that grim forbidding heap on the cavern floor.

What was there to fear? She asked; yet she knew it to be the dread of the intangible which was so overwhelming, following on the strain of so much anxiety when Cochlaeus was searching her father's house, and after that the further mental tension of watching for Tyndale's escape when he appeared to be hemmed in with danger. To her excited imagination, after such a day, the cavern was peopled with horrors. Her mind was under compulsion to think of the dead bodies close by her—to conjure up a story of unspeakable suffering, isolation, hunger, deadly fear, and the terror of the coming of the tormentors.

She thought of this while standing in the open space, one hand holding the lantern high, the other on her bosom to still the wild beating of her heart. Then came the sound of voices, and a cry which was like a challenge, all coming as a jar to her being.

She did not know the voices, for they sounded hollow and echoing in the ghostly place, having something of menace in them.

The sounds came again. Once more she heard the challenge, and she could bear the strain no longer. The lantern fell from her hand and crashed on the cavern floor, where the candle spluttered and smoked the horny sides. Her brain reeled. In the diminished light she saw something moving, she knew not what. After that she fell beside the lantern, and lay as one that was dead.

Who they were who came she did not know, nor who they were who, a few moments later, stood and gazed down at her, each one holding a lantern.

# THE NIGHT RIDE

WHEN Herman started on his errand his thoughts were divided. There was the wish that he had insisted on seeing Margaret safely through the cavern, if it had only been to give her over to his mother's care.

He had accepted her ruling, for he realized the fatal consequences if that sinister creature of the Inquisition found Tyndale. He thought of the vessel going up the river, past the castles of robber lords, and freighted with merchandise such as had never gone up the stream before, since the bundles of quarto sheets of the New Testament which Tyndale was so laboriously translating into simple English were in the hold.

Two things were fixed deeply in Herman's mind: one that, come what would, Cochlaeus must not come into touch with Tyndale; the other that his late guest, now so honored and so loved for his gentle ways and godly life, must arrive in Worms, where he would be comparatively safe, since that city was in what Cochlaeus called "the full rage of Lutheranism." And Luther, too, was there.

The purpose was a spur to him, although with the endurance of an athlete he went on and on. He was in feverish anxiety to go yet faster, and give warning to the fugitive of the men who were after him.

One thing he could not understand—that, fleet of foot though he was, he went so far without overtaking

Cochlaeus and his companions. Nor as he went did he come across any sign of the Marburg.

With a cry of dismay he pulled up when he came to a village on the riverbank. In his absent-mindedness for this long hour, thinking of so many things, and not of the way he was taking, he had travelled down the river, and every step had taken him farther and farther from the man he was so eager to serve!

An hour lost! Nay, two; for he would now have those long miles to travel back before he reached the point from whence he started, and only then would the real endeavor commence. Who could tell what had chanced in the interval?

He did not waste a moment, but swung round on the instant when he had discovered his blunder. He roundly blamed himself for his stupidity, but prayed that he might not be too late.

On he went, the speed growing greater as the urgency swirled in on him. He covered the ground so swiftly that the hour he had lost was not doubled when he came to the spot where Tyndale's hunters had been talking. He was bathed in perspiration, for the return journey had been covered in little more than half an hour.

Still, when he heard the city bell boom out the hour, he knew that Cochlaeus and the others had a lead of an hour and a half, and while he took off his cap to wipe his face, he wondered whether he could make up the loss and be in time.

The thought was like a whip to him, and he went on with untiring speed, centering his mind on that one purpose, to overtake Tyndale's pursuers.

He passed no one in that hard night's travel. More than once he plunged through the woods which ran down to the river's edge, where he found himself in a darkness so dense that it seemed almost Egyptian. He had to go slowly then, only able to guide himself by the scarcely distinguishable gleam of the water; and more than once he sprawled over a straggling root, and once again he struck his head against an unseen branch which hung low over the path.

The enforced slackening of speed was exasperating; but he took things more calmly when he remembered that Cochlaeus was in the same plight, and would have to go as slowly.

When he came into the open country again he was bespattered with mud. His doublet was torn, and he felt the warm trickle of blood on his cheek, where the jagged point of a broken branch had grazed the skin. But these were minor matters where the thing at stake was of such overwhelming importance.

By the time he had stepped clear of the forest the heavy clouds had thinned away, and the moon, while she did not altogether show her face, was casting some blurred light on the path. He was able now to go forward with a more certain step, so that he put on speed, and ran desperately, with the energy of young manhood, careless of fatigue.

He passed a village which straggled towards the river. He wondered whether he should take a boat and pass up the stream with it. He would come to the ship that way; but when he looked at the waters, they were running strong, and the boats that were moored at the landing stage were heavy ones. He left them, and went on.

In one of the meadows were some horses, standing idle, sleeping as they stood, but one awoke and turned sleepily towards him. The idea came that he could force him into service.

He hesitated. One might choose to call it robbery, but God knew that it was no dishonest motive that prompted him. Against the temporary appropriation of the horse was the life of a man whose service to the world was of inestimable worth. He could take the horse for a few hours, and see that he was returned. He could give the messenger who took the animal back a reasonable sum to pay for the unconsented hire.

Yes. He would do that. It would help him to make up the lost time through that stupid blunder for which he mentally lashed himself again and again.

He went cautiously to where the horse was standing, but he found himself in a difficulty at the outset. His hand was on the sleepy creature's mane, and then he realized that there was neither saddle nor bridle. As for the want of a saddle, that was nothing to one who had ridden bareback scores of times, but how was he to guide this silent and perhaps docile creature, who was blinking at him stupidly, wondering whether he was to be called away from his well-earned leisure to some hard night duty?

A suggestion came, and he acted on it. There was a long, thin lace scarf round his neck, and it could be made to serve his purpose. In a few minutes his ingenuity produced a bridle and bit, all in one, which would not put the horse to any discomfort. Then he sprang on the creature's back.

"On, good horse!" he cried, as he bent down to gather up the loose ends of the scarf. "God's good man is in jeopardy, and many a blessing may be lost to the world if you fail me tonight."

The horse moved forward, but with no great willingness at first. After a time, however, he seemed affected with his rider's eagerness. His rest in the field had made him fit for service, and he responded. Before many minutes had passed he was going quickly, then at a gallop in which he stretched himself out whole-heartedly.

The moon still hid her face, but she threw out sufficient light to show the way, and what was round about. As the horse raced onwards Herman's spirit rose. He began to think of possibilities. As yet he had seen no ship, nor any sign

100

of one. Nothing was moving on the river but a small craft which floated with the stream. Nor had he seen those men who were following the impatient lead of Cochlaeus. And yet it was of such supreme importance that he should overtake them, and ride beyond them.

After a time his heart leapt at the sight of a company of men, and when he drove his horse across a meadow to get so much nearer, he saw them halt, as if to wait for the coming of this rider in the night.

Suffering his horse to take his own pace, he bent low as he passed the men, so that his face should not be seen. The moon rendered him just the right service for those critical moments. She showed herself through a rift in a cloud for a moment or two, and the light fell on the men.

He knew them all. The Dean was one. Four others were soldiers of the City Guard, whom he had seen constantly for years, in their frequent perambulations through the streets, and their halberds at this moment gleamed at the moon's uncovering, but went dull again when the clouds moved by, and the country and river were once more wrapped in gloom.

Cochlaeus was there, standing apart, trying to intercept him, but Herman drew the horse aside.

"Stop!" the man cried peremptorily, and held out his hand to catch at the bridle, but Herman dug in his heels, and the horse galloped past. Who was Cochlaeus, that he should exercise his authority here, in the open meadows, far away from the jurisdiction of the Burgomaster?

The horse plunged forward, and his hoofs thundered on the path. Herman turned to look back. The group was just as he had left it—a bunch of men, and that one who stood aloof; but although he could not see he supposed that they were gazing after him angrily, because he had treated Cochlaeus so cavalierly.

On went the horse, and Herman was elated at the thought that he had stolen a march on the men who were in pursuit of William Tyndale. At the pace the horse was travelling he would overtake the Marburg and give his warning. The captain would surely do something then to get his passenger away, if by any chance it became necessary.

While the horse galloped on, taking the path along the riverbank as though the rush through the night air was welcome after a spell of rest, Herman thought out a plan which would mean safety for Tyndale. All his desire now was to overtake the ship, get on board in some way—by swimming, if in no other manner—tell his story, and then follow out this idea of his. He knew of a charcoal burner's hut on the other side of the river, hidden away in the forest, and there, with Roye to help him, Tyndale could pursue his task, the amanuensis writing while the scholar slowly dictated his translation. The printing press could do its part later, but at all events Tyndale's great work could go on.

The horse galloped on for three or four miles more, and then the moon was out again, and made the river look like a broad ribbon of silver winding in and out amid the forests and the low-lying meadows.

A shout of gladness came when Herman saw a great black object on the water, which, as he drew nearer, proved to be a ship beating up the stream, her dark sails bellying in the wind.

Was it the Marburg?

He lost sight of her presently, for a forest came in between. He slackened the pace and rode into the thicket, able to see the way because of the clear shining of the moon, so that he took the zigzag path, moving round the clumps of brushwood, avoiding the hollows, and going carefully where the straggling roots and heavy undergrowth made any progress treacherous.

He had at last to dismount and lead the horse, feeling his way almost in places, going at times at little more than a snail's pace, the horse snorting and breathing heavily with his long run.

Then the forest ended.

Standing still to gaze around ere he ventured into the broad moonlight, because he heard voices and the jingle of steel, Herman saw a broad sweep of grass which stretched from the river up a steep slope, until it came to the spot where this cul-de-sac of green terminated in the closing up of the forest. A great castle was standing there, grey and forbidding in the moonlight. On the other side of the broad grass incline was dense forest again, and Herman meant to cross to it. But on this wide strip of open grass soldiers were moving towards the river swiftly, their swords and steel breastplates gleaming in the moonlight.

Herman dropped back, for the presence of the fighting men boded evil to any whom they saw who did not belong to the lord of this domain. Many a castle on this river was the hold of a robber chieftain who preyed on the travelers on land or water, demanding tribute and often holding his prisoners to ransom.

Herman took his tired horse back into the darkness of the forest, and, fastening him in a hollow where he could not be seen, returned to the slope again, to watch the glade and see when it would be safe to move to the other side.

For a time he could see nothing of what was happening on the river, but he was full of apprehension when he thought that the soldiers were bent on piracy. By this time the Marburg must have passed the landing stage of the castle, and in that case would be safe, unless—and there he halted in his hope, and went cold with fear. Suppose that men had been placed on the watch, and, seeing the Marburg laboring up the river against the stream, had gone out in a boat to stop her, on the pretense of levying tribute, while a messenger raced up the slope to the robber stronghold to bring down the lord with his fighting men!

The consequences were too well known to anyone who lived within sight of the river, and this particular castle was often spoken of—was common talk, indeed, in the city. The ship would be gone through and robbed, if the captain and the crew were not armed and ready to make a fight for it. And William Tyndale, known, perhaps, would be carried to the castle, to be dealt with just as the wine-drinking and blasphemous master of the castle might choose.

It was natural to suppose the worst, and to suppose the worst was to anticipate what was most probable. Ribaldry would be the slightest of Tyndale's troubles. Torment was next to certainty. It might be that the lord of the castle, knowing how the Inquisitors would crave to have the Englishman in their hands, would sell him to them, if they paid a big price.

Herman thought of this. Then it dawned on him that he was thinking the worst while Tyndale's vessel might have stolen by when the moon was hidden, and by this time be far up the river, away from this robber lord's influence.

He stole in and out among the trees towards the river, careful not to be seen, and then his worst fears were realized. The Marburg was in mid-stream, and about her were a score of boats, out of which armed men were swarming on to her deck.

# THE PRISONER

HERMAN'S hand involuntarily grasped the dagger at his belt, but he realized his helplessness. He could do nothing, for here, or within call, moving up or down the slope, and out on the waters, playing a pirate part, were scores of men, all armed—men whose business it was to fight, and who, if he had gone forth to make any remonstrance, would drive their swords into him, and laugh at his mad venture. They would do it as the natural act when one had the impudence or imprudence to confront scores who knew no law but what the lord of the castle cared to make.

He watched the strange scene on the river, and from where he stood, compelled to be silent, but with a feeling of dread, he saw, in the full flood of moonlight, that the armed men were in possession of the ship. On the upper deck a man's body hung over the handrail. The man was either dead or badly wounded. That was the only token that there had been resistance to these river pirates, for the sailors, unarmed, and only a handful against scores of trained fighters, had realized how futile it was to endeavor to save the ship.

The crew were driven into a corner of the deck, and held there like penned sheep by a few soldiers whose breastplates glanced in the moonlight every time they moved. They were ready to cut down any sailor who was mad enough to attempt to break away.

Herman's teeth chattered, although the night was warm, for the thought of William Tyndale's extremity sent an icy shiver down his spine. All the bold effort to get the good man away had come to naught. There was the deadly fear of what might follow, added to the bitterness of a frustrated plan and the thought that God's Word was not to reach the people of England after all.

He resolved to do whatever remained possible. He would wait and see what was done to Tyndale—where he might be placed by the robber lord. Then to his alert mind came the thought that he might even yet be able to get Tyndale away. But how, or what the way might be, only the good God could tell.

There was no sound of fighting. Instead, the laughter of the soldiers came over the Waters. Their steel helmets bobbed here and there, and Herman knew that the men were searching the ship for anything in the way of booty—money or goods.

Presently the first things came in the shape of bales, possibly of silks, which were dropped over the side into the boats. Other bundles followed, but only what was of value, for these soldiers were experienced pillagers who spent their days and nights in this sort of work. They knew what things were of worth, and what the lord of the castle would be able to turn into gold. Boat-load after boat-load came to the bank, the booty was handed out to men on the bank, and the boats returned for more.

Herman was startled by a sound on his right hand, and, looking round quickly, he saw half a dozen men emerge from among the trees and stand out clear in the moonlight. He saw the newcomers' faces, and he dropped back farther into the shades of the forest, for one of them was Cochlaeus.

For a while these men gazed on the unexpected scene, and Herman, watching, saw how the face of the heretic hunter worked with passion—the fury of a man who thought he had but to overtake the ship, and ask for Tyndale, and he would have him in his power, but now discovered that the Englishman was beyond his reach.

They were near enough for Herman to hear what was said.

"Is this Schouts' place?" Cochlaeus asked, pointing towards the castle, and speaking in hoarse and passionate tones.

"Yes," said the Dean; "so that there is danger for us as well as for those who are on board the ship."

"Danger for us?" exclaimed Cochlaeus, in amazement. "Danger for me, an emissary of the Church?"

"Schouts cares no more for the Church than for the meanest man on board the Marburg. He has no fear for God or man."

Cochlaeus gazed at him incredulously, and when the Dean and the others drew back among the trees, he stood clear out in the moonlight and waved his clenched fists, in the impotence of his disappointment.

"Come back!" the Dean exclaimed, fearful lest this man might do something yet more rash, if he had not already betrayed their presence by his mad gestures. "You do not know this robber lord. He would flout you or the Lord Cardinal, anything and anybody that belongs to the Church, as readily as he would beat down one of his own soldiers who dared to disobey him!"

The Dean stepped forward, and, with a strong grip on the Churchman's arm, drew him away forcibly among the trees.

"I pray God we were not seen," Herman heard the Dean say.

What Cochlaeus and his companions did after that Herman could not tell, but as time went on, and he heard no

107

sound to indicate their presence, and saw no more of them, he concluded that they had gone back.

Convinced that this was so, he watched for Tyndale, wondering whether the robber lord would only concern himself with booty and let the men on board alone.

The boats went to and fro, until the Marburg's hold must have been emptied of all that was worth carrying away; and now Herman was eager to know what would follow. The man whose body had been hanging over the handrail began to revive, and he staggered over to a coil of rope on which he sat with evident pain. He was apparently waiting for the worst. The moonlight falling on the face made Herman aware that it was the captain of the ship.

Someone went to him—a tall man, clothed in the garb of a nobleman, and giving one the impression of immensity. He must have been Schouts, the predatory lord of whom the Dean had spoken. The captain lifted his face as if to answer a question, and it was crumpled and lined with pain; and even while Schouts was speaking, he fell sideways, and lay on the deck like one who was dead.

The other swung round on his heel after gazing at the prostrate man for a few moments, and, tramping along the deck, moved down the ladder into the waist of the Marburg. Before many minutes had passed a man's loud voice rang out, and the soldiers on board began to search in obscure places for something.

Were they looking for Tyndale?

The unspoken question was answered quickly. Two men came along the lower deck, and between them walked a bearded man.

It was William Tyndale.

He did not walk cravenly, although he moved slowly and with bowed head. The soldiers, with their swords drawn, took him to Schouts, whose weapon-point rested on the deck.

Something was said, although Herman heard no sound of voices, and the robber lord, turning his back on his prisoner, walked to the ship's side, the prisoner following. One by one the men came down the rope ladder into a boat, Schouts first, then Tyndale, and after him the two soldiers. As soon as they were seated, the boat was pulled to the landing-place.

Herman hurried to the spot where he had stood for his first glimpse of the grass slope. It was in his mind that he might see Tyndale more closely, and who could tell whether, in God's mercy, some-thing might happen whereby he might effect his escape? It was a wild hope, but he did not set it aside.

He passed the hollow where the horse stood quietly and tiredly, and reached the place just as Tyndale made his way among the heaps of pirated merchandise. There were half a score of armed retainers about him now, and the hope of rescue passed.

Looking out on the river, while Tyndale was kept standing to wait for further commands, Herman saw the sailors moving away from the spot where they had been penned in by the soldiers. He heard the sound of the winch, as they slowly raised the anchor which had been dropped on Schouts' demand, and before long the sails were bellying in the wind, and the ship moved up the stream.

A call came on the night air, and the company, of which Tyndale was the center, began to move. He came slowly, as though he were ill, but the soldiers, apparently realizing this, suited their pace to his. Schouts moved up the slope without waiting, but halted close to where Herman stood, to call back to the men to begin to carry the spoil to the castle.

Tyndale drew level with Herman's standing spot, and, scarce knowing why, the young man went in and out among the trees and bushes, anxious to watch the prisoner. It was a perilous venture, for a false step might cause him to make some sound, and the captain of Tyndale's guard, expecting an attack, might send some of his men into the forest to search. It could scarcely mean less than death if they found him, and what excuse could he make but this, that, having occasion to pass on through the forest, he had found his way barred by the soldiers? They would laugh his explanation to scorn, perhaps, and run him through with a sword or carry him to one of the dungeons in the castle.

The castle gate was reached at last. The draw-bridge was already down, but the portcullis had to be raised before any of the party could pass in. Herman so stood that as the moonlight fell on the face of the prisoner he saw how he cast a wistful look around him, as though this might be the last he would ever have beneath God's open heavens. Hopelessness, too, so Herman thought, was on the tired man's face, and the traces of bitter disappointment because the work on which he had been engaged might never be completed.

When Tyndale stood at the drawbridge, waiting for it to be raised, Herman heard sounds behind him, like the stealthy movements of men, and felt alarmed for his own safety. But another idea came. Was it possible that some were approaching with the intention of attempting Tyndale's rescue? But who would be so mad when, at the clangor of the castle bell, a hundred armed men would be on the spot?

Knowing that he could not be seen, he waited to discover the meaning of these movements, and what he saw surprised him. One man took his place behind a tree not more than half a dozen yards away. Another drew away from a bush and stood beside the first corner. Others crept up from the dark shadows, but not so near, within call, but standing well out of sight.

"That is Tyndale," Herman heard one say, and the voice belonged to Cochlaeus.

110

The voice of the other who answered was the Dean's.

"Then if he crosses the drawbridge, and the portcullis falls, Tyndale goes out of your power. But let him go! Now that Schouts has him in his robber den he is as good as dead. God alone knows what he may do to silence him, for I count Schouts equal to anything. You have but to think of the man to know that he is barbarity personified."

Cochlaeus spoke back in low tones which vibrated with exasperation.

"What care I for that? We want this fellow, Tyndale, in our own hands. We can only feel safe to know that he is in our care, and that, when the torture he deserves is over, we shall effectually silence him. Forever!" Cochlaeus added, almost aloud, in his virulent hate of the Englishman.

He dropped into silence when the Dean spoke sharply at his rashness in speaking for a hundred ears might catch any sound in the still night.

The portcullis rose when the drawbridge dropped, and the gate was already open. A moment's pause followed, before a word came from the captain of the guard, and the soldiers, springing from inertness into full attention, moved across the bridge with their prisoner. Before many moments had passed Tyndale had gone out of sight.

There was a hollow sound of tramping on stone inside, another command, and before the footsteps died away the gate was closed with a heavy clang, and the portcullis dropped.

Tyndale was shut up in the castle. But to what? Was it to death?

# THE FOREST RANGER

HERMAN stood in silence far on into the night. He watched the soldiers pass by continually on the grass slope, and saw as well a little army of retainers go down to the river to help in bringing up the goods that had been taken from the Marburg. He was eager to know whether among the booty brought up to the castle any of Tyndale's bales of printed sheets were there, for, if so, then all the toil of those past weeks had gone for nothing. The last load passed over the drawbridge, the portcullis dropped as the last man entered the gate, and then silence followed.

Herman had missed nothing, and he breathed with intense relief when he found that no such load had been carried into the robber's stronghold. On that count, indeed, Tyndale was not the loser.

But more important still was the fate of the prisoner.

Herman watched the castle walls as they stood there, grey and grim in the moonlight. The feeling grew upon him that Tyndale's position was a hopeless one, for this stronghold was impregnable, a death-trap from whence no prisoner could hope to escape. The towers and curtains bristled with gleaming lances and polished helmets of fighting men. What chance, then, was there for rescue or escape for anyone shut up in the stronghold of that robber noble who feared neither God nor man, who scouted all human laws, and laughed—so common rumor had it—at the bare suggestion of mercy?

Herman was puzzled to know what a man like Schouts meant to do with Tyndale, and why he had singled him out while all others on board the Marburg were allowed to go free. The Reformer's religion could have no weight with him, for he was known all the country round to scoff at anything religious, and heresy was no more obnoxious to him than the extremest orthodoxy. It was impossible that the master of the robber den had any care, or even any hate, for the Protestantism that was causing so much controversy in Europe.

Could it be possible that Schouts thought to hold Tyndale for ransom? He was too poor to find two or three hundred pieces of silver, leave alone as many golden crowns, before he would be allowed to go free. Herman knew how poor he was. If he told his story to the lord of the castle, it would be the same story he had told in Herman's home—that he was possessed of nothing, that his poverty was like the Savior's who had no home wherein at night to rest His tired head. The money on which he lived, and with which he paid for the printing of his Bible, was not his own. He was being supplied with it by some godly English merchants who, caring a great deal for the so-called "new learning," were placing the means within the scholar's reach, enabling him to live without want while he translated the Scriptures into the English tongue.

With money in some shape or form, as the one great want of this notorious bandit, Schouts would scorn the thought of counting William Tyndale a prize, who could at the most give him, when he surrendered all he had, a few gold pieces.

Herman sat on the trunk of a fallen pine tree, and burying his face in his hands, tried to think out this incomprehensible thing, that Schouts should think it worth his while to hold William Tyndale as a prisoner.

He was puzzling his brain over this when he heard some sounds behind him, as of someone moving about among the trees. A deadly fear swept through him, and he gripped the handle of his dagger. It might be some wild beast prowling, getting at the horse, perhaps, or coming for himself. Or it might be one of Schouts' men, who would run him through if he saw him, or raise a loud outcry, bringing soldiers out of the castle to carry him there as a prisoner.

He sat in silence, in statuesque stillness, scarce breathing. The darkness where he was, was dense; but he felt perturbed when he thought that the moon in the open would show him, silhouetted, as it were, to anyone behind him.

The sounds went on, always in stealth, and they drew so much nearer that he knew it was someone human, and not a prowling beast. Herman's impulse was to challenge the man, whoever he might be, but he thought it well to be silent and not betray his presence. After a while he knew from the sounds that the man was moving away towards the castle.

He breathed more freely at the thought, for the man had other things in his mind. Unexpectedly the stranger stepped a little into the open, where the moonlight cast his shadow on the grass, and an exclamation of amazement sprang from Herman's lips.

"Roye!" he said, in subdued tone, just loud enough for his voice to carry to the man who stood gazing at the castle.

Roye started at the unexpected call, and dropped back among the trees.

"Who is it?" he exclaimed, in a tone which betrayed his anxiety.

"Herman Bengel. I am here."

A moment later he had sprung from his seat and was trampling among the brushwood, the low hanging branches of the trees rustling as his body swept against them.

"Have you seen Master Tyndale?" Roye asked, the moment they met in the darkness, where they barely saw each other's form.

"Yes. He was taken into the castle. But why should the robber lord take him there, a prisoner, more than any other on board the Marburg? Yourself, for example?" Herman asked in a puzzled tone. He scarcely paused, for another thought had come.

"It could never be that the robber lord had some inkling that Master Tyndale was on board that ship and was thinking to carry him away to some safe place, just as was done once with Martin Luther, to hide him from his enemies."

It was a new idea. There was something like hopefulness in Herman's soul when he considered the possibility, but the hope was dashed at once when Roye spoke.

"Would God it were so. But this man, this bandit lord, I heard the sailors say, when they were speaking about him as we were beating up the river, has no fear of God in his heart. He scoffs as much at the Reformers as he does at the Catholics. The idea is to sell my master to the tormentors if they will pay the price."

"God forbid!" Herman cried, smitten with horror at the thought. "It cannot be!"

"Why not?" asked Roye. "Others have done it. The Inquisitors have bought the prisoners in these bandit castles by the score, paying big sums of money for them, to have the opportunity of dealing with them in the torture chambers of what they call their Holy Houses. Schouts must have heard that Master Tyndale is badly wanted, and he believes he has a prize."

They stood and talked in whispers. At odd times some creature slunk past them into the forest depths, out of their way; but nothing human came near them. Feeling oppressed with the hopelessness of the position, they turned back into the forest, Herman leading the way to the hollow where the horse was tethered. Their idea was to go back to the city and tell the story of this disaster.

After a while they felt the stress of hunger, and, seeing a light down one of the forest avenues, they went towards it and found a hut, from the window of which the light was streaming.

"Who goes there?" came the cry when Herman knocked loudly on the door; then someone passed the window, and Herman, seeing the face, knew him.

"'Tis Otto Engel!" he cried.

"What if it be?" was the man's half-menacing answer, for he heard the words. "I asked who was there, not who was I!"

"I am Herman Bengel."

"What?" was the incredulous response. "Out in the forest at this time o' night? What art doing here?"

"Knocking at Otto Engel's door, to ask if he will sell two hungry men some food."

The ranger laughed.

"That's good! To come to a friend to buy a meal!"

By this time the bolt was drawn and the bar dropped, and now the ranger filled up the open doorway, a giant, so he seemed, by contrast, even to those outside, who were both beyond the average size.

"Come in!" he cried, drawing back to make room for them to enter, and thus allowing the light to fall on the faces of his visitors.

"One is Herman Bengel. I know that much," he said, as they passed into the hut. "But who is the other?"

"I'll tell you when the door is shut," Herman said in a low tone. "It is not well to shout a man's name, nor even whisper it—not this man's, at all events, even in the depths of the forest."

"Ha! some criminal escaped from jail, and you think to bring him here for me to hide him?" the ranger said jestingly, to tease Herman.

"Just as you will. But can you lodge this horse?"

"Yes. Come this way," was the hearty answer. Laying a hand on the queer bridle, but saying nothing, he led the horse to the other side of the hut, where he placed him in a snug stable and gave the tired creature a plentiful supply of food and water.

Before long the two men were sitting to a meal which Engel set before them, so appetizing that in spite of their anxiety they ate with keen relish, the ranger plying them with food till they could eat no more.

"Now for this story—the reason why two men should be 'out in the forest at this time o' night," the ranger said, when he had cleared the table.

Herman gazed about him before he answered. He got up from his stool and walked round the hut, looking into the corners, and opening an inner door to assure himself that no others but themselves were there.

"Nobody's here, Herman," said Otto Engel, who was watching his movements, and guessed his purpose. "I live here all alone. I've neither wife nor child, more's the pity!" he added sadly. "Those creatures from the Holy House in your city came out here one day, and took my wife. And the little one pined away, and her mother never came back."

The big man paused in remembrance.

"What brings you here, Herman?" Engel asked, more quietly. His hand trembling hand rested on the table, and his face twitched with emotion.

"William Tyndale is the cause of our being here tonight," Herman said, returning to his stool again, satisfied now that he could speak as freely as he pleased.

"Tyndale?" cried Engel, his face full of surprise. "Do you mean the Englishman?"

"Yes. I'll tell you all about it, Engel."

Herman told the story from the day when he and Margaret met the tired traveler in the meadow, down to the capture of the Marburg a few hours before.

"Is that all?" Engel asked, having listened with parted lips.

"All? Isn't it enough?" exclaimed Herman.

Silence followed. Each man was busy with his thoughts—Herman and Roye wondering how far their dread concerning William Tyndale might become a certainty, and the prisoner should be handed over to the tormentors; Otto Engel ruminating on the memory that never left him, but wondering as well what he could do to set the man free who was daring so much for the world's uplifting.

Herman had not mentioned his and Roye's fears as to what Schouts would do with his prisoner, but Engel's own thoughts had travelled in that direction.

"My lord, in the robber's castle yonder, will make a pot o' money out of William Tyndale!" he ex-claimed, breaking the long silence, and jerking his thumb over his shoulder.

"How?" asked Herman, startled at the thought that their fears were likely to become a reality.

"How? This Cochlaeus will offer Schouts a big sum, and the two will haggle over terms. Perhaps they'll spend days in making offers and rejecting them; but I can see the end as plainly as I see this fist of mine. The Inquisitors will get William Tyndale into their toils, while Schouts will get his price. Don't I know?"

Silence followed again, save for the sounds of the sleeping dog on the hearth, who barked in his dreams, and the blazing and crackling of the pine-log fire.

"I will spoil their wicked game for them!" the ranger exclaimed presently, shifting his great feet and turning away to the fire, so that the blaze of it lit up his face, usually so ruddy, but now pale, yet full of determination.

"What do you mean?" the others cried in their surprise.

"What I said," came the answer almost curtly. "I'll spoil their wicked game for them."

"How?" cried Roye, coming to the ranger and laying a trembling hand on his shoulder. "In God's dear name, Otto Engel, tell us what you mean," he went on eagerly.

"I scarcely know."

The answer came in a tone which showed how greatly perturbed he was.

"I must have time to think. I must sleep on it, and then, please God, we will do something. Go and lie down yonder, both of you, for we'll want some quick brains to puzzle this thing out. It will take some thinking to frustrate a man like Cochlaeus, but we'll do it. We'll spoil their wicked game for them, and we'll defeat the robber lord somehow."

Engel waited to say no more. Blowing out the lamp, so that the only light inside the hut came from the flickering flames of the fire, he threw himself on the hearth after a brief and silent prayer; and as if he only had to will it, he went off into a heavy sleep. The others followed his example, lying on the bed of leaves in the corner, and before long all were asleep in the ranger's hut.

# A DARING DECISION

THE sun had been up for some time before any of the sleepers began to stir, and when Otto Engel stretched himself and yawned, and, doing so, awoke the others, he had no sense of shame for being a laggard with the day so far run on. It was his custom to sleep away so many of the hours of daylight, for he was very much of what he called himself—a night-bird, who must needs walk about his business while the world was sleeping. That night wandering was a part of his duty as ranger of the forest.

"I'll get you some breakfast," was his first word, when Herman sat up and stared around, wondering where he was; and before long the three men and the dog were eating what for two of them was a late morning meal.

"I think I'll find my way home," said Herman, who was depressed and ate but sparingly. Roye, too, sat playing absent-mindedly with his bread. "Nay, you must stay here today, if anything is to be done to help William Tyndale," the ranger cried, tossing down his knife and wiping his mouth with the back of his hand, while he shifted back his stool to cross his knee.

"How can we help Master Tyndale?" Roye asked gloomily.

"I'll tell you before the day is gone; but the thing wants a deal of consideration. If you care to stay, you are more than welcome, and, what is more to the point, your assistance will be valuable. Whatever I may decide, I won't be able to do anything single-handed. I know that much, so that William Tyndale's largely in your hands."

Herman watched the stalwart forester.

"What do you think is possible?" he asked.

"I don't know any more than the man in the moon, as people say. I shall have to think the thing out. My real idea is to get William Tyndale out of the hands of Schouts, if you must know, and defeat Cochlaeus as well. So now you know. Lie by, and don't show yourselves," he added.

By this time Engel was standing at the door, with the dog at his heels ready for duty with his master. "When I have thought this thing well through I will come back and talk it over with you. It may be a couple of hours. It may be a great deal more. But I'll come, and if you are here, so much the better. Burn it into your mind, Herman Bengel, and you, William Roye, that we are going to get Master Tyndale out of that devil's den."

He went out, pulling the door after him noisily, and walked down the foot-beaten track. He halted before he had gone many yards, and, returning, opened the door again.

"Help yourselves to food when you feel hungry," he said, standing in the entrance with his hand on the latch. "There's no need for stint, since the larder's full enough. I may be away some time, for, if you don't mind, I'll take that horse back, and set him adrift in the field where you found him. It would be awkward for me if they found him in my stable. Shall I do that?"

Herman nodded.

The forester had more to say.

"Put the bolts in the door to keep intruders out. I don't want any of my friends yonder to come and find you here." He jerked his thumb over his shoulder towards the castle. "They come sometimes for a chat, and so I get to know things. If any of them come, keep quiet, and don't open the door. They'll think I'm on my rounds."

He stalked away to the stable, and Herman, as soon as he saw him ride past the window on the borrowed horse, drove in the bolt.

The hours went slowly, and to those who were shut up in the forest hut, compelled to be idle, they seemed interminable. They talked over the possibilities at which Otto Engel had hinted so confidently, but in the slow passing of the hours they began to grow hopeless over Tyndale's affairs. They speculated as to what the forester might be able to do, but their own memory of the drawbridge and portcullis, and the armed men on the walls, drove them to the conclusion that his scheme was a wild and impossible one.

Again and again Herman went to the window, and looked out to the forest, hoping to see the forester, but there was no sign of his coming. He saw the giant trees rearing their proud heads to the sun, which at some spots found its way on the pathways and undergrowth. Some wild boars rushed by at odd intervals, and a dark-grey, grizzled lynx chased a poor creature among the branches, or dropped to the earth on an unsuspecting victim. It served to pass the time to watch from the window all that went on in the forest—the wolves that passed, or a bear that shambled along, but halted at an ant-hill to scrape out the nests and lap up the eggs.

But the all-absorbing matters were those two—the rescue of William Tyndale, and Margaret, who in less than a week was to be his wife. He shivered at the thought of her journey through the cavern, with its loneliness and those tokens of death from which she had shrunk even in his company. What must she have felt when she was moving in the cavern alone?

The hours went on—the longest he had ever spent. The morning passed. The sun changed his position, and cast long, slanting shadows, and presently the afternoon began to grow old. Then evening came, and the forester had not returned.

They began to be anxious for his safety, and fears of many sorts were talked about. Had he shot some wild creature, and in the brute's agony had he been mauled and torn? The anxiety became so great, when the shadows grew dense and night was falling, that Herman drew the bolt, intending to go out and search for the absent man; but Roye, as much distressed, but cautious, dissuaded him.

At last they heard the heavy stamp of feet on the path outside, and then the scratch of a dog's paws on the door. Herman's hand went to the bolt, but he waited for another sign, and when Engel spoke quietly and lifted the latch he opened the door.

"I put the horse back in the meadow!" the forester exclaimed, lowering himself stiffly on a stool, but he had barely done so when he straightened himself and went to the cupboard to get food for himself and the dog.

"Sit down," cried Herman. "I'll do that."

"I've got to the bottom of my scheme," said the tired man, glad to be seated. "I'll tell you all about it as soon as I find myself in front of food. But we'll see to the dog first," he added, the moment Herman set the meat on the table.

"I've found a way for getting William Tyndale out of that robber's den, so that we shall surprise both Schouts and Cochlaeus, and spoil their plans!" Otto Engel exclaimed, his mouth full. He was eating ravenously, for he and the dog had gone all the day without food. In his wanderings he had threshed out that difficult problem of deliverance. "I can see my way, and we'll have him out of it before I'm very much older," he added, when he had swallowed a draught of water and had given the dog another great helping.

"You can?" the others cried, startled by the forester's words, and impressed with his confidence.

"Yes, I can!" mumbled Engel, who seemed to grow hungrier as the moments sped.

"And what's your plan?" asked Roye, drawing his stool up to the table, where he leant forward and gazed at the ranger. "Is it sure?" he went on, laying his hand on the other's arm. "Or is it possible that you may fail and leave us to our disappointment, and my master to his death?"

His face was pale and his voice eager and tremulous, while his eyes gleamed as though they were not far from tears.

The ranger swallowed his mouthful, and then he answered as earnestly as Roye:

"Neither of you shall be disappointed, please God, if you choose to throw in your lot with me and make this venture. You will possibly say 'tis a desperate thing to do. You may even deem me mad. I know not what you may say or think when I tell you what I mean to do. God only knows what you may say about it—that it is like putting one's head into a noose if by any means the plan should fail."

Engel's meal was ended now, and, getting up from the table, he carried his stool with him and sat before the fire, and sprawled his crossed feet to catch the warmth of the burning logs.

"I suppose nine out of ten, not knowing what I know, would say it was a madman's venture, but I'll tell you exactly what is at the back of my mind, and you shall say 'yes' or 'no,' according to what you think when I have had my say."

The others pulled their stools to the fireside and listened; but while he unfolded his plan they thought he must be mad. Yet when they looked at his face they felt they were mistaken. He had evidently planned the whole thing out, basing this desperate scheme on his knowledge of the castle and not on mere supposition.

They shrank from the venture which the forester proposed, for there could be but one ending to it, without benefiting William Tyndale in the slightest degree. On the very face of it, it was doomed to failure, and it might end in death for them all.

"You are only telling us of the bare possibilities, Otto!" Herman exclaimed, when the ranger had ended. "You surely do not mean that we shall make such a wild attempt?"

The ranger swung round on his stool and faced Herman, but did not speak until he once more turned to gaze into the midst of the burning logs, leaning forward as though he saw pictures among them.

"I am telling you of something more than possibilities," he said presently. "I count what I propose as a certainty, and I mean to try my plan. I shall be glad to have you with me, but if you are afraid—and it's not to be wondered at if you are—I will do the thing alone; only the task will be so much the harder, and the risks will be greater because it will take so much longer time. God helping me, the man on whom so much depends shall be freed!"

Engel sprang to his feet, overturning the stool, and paced the floor, walking round by the wall and past the door and window like a caged beast, back and forth again, as though to walk off his excitement.

"I mean to try it!" he exclaimed. "I've been kneeling a lot today in the forest to pray about it, and I believe God has shown me the way. It would be woe to me if I did not do my best for the good man after that."

He was moving about restlessly, not pausing while he spoke.

"I can't imagine how you mean to get inside the castle," Herman said, incredulous. The scheme was such a preposterous one.

Engel went to a cupboard on the farther side of the room, and, feeling about in the darkness, he brought out a sheet of paper, which he smoothed out on the table.

"I'll get a light," he said, and when the candle was burning he spoke again. "You are both able to lay some claim to scholarship, I suppose; so you will understand this plan with a bit of explanation. It's a plan of Schouts' castle, but he doesn't know I've got it, or he might hang me over his gate."

He bent over the sheet when he had covered the window, so that none might look in from outside. Then, with his forefinger, while the others bent over, he opened out the scheme more fully. He showed them the point where he would go in, where he would go when he was once inside, and how he meant to get out with William Tyndale, and the others, with the plan so plainly before them, saw that the scheme was possible, provided there were no accidents to mar it.

But it was a desperate venture, to say the least, for three men to pit themselves against the robber lord, and expect to snatch their friend from the clutches of one who had scores of servitors, every one a trained fighting man who had no fear of God or man, and, like the Norse warriors who had in them the Berserker spirit, would go to the battle when the call came, and fight with frenzied and merciless fury. The bare suggestion was little less than madness.

After bending over the table so long, the forester straightened himself and gazed down at the crumpled sheet of paper which was resting on the table among the crumbs and broken bread which had not been swept away. Herman and Roye glanced up at him, and saw the resolute look on his face and the total absence of fear. The first to speak was Herman.

"Otto Engel."

"Well?"

"I shall go with you."

"So will I!" Roye exclaimed. His pale face showed that he did not speak lightly.

The ranger put out his hands and gripped those which were stretched out to him.

"I counted on you both," he said quietly.

"When shall we start?" Herman asked.

"Now."

Roye turned his back on the others and gazed into the fire, but a few moments later he swung round again.

"I said I would go, and so I will. But 'tis too great a venture without asking God's help before we start," he said, dropping on his knees at the table. The others did the same, and buried their faces in their hands while the elder man prayed concerning this dangerous enterprise, and asked that William Tyndale might have a safe deliverance.

"Now I can go in double strength," cried the ranger, still on his knees; and there was something exalted in his tone and a look on his face that is rare with men. "Please God, we'll have that dear man here before the dawn comes!"

He rose to his feet, and, looking to his weapons, bade the others do the same. Telling the dog to keep safe watch, however long they were away, giving him a big bone to wile away the hours and placing food within his reach in case the creature should grow hungry, he blew out the light, threw open the door, and walked into the night.

The moon was already showing her face in fitful gleams where the leafy canopy of the forest was broken here and there; but even thus it seemed dark at first. They moved in stealth, not knowing who might be abroad. Once they saw a pair of shining eyes in the thicket, but at a sharp word from the ranger and a menacing movement on his part, the beast moved off, snarling, yet frightened, for three men were too many to meet in fight.

"'Twas a wolf, and he's a desperate coward when you get him in a corner," Engel said carelessly.

The slow going in the forest took more than half an hour of their time, but at last they reached the open, where the green slope swept, up which William Tyndale had been taken, as a prisoner.

All was silent now, and the moonlit sweep of grass had neither man nor beast on it.

Away to the left were the silver-shining waters of the river, but it was clear. No craft moved up or down, and nothing tempted the bandit lord from his warm banquet-hall. Presently, however, Herman and his companions caught the glint of steel, and then they saw a soldier come from behind a bush and pace the bank, doubtless on the lookout for any vessel that gave promise of plunder.

"Were it not for the trouble that would come, I would go on my knees here and pray that some craft might pass which would bring Schouts and his cut-throat soldiers out tonight," the ranger muttered. "'Twould go some way towards lessening our own danger."

"Many a poor man would lose his life tonight if we prayed like that," said Roye seriously.

"Yes. That's the worst part of it. One benefits so often at the price of another's irremediable loss," came the ranger's grave response. "Ah, well! We'll take it as God sends it!"

He led the way along the edge of the ascending slope, but well within the shadows of the trees.

The castle stood on the brow of the hill, and those who were on this desperate errand saw the massive towers and wondered how an enemy could hope to scale the walls and capture the place. Standing for a while, since there was ample time, Engel told his companions what the castle was like inside, so that they might not be altogether unprepared for what they would see during their venture.

"You pass the gateway which those two towers defend. Then you are in the first or lower ward, which is defended by as many as eight strong towers, and separated from the second ward by another gateway with a portcullis.

"In the second ward is a dungeon tower and a prison chapel, but William Tyndale is not in that part of the castle. I found out so much when I was abroad today. You go out of the second ward by a long flight of steps to the third and fourth wards, which are surrounded by a steep rampart and a wall, I know not how many feet thick, nor how many high. Then you come to the very heart of things. There is the King's Tower, where Schouts is lodged. There's the Queen's Tower, where his lady has her quarters. The kitchen and the chapel and other places are near. Well, it's in the King's Tower we have to go, for Master Tyndale is lodged there, and because I have a friend in court, I know just where."

The ranger stopped talking abruptly. They were approaching a broad and open path which ran through the forest, and they caught the sound of men's voices.

Standing back where none could see them, they waited, wondering at the meaning of these unexpected sounds. A minute or two later the lights of lanterns appeared on their right in a dense part of the forest. These came nearer and nearer, and not only were there the sounds of men's voices, but of horses' hoofs, their snortings, and the jingle of their trappings.

Before long a dozen horsemen moved past those who were standing in the shelter of the bushes—two men, fully armed, going first, their drawn swords glancing as they rode out to the grassy slope. Then two others at whose sides swords hung in their scabbards, and behind them a number of well-armed men.

None of the watchers could tell who they were, for the heavy foliage hid their faces; but when the cavalcade swept round towards the castle, Herman gripped Roye's arm.

"Do you know who they are?" he whispered eagerly.

"Ay, I know," Roye muttered. "One is Captain Berndorff of the City Guard, and the man riding at his side is Cochlaeus!"

# WITHIN THE CASTLE

THE cavalcade halted at the drawbridge, and a horseman sounded a trumpet which brought a soldier to one of the towers over the gate.

The watchers had gone forward among the trees, keeping pace with the horses, and now saw and heard all that passed. The soldier demanded their business, and the response came from Cochlaeus.

"Tell my lord of Schouts that the Deacon of the Church of the Blessed Virgin wishes to confer with him on a matter of the first importance. Say that I have ridden out from the city for that purpose."

"Bad hours for a Churchman to keep," the soldier remarked insolently, and laughing. He waited, to know whether Cochlaeus had more to say, but, when he found that no answer came, he turned away. More than a quarter of an hour passed, and then the gate opened slowly, the portcullis was raised, and the drawbridge dropped over the moat noisily.

"My lord says that the Deacon of the Church of the Blessed Virgin may enter," said the warden surlily.

Berndorff, hearing what the soldier said, gave an order, and the horsemen moved forward. Already the feet of the first two horses were on the bridge, but the soldier caught at the bridles.

"Nay!" he cried. "I told you that my lord said that the Deacon might enter. I ought to have said, and no other! All else must stay outside and cool their toes, or ride away, just as they please. But as for going in, no!" the soldier exclaimed roughly.

"An insolent varlet!" cried Cochlaeus, riding forward. "Is that how you speak to a dignitary of the Church?" he asked angrily.

"I speak as my master bids me, and, whether it be insolent or not, I stand by my orders," was the sharp retort. "These must wait until your business is done and you come forth again."

Cochlaeus was irresolute. In his own mind there was the fear that he might be detained by the bandit lord, and held for heavy ransom, since it was known that the treasure coffer of the Church of the Blessed Virgin was a full one. Schouts was known among the Churchmen to care nothing for the maledictions of the Church; and while he may have thought seriously of armed men standing at his gate in considerable numbers, he had no fear from such as were in the community to which Cochlaeus belonged.

"'Tis an insult," he cried angrily.

"That's for my lord to say, not for me," the soldier answered, with indifference.

"'Tis inhospitable as well," the Inquisitor ex-claimed, "not to allow my attendants shelter at such an hour, but they must stay outside!"

"Where lies the lack of hospitality?" came the curt rejoinder. "You come hither at your own suggestion, and not as my master's guest. Would you suppose that he would suffer any to enter his stronghold who chose to pass this way? He can surely say whom he will see, and refuse if he cares?"

The soldiers behind Cochlaeus sat grimly in their saddles, but they understood. Schouts was not likely to admit any armed men who might prove awkward if once they got across the bridge and held the gate, keeping it wide open for hundreds to come who might be lurking in the forest for surprise. And as for Cochlaeus, were it not for their own honor as soldiers in the service of the Burgomaster of the city, they would have been well content to see this heretic hunter lying stark and still on this same bridge to which he had come to parley with the robber lord.

"What must I do?" Cochlaeus cried angrily, irritated by this undisguised insolence. It was an intrusion on his dignity which he would not have brooked elsewhere. But here was a lawless lord's stronghold, and the master of it was known up and down the river as one who was a law unto himself, and dictated terms, especially within his own domain.

"What must you do?" the warden responded in surprise at the question. "Come in alone, or go away again, just as you may please. I have my lord's orders, and I won't go from them. Nor dare I. None of these soldiers, therefore, may enter. My lord will have none of them inside of his castle. He said so when I took your message to him."

The soldiers on the drawbridge moved their horses back, and stood with the others, while Cochlaeus, going forward in an ill-humor, rode in at the dark gateway. Then his temper gave place to fear, for it dawned upon him that he was placing himself in the power of a man who might retort on the Church to which he was an inveterate enemy, and hold this heretic hunter for ransom. His face paled, and his hand trembled on the rein when the drawbridge began to rise and the portcullis rushed down, the sound of the loud rattle of chains coming as a reminder of the helplessness of his position, and how completely he was in the power of the bandit lord.

"Caught like a rat in a trap, I'll be bound," muttered Otto Engel, who, like his companions, was watching all that passed, and trying to gauge how far this night visit of Cochlaeus was likely to affect the prisoner in the castle. "Ay, like a rat in a trap! God grant he may never come out alive!" he said, when the gates clanged together. "But come, friends. Let us be on the move, lest that Inquisitor has come to buy William Tyndale, and will pay Schouts' price. Then there is no saving the poor man."

The ranger moved away at a run, winding in and out among the bushes, leaping over little runlets and brushing through thick undergrowth; but his comrades kept pace with him, so that when he halted under a gnarled oak, whose great branches hung so heavily that he had to stoop to pass beneath them, the others were but a little way behind.

"Is this the place?" Herman asked, bending low to look for Engel, who was completely hidden.

"Yes. We'll waste no time now we are here," said the ranger. "Stand there awhile and get your breath," he said to Roye, who was panting with his run. "I will go first, and what I do you must copy."

Getting a foothold on the trunk of the tree, he climbed among the foliage and disappeared. Herman could hear him mounting, the rustle of the branches telling how he was moving.

"Art coming?" Engel asked presently, in a tone which warned the others to be cautious.

"I'm coming," Herman whispered back, but he turned to Roye. "You had better go next, then I shall know that you are safe. I am used to climbing trees, but possibly you are not."

"'Tis true," said the elder man, but he followed Engel, and before long word came in the darkness that he was safe.

When Herman stood with the others in the great fork, which formed a natural platform, the ranger dropped on his knees, and felt about in the darkness with his hand.

When he had found what he wanted, he began to descend into the body of the tree, the trunk proving to be hollow. The others could hear the sound of his feet, as though he stepped on iron. The fancy became reality when Engel produced a light, and while he held a lantern in his hand, they saw him below, waiting for them to follow.

"Put your feet on those irons, and hold tight with your hands, or you may get a nasty fall," he whispered, pointing to some iron loops which had been driven into the inside of the tree, forming what was equivalent to a ladder. Herman descended, feeling with his feet for footing as he went, Roye following closely.

Looking around them curiously when they stood in a group, they saw all manner of insects crawling about, startled by the light and this unwonted invasion of their domain. Many of them left shiny tracks behind them, while some insects, attracted by the lantern, flew against its horny sides.

It was an unpleasant sight, but they had other business on hand, and they went about it with that quick glance at their surroundings.

Handing the lantern to Herman, the ranger bent down and prodded the floor with his hunting knife. At every prod there was an answering metallic sound.

"That's iron," said Herman, who was watching eagerly.

"Yes. Don't you remember what the plan showed you?" Engel replied. "Ha! This seems to be what I want."

He had driven his knife into a crevice, and, scraping the earth away, as he moved along, with the point, he marked out a square space. Driving in the point of the tempered steel, he raised an iron plate which worked on hinges, and, getting his hands to it when it had come a little way, he threw it back against the tree's side, and looked into a hole, the bottom of which was lost in blackness.

Here, again, were iron clamps by which Engel descended carefully, for some distance, until his foot touched solid ground. Herman followed and found himself in a cavernous space.

Gazing around, they found that it was what they expected according to the plan. Here was a great chamber, low-roofed, and narrowing down on one side to a passage whose walls gleamed in the light of the lantern.

The walls were veined in all directions, and the yellow color suggested gold; but this was no time for close examination. The matter in hand was the finding of William Tyndale, to wrest him from Schouts' harsh keeping before he had time to sell him into the hands of those for whom Cochlaeus was acting.

"Yonder is the passage," said the ranger, walking the next moment across the floor with the others so close at his heels that, when he halted unexpectedly, they bundled against him.

For some distance the passage ran level, narrowing down occasionally, so that Engel had to turn his burly form sideways and squeeze himself through; but after a time the floor sloped downwards, and so steeply at some points that the footing was treacherous. It was made more so by the moisture which oozed through the rocky ceiling and trickled down the walls to the ground on which they trod.

"We are under the moat," whispered the ranger, who stumbled while he carelessly turned to speak, and barely saved himself from a heavy fall.

Having passed this slimy, moss-covered floor, they found themselves on an ascending path, and there they paused; for at this point the real danger of their daring venture began.

"We are inside the castle," whispered Engel. "What say you? Shall we all go forward, or will you both stay here while I go forward to see how the land lies?"

"Let us go on farther," Herman proposed. "We ought not to be so far separated if one of us should choose to stand back. As far as I remember the plan we have fifty yards or more to go before we reach the corridor. There is, moreover, a door at the end of the passage, if the plan is true."

"It's true enough, so far," said Engel, "and why not be correct all the way through? I've heard my father say so, and he knew, for he had tried it more than once."

The ranger was moving forward while he spoke, throwing light on the treacherous path with the lantern.

For more than fifty yards they went their way, touching the slimy walls at times, and treading on softness they would have shuddered at, but for this matter on their minds, and of such supreme importance.

Suddenly they came to a full stop, for a wall was in front of them, to all appearance solid rock, and impassable. But instead of dismay there was a stifled sound of satisfaction. It was what the plan had marked.

Herman began to look about this rocky face, smoothing his hand over it lightly, but for a time he failed to find what he was searching for. Then he exclaimed in a tone of satisfaction, just as the fear was coming that they had been misled:

"I have it!"

He felt a tiny knob of rock, and, pressing on it, the wall began to move away slowly and heavily, but without a sound. The moment he took his hand away, the rocky door stood still, leaving a crevice sufficiently wide for them to peep through.

Hiding the lantern's light so that it should not betray them, they saw a long passage, three or four feet wide, but almost in darkness. The only light it contained was that of a smoking lamp hanging on the wall far down the corridor.

"Shall we venture?" asked the ranger.

"What use was it to come so far, and not go farther?" Roye asked almost testily. "We have to get my master out of this."

While he spoke he put out his hand and pressed the door farther open. Then, brushing past the others, he stood in the passage. Engel and Herman followed. Thrusting the door back into its place, careful not to send it too far, for the latch to catch, they looked at it in such dim light as there was, and saw that it fitted into the roughly built wall so well that none would suspect the presence of a door when thrust back completely. It was clear to them that it was a secret entrance and exit, the existence of which had probably been forgotten.

"Now for the next thing," said the ranger, glancing up and down the passage anxiously. "Put your minds on that plan in my home, and you will remember we had to take the first turning to the left. It comes half-way between us here and that light yonder."

He led the way, going softly and cautiously, ready for advance or retreat, as things might chance. Ere many yards had been traversed they came to an opening on the left, and it led up some winding steps, past doorways from none of which came any sound or sign of life or light on the other sides. The stairway opened on a long corridor, broad and pretentious. Some of the doorways had heavy curtains hanging over them, and one into which they peered, since the door was wide open, showed the great banqueting hall, with tapestries on the walls, casques and bucklers, antlers, and many other relics of the chase in the forest. Across the hall at the upper end ranged the high table at which the lord of the castle sat, and the other tables ran down by the walls, leaving the central space clear.

To linger was dangerous, and yet the nearer way to Tyndale's cell lay through the hall.

"I'll not venture," Engel muttered, listening intently for any sound of approaching voices or footsteps, and realizing, like the others, that in this escapade they were almost challenging death. "We'll go round, for who can tell what men may come into the place when we are half-way across the floor of that hall? We should never get to yonder door, nor any other door, except a dungeon one."

He turned away, hugging the wall as he went, and always keeping an eye on the hanging curtains at the doors. His idea was that, if someone came into the passage, he and his comrades in this deadly venture might get into hiding until the danger had passed.

Every sound thrilled them, for the peril was so great. And yet they moved onwards, bent on getting Tyndale away, if it were possible. After a time they came to a corner, and glanced along another corridor shut off with heavy hangings.

Should they venture? There was no hiding place nearer than a doorway a dozen yards farther on. And here Engel knew his way thoroughly, for, being hail-fellow-well-met with many of the retainers, he had often been there, and was always welcome. He knew that if he could pass that door in safety he had but one more to go beyond, and he would be at the steps which descended to the place where, so Sprenkel had told him when they met in the forest in the afternoon, the prisoner had been placed.

The danger centered at that door, and Engel half wished he had come alone, so that his movements should not be hampered. One could move where three would find it impossible and dangerous.

"Roye," he whispered, while they were hidden in the curtain, "one can move freely, and perhaps two; but three are too many.  It adds so greatly to the fear of discovery. What say you to going back to the secret door and staying in the passage, keeping everything in readiness when we bring William Tyndale with us?"

"Is there likely to be any fighting? for, if so, I can do my share," said Roye readily.

"There will be no fighting. It's a matter of stealth, and three are too many. One may blunder and spoil everything. We shall all be waiting for each other."

"I'll go back, but not willingly," came the reluctant response. "I wanted greatly to be one of those to go to my master, but I see the difficulty."

Roye turned on his heel.

"Can you find the way?" Engel whispered; and Roye, answering quickly, went back softly. They watched him until he disappeared at the steps.

"He's brave enough," the ranger said sincerely, "and I like the man's spirit. There's no doubt as to the love he has for his master, and he's sore at heart at turning back. But three are too many."

Engel and Herman made a hurried progress down the dimly lit corridor, making for one of the doors, but they hid themselves among some curtains almost in panic, for a page-boy came into view at one of the corners, whistling gaily as he walked along carelessly. He passed on, unsuspecting, not even looking at the heavy curtains.

As for those in hiding, they almost forgot the boy in the intensity of their surprise at what they saw. From among the folds in which they stood, they looked into a gorgeous chamber, and at the table, in the center, so seated that the flaming logs upon the hearth lit up their faces, making the lights of the candles dim with the red glow, were two men.

One was Schouts, the robber lord. The other was Cochlaeus. Both had wine goblets by their hand and were talking seriously.

# THE MAN IN THE DUNGEON

"WHAT will you give me, Deacon, if I hand you over this prisoner of mine, whose name, you say, is William Tyndale?"

Schouts lifted the silver flagon while he spoke, and filled his goblet.

"Two hundred and fifty golden crowns, my lord—the price that is set on that fellow's head," Cochlaeus answered.

"What!" cried Schouts, in sharp surprise, with the goblet halfway to his lips. "You would make a crafty bargain with me, and pay me as much as you would pay one of my retainers if they chanced to find this lean-faced Englishman?"

Schouts laughed scornfully, and instead of drinking he brought down the goblet heavily to the table, spilling the wine on his hand.

"'Tis a big sum, my lord. Two hundred and fifty golden crowns."

"It may be, Deacon, but I should get as much from this fellow's friends in Hamburg, for since I got hold of him I am told that some English merchants there have some regard for him, and are finding him money for this enterprise of his, this writing of pestilent papers. I shall go to them, perhaps tomorrow—perhaps tonight—and tell them how anxious the Churchmen are to burn their friend, but they only value him for fuel to an Inquisition fire at two hundred and fifty crowns. They will give me five hundred without a word, I'll warrant you, and think they got this Tyndale cheaply. But I'll not take five hundred from them, nor from you. The price for that Englishman in my dungeon is a thousand crowns, down here on this table, if you are the purchaser. Then you may torture him to your heart's content, or burn him, just as you are disposed."

"A thousand crowns!" cried Cochlaeus, gazing at the robber lord in blank amazement, and in his movement of surprise unwittingly overturning the wine goblet near his hand. "Who would give you such a preposterous sum? No one!"

He brought his clenched fist heavily on the table while he spoke.

Schouts laughed, then drank off his wine, draining his goblet and filling it again before he answered.

"I said a thousand crowns, and golden ones. And if nobody will give me that much, no one has him but myself, and I shall keep him. He won't cost much for his food, and I shall get a bit of satisfaction out of it all. I shall know, for instance, that you and your torturing crew in those Holy House cellars where you keep your racks and your thumbscrews are consumed with anger because you cannot work your will on that man you want so badly, and won't buy at my price."

Schouts sipped at his wine two or three times, staring at Cochlaeus, half amused at the look on the Churchman's face.

"I shall keep him for a time, and he may bring me in a good sum before I have done with him. His friends may go beyond the thousand when they know where he is."

"I can't believe it!" exclaimed Cochlaeus, in a tone of incredulity.

"Can you not?" cried Schouts. "Look you, Deacon Cochlaeus! If this man goes out of my hands, whether to his friends or to his foes, he will not go until I see a thousand crowns of gold on this table. Now you have my answer. I won't take nine hundred and ninety-nine. It shall be a thousand; and when you have brought me that many you may do as you please with him, for then he is yours, body and soul."

The robber had stood up, and, pushing back his chair, so that it fell to the floor with a noisy clatter, he went to the hearth, and, having kicked the logs together with his boot, stood with his back to the fire and looked to see how this emissary of the Inquisition received his ultimatum.

"Say seven hundred and fifty, my lord," ex-claimed Cochlaeus, now standing. "A thousand crowns is such an enormous sum for a penniless man."

"'Tis William Tyndale's price, whether he is penniless or rolls in wealth," came the dogged answer. "And, as I said, I won't take a golden crown less, not even nine hundred and ninety-nine."

Cochlaeus paced the floor to and fro, his feet treading on some magnificent carpets which must have come from Turkish looms. He had no thought for all the luxury that was round him—the spoils of many a piracy. His thoughts were on the man for whose purchase he was bargaining, whom he longed to see crouching in one of the dungeons of the Inquisition, presently to be bound on the wheel and broken, or put to some other torture, and, if he had his own way, burnt in the open market-place of the city which he had dared to pollute with his shameless sheets!

But the price! This robber lord had the audacity to ask a thousand golden crowns, and as he had already protested, the sum was preposterous. Yet, before he came away to hunt down the arch-heretic, who was dealing such deadly blows at Mother Church, and spreading far and wide his pestiferous books, his fellow-Inquisitors had told him that a thousand, or even two thousand, golden crowns would not be too much if it would bring Tyndale into their power. They would be able to silence him forever, and he would not then seduce the people to heresy.

Schouts stood with his back to the blazing logs, and watched the Churchman with a sinister look on his face, as he moved backwards and forwards, debating this question of payment to the bandit lord. As for the lord of the castle, he was smiling to himself, although his face was stern, to think that he was wringing out a thousand golden crowns from a Church for which, in his godless way, he had the most profound contempt.

"Well, Deacon, what decision?" he asked abruptly, when Cochlaeus seemed no nearer to it.

"I cannot decide," the Churchman protested. "The terms are so exorbitant. Who ever heard of such a sum—a thousand crowns—for one of Tyndale's stamp?"

Schouts laughed.

"I've more to add, and that, too, may prove preposterous!" he exclaimed. "I forgot, when I fixed the price for my prisoner, that I must have a full pardon for every sin of which I stand convicted—my robberies, what you and many another call my murders, my wanton insults—to quote you again—to some of the Church's high dignitaries—for everything that you and yours may count a sin! That and the thousand crowns! So now decide, and quickly, for I want to be gone."

He was going to say more, but there were quick steps on the stones of the corridor, and then a man came in without ceremony, and, breathless with haste, strode to where Schouts was standing.

"My lord," he cried, not heeding the Churchman, who had paused in his restless walk to hear what Schouts had to say, "there is a ship coming round the bend. She is the same you bade me keep a sharp look out for."

The man held his hands to his sides, and sought to regain his squandered breath, but Schouts, filling his goblet with wine, gave it to the soldier, told him to drink, and follow him quickly.

"I will talk with you later, Deacon Cochlaeus," Schouts exclaimed, facing his visitor; "but I must see to this business at once. But bethink you of what I said. A thousand crowns and absolution, or nothing." He halted at the door, and the confusion on the face of the Churchman so amused him that he burst into loud laughter. "By the way, twelve hours hence my price will he raised. Maybe I'll ask for fifteen hundred crowns."

He pulled the door after him, and walked swiftly along the corridor, looking to his weapons as he went.

The great bell of the castle clanged a few moments later. The sound of it travelled to the building's farthest depths, and away beyond the walls, into the forest itself, for, as Otto Engel whispered, he had often heard it in his hut, and knew that there was murder afoot.

Those who hid behind the curtain heard the tramp of men, and before long they came by in haste. They were taking the shortest cuts to be in time to form up and receive the commands from their lord, who was bawling out his orders in the courtyard. Some, to save time, rushed through the room in which Cochlaeus stood—in at one door and out at that where Herman and the forester were hiding. They were buckling on their swords as they went, and, careless of the Churchman's dignity, brushed past him, almost overturning him in their haste. Cochlaeus' jaw dropped when the last to pass through the chamber was a priest, who did not look his way, but hurried on with noisy cries and oaths and drunken laughter.

147

Before long the clatter of men's feet was heard outside, and a horse's hoofs beat on the stones, then thundered on the drawbridge when it was lowered. Herman and his companion knew what it meant, for the robber lord and his retainers were on the way to another daring act of piracy.

"God be praised!" exclaimed Engel, in a low tone. "'Tis our opportunity. Our prayers are going to be answered," he whispered, but even then the voice thrilled with exultation.

Gripping Herman by the arm, he drew him from the curtains, and hurried with him down the passage they had traversed before, to the open door of the banqueting hall. There they paused to look in cautiously, to discover whether it was empty. No one was there, and, taking the risks, they went through it at a run and out by the door at the other end.

When they passed the kitchens they, too, were empty. Not a sound was heard, save what was distant, for the bell was no longer clanging, and every man within the castle, throwing aside his task, whatever its nature, was gone, either to take his stand on guard at the drawbridge or above the gate, or to descend the slope to the river, to deal with the doomed vessel that had been daring enough to venture past in the dark night hours. She was going to pay the price of her mad audacity, and the robber lord was there to extort it to the last penny.

Going along the deserted corridor, Herman and the ranger came to some steps, down which they went swiftly after Engel had snatched at one of the few lamps that were hanging on the wall. The steps were black as night, but with the lamp's aid now they went down and down, until they came to a sudden stop at a blank wall. But here they saw that on the left were other steps, breaking off at right angles, and descending they came to a door studded with nails and sheeted with iron, crossed with bolts and bars.

"'Tis here," whispered Engel. "And here's the key, just as Sprenkel said."

A great key hung on a nail near by the door, and the ranger, taking it down, thrust it into the lock. When he twisted it, the bolt went back with a scream which seemed dangerously loud in the quietness of the castle depths. Herman, meanwhile, was busy, for they both knew well how precious the moments were, and what they were to do they must do quickly. He pulled back the bolts and dropped the bars, and, thus free to move, the door was thrust open into darkness.

"Are you there, Master Tyndale?" Herman whispered, stepping down into the dungeon.

"I am here. Who are you?"

The question came in tremulous tones, which gave the two strong men at the door the impression that the voice was that of a weakened man.

"'Tis Herman and a friend. Come at once. We want to get you away from this robber's castle, and the moments are precious."

Engel stood with the lamp lifted high, to see where the prisoner lay in this dank dungeon. The uneven floor was full of pools, and the walls ran with moisture, while, in the momentary silence, before any more was said, a drop of water fell with a musical note into one of the pools, and made the broken surface shimmer in the lamplight. Herman's eyes were quick to see the misery of the place. There were crawling creatures on the floor and the walls, and dull green moss coated the floor.

That, at first, was all he saw; but presently he saw William Tyndale kneeling on a spread of damp straw in a corner behind the door.

He was looking their way, uncertain as to those who had come to this fetid cell; half wondering whether it was

149

reality, or that he was dreaming that he had really heard Herman's voice. Herman caught the gleam in his eyes from the lamp's light, and went forward. And still it seemed to the prisoner such an incredible thing, till Herman was really near him, scuffling his feet among the straw, and flinging a strong arm about his shoulder, kissing the cold cheek, and telling him that he and his comrade had been searching for him, meaning to get him away.

Tyndale put out his manacled hands to grasp those of the young man who had been tender and loving as a son for the past months.

"'Tis wonderful!" the prisoner exclaimed, trying to rise from his kneeling posture. "You might almost have heard the words of my prayer when you came to the door. Out of the depths have I cried unto Thee, O Lord. Bring my soul out of prison, that I may praise Thy name. And think of it! The Lord heard my supplication, and made haste to help me!"

Herman bent down, and, throwing his strong arms about the kneeling prisoner, lifted him to his feet; but Tyndale could not stand without the young man's aid.

"I am very weak," Tyndale said, in a trembling tone. "Since I left your home I have not touched a morsel of food, and none has been brought to me."

For the first time they heard the clank of chains, and when Engel lowered the lamp he saw that Tyndale's feet were in irons.

"The cowardly hounds!" he exclaimed.

"God do so to me, and more also--"

But Tyndale checked him.

"Say it not, friend. God can best requite what has been done to me. But can we not go away, since, as you said, the moments are very precious? I should feel the stroke of my misfortune in double measure if you met with trouble in your desire to help me."

The forester looked carefully at Tyndale, at his hands and feet, and then, to his confusion, saw that there was a chain about his body which fastened the prisoner to the wall, so that at the farthest he could not get more than a yard or two across the floor.

"Herman, hold this lamp!" he cried. Then, passing closer to the wall, his lips shut tightly in his frenzy of determination, he gripped the chain with his strong hands and strove to wrench away the iron ring at the wall.

It was a task beyond his power, and Herman, understanding his purpose, set the lamp down on the floor and went to his side, to grip the chain as well. Then, with their strength combined, they tugged and tugged at what seemed a hopeless task. They pulled and strained, planting their feet against the wall, until the veins in their fore-heads seemed to stand out like whipcord.

"It's coming!" said Engel exultantly. "See! The iron is moving in the wall. Again! With all your might, Herman! We won't be done!"

The pull was the supreme effort of their strength, and the iron ring broke open, and the chain was set free, so suddenly that the two men fell backwards heavily on the floor among the pools.

Scrambling to their feet, scarcely waiting to rub their bruises, they went forward to where Tyndale sat in his weakness.

"Take up the lamp, Herman," said the forester, "and show the way. Tell me where the risky places are, so that I take no false step at all."

Herman asked no questions, and Engel, bending low, took Tyndale up in his strong arms as a woman might take a child. Making light of his burden, he followed at the younger man's heels, and, although the steps were treacherous with slime, he almost pressed Herman forward. For the younger

151

man was going cautiously, not knowing what danger might suddenly confront them.

The castle seemed to be silent, and no sound was heard save that of their own hurried footsteps in the passage and the faint and occasional clinking of Tyndale's fetters.

"Make for the secret passage," Engel whispered, panting a little with his burden after having climbed the treacherous steps so quickly. "Go ahead, and see whether the way is clear. Put the lantern down, anywhere, for if anyone saw a moving light it would awaken suspicion, and we don't want to run the risk of being challenged. If you hear any sound, stand by and see if it means danger."

Herman blew out the light, and, setting the lantern on the floor in a dark place, he went forward at a run, on his toes, alert and urgent; but no one crossed his path. When he peeped into the banqueting hall it was empty. For any sound or sight in that dangerous venture the great castle might have been deserted by everything living except himself and his companions. It was so wherever he went, and at last he came to the door in the wall.

Roye had drawn it after him, just as closely as he found it, to prevent suspicion in the mind of a possible passer-by and Herman stood by, without opening it, waiting for Otto Engel to come up with his burden. He turned the corner sooner than Herman expected, but in the dim light it was easy to see that the load he carried was growing heavy, as much almost with nervous strain as with the actual weight; for this daring enterprise was so beset with danger that the forester had lived what seemed to be hours of anxious thought in those brief minutes which passed between the dungeon and the secret door.

He knew that if they were seen by any of the castle soldiers or servitors, and caught red-handed, as it were, and with a helpless man in chains, he and Herman would scarcely escape overwhelming odds. What, he asked himself, as he carried William Tyndale, worn down with weakness and privation, and feeling him growing heavier with every yard he covered—what if one of the page-boys or some of the women should be moving about and, seeing them, run away, screaming out an alarm! Only God could tell the consequences, and it might well end in death for each of the three.

The forester was within three or four yards of the place where Herman was awaiting him, when he caught the gleam of steel in the younger man's hand, and saw by the light of one of the lamps on the wall that he was bending forward and gazing along the passage. He went even more softly than before, and with his intensely quickened hearing he heard the sound of someone singing—a boyish voice shouting out the robber's song.

Although he had been feeling overborne with his burden, and the sweatdrops were on his brow, the forester hurried forward. He might have had no burden in his arms at all, so swiftly did he bound over those last few yards.

"Open the door!" he exclaimed, reckless now; for if he could pass through the doorway with his burden and the door could be pulled into its place again, he thought their safety was assured.

It was not necessary to say, for Herman dug his finger nails into what little edge there was, and pulled the door open, so that he looked into the dark, forbidding gap. Dark though it was, the forester did not hesitate, but hurried in.

Waiting for the moment when he could follow, Herman kept his gaze fixed on the distant end where there was a possible corner which the boy would turn at any moment. The passage was still empty, although the sound of stamping feet grew plainer, rattling to the rhythm of the song. The relief was intense, to know that William Tyndale was carried into the secret way without being seen. It was now his own turn to enter and it must be at once.

He stepped into the blackness, careful as to where he placed his feet, and began to draw the door after him. At that moment Roye came near to him with his lantern, and in the swift glance he took along the passage, Herman saw that a sharp line of light from the lantern fell across the floor of the passage, and on the opposite wall. At that same moment the boy turned the corner and came into view. He must have seen the line of light, for he halted suddenly, and the song gave place to an exclamation of wonder and half of alarm. In his own keen thought Herman pictured the boy gazing along the passage with startled eyes; but he did not wait to see what happened. The opening in the wall closed up with a soft thud, and as he looked, Herman saw that the latch had caught, and the entrance was securely blocked.

How much had the boy seen? Herman asked himself, wiping the dampness from his forehead, for this narrow escape had startled him. Surely, only the flash of the line of light, for he had entered so speedily, urged on by the dread of discovery.

"Where are the others, Roye?" he asked, only seeing him, as he turned his back on the door.

"We're all right," said Engel, and Herman saw him close by in the passage, and, having set his burden gently on the floor, he was wiping his face and neck with his cap. "Did anyone see you?"

"No. The boy swung round the corner into the passage, a long way off, but he could not have seen more than the flash of this lantern across the floor just as I had stepped in and was pulling the door into its place."

Herman said it bravely, but this experience had tried him greatly, and now he stood with his back against the wall, in something like helplessness, and his knees were trembling, while he felt his lips quivering.

They turned their attention to Tyndale, and going on their knees beside him they sought to discover how much he was in need of help, and what likelihood there was of getting him away. The man for whom they had dared so greatly sat on the rocky floor, fettered heavily, his back set against the wall of rock, and his head bowed so that his chin rested on his bosom. But his thin hand was lifted to take theirs, while he thanked them for their splendid service.

Herman held him by the hand, while all three watched him anxiously. In that uncertain light he looked to them like a dying man, and he seemed to guess their thoughts.

"I am very weak and ill, Herman," he said quietly; "but you came in time. I shall not die, but live, for God has brought me out of the depths to give me the opportunity to complete His work."

Weak though he was, on life's borderland, as it seemed to his companions, there was a thrill of exultation in his voice. He spoke as one would speak who had unshaken confidence in the success of his mission.

Still watching him, they felt that his condition was serious. They saw in him a man capable of high and prolonged endurance, but the strain of the past few months, when he was compelled to remain in the house in hiding, and especially during these last few days, when he was seeking to get away from his would-be tormentors, had borne him down, and he had come to the end of his reserve strength. Yet, to their amazement, he was exultant and confident, and they realized in those moments of watching that William Tyndale was a man whose character had been matured in the hardest of all schools, annealed in the furnace, and not forgetful, although the chains were about his hands and feet, of the Hand that was strong beyond that of men, and had brought him out of the dungeon depths.

"Is my wallet all right, Herman?" Tyndale asked anxiously, too weak to look for himself; too weak, indeed, to lift his hand to feel for the strap across his breast.

Herman saw it hanging about his shoulders by the leather band, and told him it was there. He gently guided his hand so that he might feel it; then brought the wallet round for him to see, and have it in his lap. In spite of his chains, Tyndale hugged it to his bosom.

"I should have been bereft indeed if I had lost these treasures," he muttered. They were his stock-in-trade, as he had said at other times half humorously. His books were in the wallet—those precious volumes from whence he drew the material for his translated Bible.

But the watchers were anxious and perplexed, not knowing what next to do, now that they found Tyndale so near to collapse, and, in spite of his exultation and confidence, so near, as they thought, to death. What if, after having ventured so far, they had a dead man on their hands? Or if not that, how were they to get him away? And where should they lodge him until he grew stronger?

# IN THE CELL

WHEN Margaret came to herself, after she had fallen in a senseless heap on the cavern floor, she found herself in darkness, and lying on some straw.

Sitting up, she began to link up slowly with the past, so that she recalled her desperate venture into the place which had so much in it to terrify her. With this came the remembrance of the voices she had heard. She recalled it all, and the dread returned, for surely she was lying in the same place, and her surroundings were distressing as before.

These were her thoughts; and, presently, she determined to move away, to get into the outer air again; anywhere, rather than endeavor to find her way along those forbidding passages which led to Herman's home.

She rose to her feet and moved cautiously, with her hands stretched out before her, lest her face should beat against something in the darkness. She had not gone far before she touched a wall, and it felt cold and damp.

Still going carefully, one hand moving along the wall, or what she supposed to be the rocky side of the cavern, she shivered at the thought of what her feet might presently touch—those forbidding skeletons over which, when she first came with Herman, she had thrown her cloak in reverence for the unknown dead.

But with the dread there was another thought, and one of surprise.

This rock, or wall, which she was touching, was wet, and the air had a clammy feeling in it. Her hand became so damp that she caught up her skirt to wipe it. She shuddered when she felt her way on again, thinking to get to the opening to the river, for her hand touched a chill and slimy substance, and then it moved.

What did it mean? The rock which she and Herman had gone round was dry; the floor was crisp and dry as well. Thinking of this, she bent down to feel what the floor was like, and it was wet.

She was bewildered. Was she in the same place, or had she wandered somewhere else in a state of semi-consciousness, in a sleep-walk, perhaps? Determined to solve this problem, she moved on, and then her hand touched something which brought a cry of wonder to her lips.

There was a break in the wall, and her hand went out into the open air, but as she moved her hand farther it struck against something, and her fingers closed over a cold iron bar. There was another, and a third. Running her hands up and down the bars, she came to a stop at the top; to another stop at the bottom. Looking before her, she saw something glinting, and, watching it, she knew it to be a star. In her growing astonishment she saw another, and yet one more; then many. There was a moon somewhere, but hidden behind the clouds which again and again rolled by and shut away the stars.

It began to dawn on her that she was not in the cavern. She continued her progress along the wall, and came to something, the discovery of which brought a cry of anguish to her lips. It was a door, cold to the touch, and sheeted with iron, rough on the surface, as though the rust had formed on it because of the dampness of the place. As her soft hand ran over it she felt iron ribs crossing the door from left to right, and solid studs like the square heads of great nails.

A greater horror came to her than if she had found herself shut up in the cavern near to Herman's home; for now she knew that she was not in it.

This was some other place—but what?

Determined to assure herself, she stood with her back to the door, and walked forward slowly, groping in the darkness, with her hand stretched out before her. She had not gone far before her feet brushed against something which rustled, and, stooping, her hand touched some spread-out straw. Once more upright, she moved across the straw, and came to the wall.

The truth dawned on her now, and she sank on the straw with a sense of horror, hopelessness, an indescribable fear—she knew not what to call it. But this she knew, that she was in prison!

She buried her face in her hands and, shuddering, tried to think this thing out. Why should she be in a prison cell, and not in a cavern with an outlet to the open air, where, when she came to herself she might have waited by the river till the day dawned, and she could have gone to the city gates, and so to her home?

She recalled the voices which had startled her in the cavern. To whom did they belong? Were they river robbers? And was it possible that they made the cavern one of their hiding-places? She began to put the thing into shape. These robbers had found her, and had carried her to some inner place, thinking to deal with her later on, when they had time.

It was a terrible plight for a delicate girl to be in, and she prayed for God's shielding if she had fallen into the hands of desperate and disreputable men.

Another thought gripped her which seemed more terrible than the other. What if those voices belonged to the emissaries of the Inquisition, who had gained an inkling of the fact that William Tyndale was hiding hereabouts, and had

159

come to search the cavern on the chance of finding him? If that were so, then they had found her while she was unconscious, and had carried her to this cell. It was fearful to contemplate the possibility, that this was one of the dungeons in the place which was known throughout the city as the Holy House.

Margaret crouched on the heap of straw until the light of the day-dawn began to creep through the barred window. When she lifted her white, drawn, tear-stained face, and gazed around, she saw that it was as she feared. She really was in a prison; and from what was there, it surely was a part of the Inquisitors' House. When her eyes ranged round the damp walls, where the morning sun came in brokenly, and made the lines of trickling moisture gleam, she saw a great crucifix hanging opposite the window, so placed that the prisoner could not fail to be reminded of the religion and the Church to which she was supposed to be a renegade. The size of this one in the cell was disconcerting, for it was as large as life, as though the Inquisitors meant that the figure of the suffering Savior should be intrusive.

The long hours went, and Margaret was left to her loneliness. No one came with food, and nothing had passed her lips for all the hours that had gone since she left her home on her father's errand to bid Tyndale leave the city. She looked about to see whether the usual prison fare was in the cell—the bread and water; but none was there.

Nothing living came, save a bird that hopped about on the windowsill, between the bars, and peeped in at the prisoner. Standing in the line of light, the little creature sang his song, but Margaret gained no cheering from it, sweet though it was. There was liberty for that pretty bit of feathered life, which only served to make her feel the misery of her own imprisonment.

The bird flew away, and Margaret's loneliness grew on her. Hunger had begun its torment, and thirst as well. Was this to be her treatment? Had they who brought her here discovered that she was a friend of William Tyndale, and now they meant to leave her to hunger and thirst and loneliness until she died?

That thought brought her from her crouching attitude on to her knees; and then, with her hands clasped and her head bent low, she prayed. She asked for deliverance. She knew not how it would come, but God, she was sure, would find the way. Then came the alternative to her prayer, but she paused and wondered whether she could take it. Could she ask for deliverance, but then say, "If it be possible let this cup pass from me; nevertheless, not as I will, but as Thou wilt "? She sobbed, for it was so hard to say, "Thy will be done."

For a time she paused at that point, undergoing the struggle, shrinking from it. She was half rebellious at first; but presently the full surrender came; and the words rang out, "Not as I will but as Thou wilt." If she was to go the way of the martyrs, she pleaded that she might be true, and go on to the end of her martyrdom.

It was late in the afternoon when she heard a sound by the door. A key was thrust into the lock from outside, and it screamed as it turned. Then came the thrusting back of bolts, so many of them, Margaret thought bitterly. What could a girl do, that she should be kept in durance by an iron door, with lock and bolts and bars?

The door opened outwards, and, watching intently, wondering who was coming, she saw two men, cowled and gowned like the Familiars she had sometimes seen in the streets. Neither of them spoke, but one who carried a jar of water in one hand and a loaf in the other, set the water at her feet and tossed the bread on the straw. He turned away in silence, going back to the door with muffled tread, where he waited, without a word.

Margaret sprang to her feet, and, going to him, caught at his coarse, black robe, but he tore her hand away, still without speaking.

"Why have you brought me here?" she cried, and her face was full of eagerness.

The man made no reply, but stood looking at her, unmoved, apparently, in spite of the traces of her grief on her face.

"Have you no answer for me? If you brought me here, what was your right? And what was my crime that you should bring me to this horrible place?"

She spoke impulsively and boldly, like one who was fighting for her life, and was taking the chance now that it was here.

The man was silent and still, as though he had been stone, and the girl gazed at him in wonder.

"Do you not hear me?" she cried.

She clutched at his robe and shook his arm, as if to compel him to do something that was human, and not stand there in baleful silence as though he were made of stone. He caught her hand in his, and with a rough wrench that made her cry out with pain, he tore it away from his robe, and thrust her from him with such force that she staggered and fell heavily on the straw.

The other Familiar was meanwhile passing round the cell, looking at everything intently, and especially at the window bars, as if to satisfy himself that they had not been tampered with, and that there was no possibility of the prisoner's escape. He, too, was silent, and, going to the door when his investigation was ended, he passed away with the other. The door closed noisily, and those sounds which followed made Margaret feel the more how impossible it was to hope for escape.

For a time the bread and water remained untouched, but hunger and thirst compelled her to eat. The coarse black bread, the like of which she had never eaten before, was so dry that she had to soak it in the water. The food satisfied her hunger and took away her sense of weakness, but there was the long night coming, with its loneliness and uncertainty, perhaps its, horrors.

The darkness began to enshroud the place, so little was the opening through which the sunset light could come. Somewhere outside, Margaret could hear the birds singing their evening songs, but these grew less and less until the last note came, and the silence of the night began.

Gradually what was in the cell grew indistinct. The image of the Savior on the cross faded away; and although she had watched it disappear, bit by bit, there was nothing of the crucifix at last for her to see. She turned to the window, but that, too, with its bars, lost its shape, and the night came on so blackly that she would not have known where to look for it. After some hours had gone the cell began to look less dark. The things that had been hidden began to appear, dimly and indistinctly, until the moon came away from the horizon and later shone out clearly while she took her silent night ride through the heavens. This silver light, stealing in, made the cell seem less lonely.

At last, after shaking up the straw, to lie more easily, she threw herself down upon it, after prayer, and fell into a dreamless sleep. When she awoke it was day, and the world was alive and beautiful in the sunshine, although she had no token of what was going on save from the songs of the birds. In the cell itself there was silence but for the scramble of a rat at odd times across the floor. Then she knew what the creature's errand was, for it had eaten some of her bread. All else was quiet, and the stillness of the house to which her cell belonged was such that it appalled her. She would have welcomed the slam of a door, or the sound of a human voice, however harsh, or the tramp of a man's feet.

The thought came to her that possibly a part of her torture was this intolerable loneliness. What might it not mean to her if it continued many days and nights?

# SPOILING THE EGYPTIANS

WILLIAM TYNDALE was so weak and ill when Engel had carried him as far as the cavern, and set him down there, that they wondered whether they had brought him from the dungeon only to see him die. Kneeling at his side, the forester watched him seriously, and then it struck him that what Tyndale wanted was food.

"Stay here, Herman, and you, Roye, and keep watch, while I go to my but for food," he said, looking up at the others, who were gazing down at the overwrought prisoner.

Herman was alert in an instant.

"'Tis a long way, Otto, and the shortest time before you could return would be more than an hour and a half," he protested ; but Engel responded almost impatiently:

"I know that. But if I stay here he will die; and how to get him hence unless he can put a foot forward for his own helping, which is not possible, I do not know."

"Let me go back into the castle and look for some food!" Herman exclaimed.

The forester was aghast at the proposal.

"Then we shall have two dead men on our hands, or at all events one helpless, like this poor one," pointing to Tyndale, "and a dead one, which will be yourself," he cried.

"I think not," said Herman sturdily. "I will go cautiously, and I know my way about by this time. There was some food on the tables in the banqueting hall—a meal, doubtless for the retainers, all ready, but the men had not come to it because of that summons to the river."

The forester demurred. The proposed errand was too full of danger for his assent to be given with readiness.

"I mean to go," said Herman, in such a tone of quiet determination that the other felt that it would be useless to attempt to hinder him.

"Very well, then. I admire your boldness, but I think it next door to madness!" exclaimed Engel. "Take the lantern with you."

"No, I won't do that. I can grope my way along the passage, and when I am once on the other side of that door I shall be safer without a light. While I am away, why not see whether it is possible to break away those fetters from Master Tyndale's limbs? Stay here, Roye, and help Engel in doing what can be done for the dear man's comfort."

"That's easily done," said the forester, smiling, and he brought out a file which he had hidden away somewhere. "Sprenkel told me it was just possible that Master Tyndale would be fettered, since it was Schouts' custom to put all his prisoners into irons. That's why I came prepared. Go on your errand quickly, and God speed you. I will start on these irons at once."

While Herman was groping his way along the passage the forester worked hard to relieve Tyndale of that incubus which made free movement an impossibility. But his mind was on the younger man's danger, and he thrilled at the almost certain consequences.

"He must not do that mad thing," he muttered, rising from his knees and tossing the file on the floor.

"He must not, my friend," said Tyndale weakly, rousing himself from his stupor.

Engel did not pause, but hurried along the passage with the lantern in his hand, leaving the others in darkness.

He overtook Herman as he was smoothing his hand over the stone door to find the knob which would open it.

"What's wrong?" Herman asked anxiously. "Is Master Tyndale dead?"

"No. But he has spoken, and he thinks with me that you must not attempt this mad thing."

"I shall attempt it, nonetheless, Otto. There's food to be had, and I mean to get it. The good man's life is worth the risk. The world has need of him."

Herman fingered his dagger while he spoke, and Engel, seeing the gleam in the other's eyes and the determined look in his face as the light of the lantern played on it, knew that it was vain to endeavor to turn him from his purpose.

"Go softly, then," he whispered, while he, too, felt about for the hidden spring. "Ha! it is here. I'll hide the light first, before we open the door."

He turned and saw a niche in the rock where the lantern light would be completely shaded, if anyone chanced to be in the passage. Then, with his hand again on the spring, he thrust the door away, barely, while the two men peered through the slit.

The passage was dark and silent. There was no sound save the distant shouts of men who were calling to each other in connection with the night's piracy.

"Slip through and look the other way," the ranger whispered, and Herman, venturing stood in the corridor.

"Go back and file away at those fetters," he whispered back.

"Roye is there, and as I came away, although I was leaving them in darkness, he was beginning to work at them for dear life," the answer came.

A moment later Herman was alone, and the door was drawn into its place, as it had been before, when the search

167

for the dungeon was being made. The passage was dark. The page was somewhere in that part of the castle still. He must have thought he had been dreaming about the streak of light across the floor, for now he was whistling lustily, and breaking off for an occasional snatch of song. The increasing faintness of these sounds assured Herman that the boy was going farther and farther away, somewhere in that part where the steps led down to the now empty dungeon.

Going forward to the banqueting hall, taking every step in stealth, alert for any sound, and ever on the watch for any token of approaching danger, Herman came to the place where he thought the door of the great chamber should be. He paused when he saw a narrow line of light on the floor of the passage, and, going nearer to know what it meant, he found that the light was streaming through a slit in the doorway of the place where he had seen the food.

When his hand touched the door, he paused to listen, to glance both ways along the corridor; but there was nothing to indicate that anyone was moving about. Growing confident, he pushed the door a little wider open and peeped in. The chamber was empty, and it was all as he had seen it before. Food lay on the tables set there, either for supper or in readiness for the early morning meal. It seemed to Herman that all he had to do was to step in quickly, take a, dish of bread, and one of the roasted fowls from one of the tables.

It was a bold thing to do, but so was everything he had been doing in this night's enterprise. He thought of William Tyndale's need, and knew that, unless he did something such as this, his escape would hardly be possible, seeing that he was so weak.

Opening the door widely, that his movements might be unhampered, he walked to the table, going so rapidly that his feet, with all his attempt at stealth, fell with what seemed to him sharp, loud taps upon the tessellated floor. He was within a yard of the spot where he could lay his hand on the things he wanted, when his heart leapt at what he saw. The door at the other end of the banqueting hall opened, and someone entered. In a moment Herman pulled his cap low over his eyes, throwing a shadow on his face.

The man who stepped in was Cochlaeus, and as he stood just within the doorway, and the light fell on him, Herman saw that his face was a frowning one, as though he took offence at the treatment that was meted out to a man of his quality and importance among Churchmen—that he should be set aside to await the lord of the castle's leisure while he busied himself with piracy.

The impulse came to turn at once and walk away, hoping that Cochlaeus would not see and recognise him. Before he came to a decision, the Deacon looked up and saw that someone was in the hall.

"Hi, varlet!" he cried peremptorily. "Come and wait on me! This lord of yours has no respect for those who come to see him, for he must needs go on with his godless pursuits, while I am wasting my time, and faint with hunger."

The words came angrily, but so far it was plain that Cochlaeus had not recognized Herman. He was intensely relieved. Could he not play a bolder game?

"Sit, sir, at my lord's table, and let me wait on you," he answered, in a simulated voice. "But I must carry this away first, lest there be trouble at my slackness."

He went forward to a table, and easily, recklessly, indeed, he caught up a great dish of varied meats when he had placed a fowl there, and heaped bread on it. With this he turned his back on Cochlaeus, and walked to the door by which he had entered.

"Be quick, fellow!" cried the other, who by this time had seated himself at the cross table where Schouts always sat. "I told you I was starving. Canst not serve me first and see to that later?"

The man's voice rang down the hall impatiently.

"I dare not! 'Tis more than one's life is worth in this castle," Herman called back with assumed ease; but his heart was beating tumultuously. With a swift look up the banqueting chamber to see that none had been watching him besides the heretic hunter, and then with glances as keen each way in the corridor, Herman went at a run, regardless of his sounding steps.

"Here," came the ranger's whisper, as the door opened wide, and Herman; with an ejaculation of thankfulness, stepped through the doorway. He heard the thud of the heavy stone coming into its place, and the click of the latch before he turned.

"Safe again, and God be praised!" exclaimed the forester, reaching for the lantern and looking at the load which Herman carried. "And successful, too!" he cried, a ring of satisfaction in his voice.

"There's plenty for us all," said Herman quietly, now realizing the strain this bold venture had placed on him. "Lead the way, Otto, and let us get back to Master Tyndale."

He felt that for a little while, at all events, he did not want to speak. His mind was not so much on the danger he had faced as on that man who was the instigator of all this trouble and he marveled at his escape from recognition since more than once he had confronted Cochlaeus in the city, and had been compelled to do business with him. Each step in that short walk towards William Tyndale served to restore his confidence, and as Engel went before him silently, holding the lantern low down, so that the light fell on the path showing him where to tread, he was becoming his old self again.

"Wert seen at all?" asked the ranger presently, wondering at Herman's silence.

"Yes, and by Cochlaeus."

"What! By Cochlaeus?" the other cried, gasping out the words, and turning round so unexpectedly that the dish Herman was carrying was barely saved. "Did he know thee?" he exclaimed, staring at Herman and lifting the lantern to see his face.

The question amused Herman, and he chuckled.

"He came into the banqueting hall while I was there. The fellow had a scowl on his face."

"I never saw him without one," Engel ejaculated.

"Ha! But it was a more than usually savage one this time, for he was hungry. But go on. Think of Master Tyndale's need. I can tell it as we move forward."

The forester led the way again, and Herman, went on with his story.

"His dignity had been offended because Schouts had gone to his pirate work, instead of pursuing that bargain concerning Master Tyndale. He took me for one of the varlets, and bade me serve him with food."

Herman stopped and laughed aloud, and the ranger, turning, saw his face and laughed with him.

"Didst take him any?" he asked.

"Nay, he's there, waiting for me," Herman cried, moving forward.

They laughed until the place rang, for there was no need for restraint since no one inside the castle could overhear them. Tyndale, who had been sitting in helplessness while Roye was filing at the irons in the dark, and feeling his work with his fingers, heard the sounds of laughter, and it was cheering to him.

"There is good news, Roye!" he exclaimed. "They have met with no mishap, for which I thank God, or they would not have come back in such high spirits. And I would be glad to have food, for I feel faint."

171

He spoke weakly, but when he saw Herman and his companion, coming back with the lantern, which the forester held aloof, he saw their faces and the dish in Herman's hands.

"You seem merry," he said, but already better for the assurance that some of the danger had passed.

"We are!" exclaimed Herman, stepping forward quickly. At Tyndale's side he dropped on his knees and set the food on the floor. He wondered when he saw that already Roye had taken the irons from his hands and had begun with the rings about Tyndale's feet.

"Drink first," said Herman, and by this time the forester had gone to Tyndale's other side and had him in his arms, holding him up while the younger man put the flagon to the sick one's lips. He drank a little, and then with care they fed him, and to give him confidence, as well as to fall in with his wishes, they ate with him, for Herman had brought enough and to spare.

When they had eaten, and Tyndale seemed already so much better, they faced the difficulties of the present and the immediate future. Tyndale had been brought out of the dungeon, but what should the next step be? It would soon be known that he had escaped, and the forest would be searched through and through, not only by Cochlaeus and the City Guard, but by the robber lord who had lost a prize that was worth to him at least a thousand golden crowns.

"If I take you to my place, Master Tyndale, they may go there, and they would not fail to find you, and then!"

The forester shrugged his shoulders and thought of the end of this man for whom they had dared so much, to say nothing of their own penalty for aiding him.

"What can be done?" asked Tyndale quietly. "It seems to me that I am compelled to take the risks."

The future appeared very black as they talked over a dozen plans, every one of which had a spot in it of weakness and the certainty of a disastrous ending. But presently the forester, who had done as he was wont to do when in perplexity, came back to the little group after having walked to and fro, wrapped in thought.

"What say you if I leave you here with the others to bear you company, while I go about my business as though nothing had happened? I might even play my part and help the people at the castle—ay! and that rascal, Cochlaeus—in their search for you. But I warrant you 'twill be a vain one. I'd be very diligent for the Churchman."

The cavern rang with the forester's laughter, and he laughed till the tears came, and his body ached when he thought of the chase he would lead them if they suffered him to share in the search.

"I'll bring you food in plenty from time to time, and meanwhile I can think things out and see how we can contrive to get you away. Art willing, Master Tyndale?" he asked, becoming serious.

"I am willing," came the answer; "but I am loath to keep these with me cooped up in the darkness----"

"You shall have light in plenty," the forester interrupted.

"But Herman—think what it means to him, with Margaret Byrckmann waiting for him and wondering what has become of him.

"I'll send her word," said Engel seriously.

"Had I but paper and ink, I could have gone on with my work," said Tyndale. "I should have been using up my hours, and this task would be so much nearer to completion. Roye could have written while I dictated."

"So he shall. I know a priest who is a man of letters, and I can tell him some story which will induce him to give me both pen and paper," said the forester, disposing of that difficulty.

"As for me," said Herman, longing though he was to go back to Margaret, if only to see her for an hour, but feeling that, so far as duty went, it was here, by Tyndale's side—"as for me, I shall stay and keep watch if Otto Engel will only set you going on your work, Master Tyndale!" he exclaimed earnestly.

Engel went just before day dawn, but he came in the middle of the afternoon with a basket. It contained food, for which they were grateful, but Tyndale's eyes gleamed at the sight of a bundle of paper, some ink, and a store of quills.

"Thank God!" he ejaculated. "Ay, and my dear friend, thank you as well, from the bottom of my heart. There need be no hurry now, for with light and these I am as well off here as in a palace. What care I for comfort if my hand is not stayed in my God-given task?"

His eyes gleamed with pleasure as he turned over the sheets and drew out the books from his wallet. But he thought of Herman.

"My son, since I am safe here, you may steal away at night, and you know your way by that secret entrance to your home; and after that it will be easy to pass through the streets to where the girl you love dwells with her father."

Herman took his outstretched hand in his.

"I'll think about it," he answered softly, the love-light in his eyes. "I should like to go, but my duty is here, and she knows I am with you."

"Is there any news of the castle?" Herman asked a moment later, turning to Engel, who was trimming the lantern.

"News?" exclaimed the forester. "I should think there was. Schouts came to terms with Cochlaeus when he had cleared out the ship and sent her away empty, and then, so Sprenkel told me, they went to the dungeon so that the pious Churchman might see his prisoner. I'd have given something to see them going down those slippery steps, and would have hoped for them to fall. But I would have given a week's wages to have seen their faces when they stepped into that horrible dungeon and found that the prisoner was gone!

"Sprenkel was with them, and he told me that Cochlaeus stamped about on the filthy floor, beside himself with rage. He swung round presently and faced Schouts like a madman, then shook his fist at him, and declared that he had been playing with him. And as for Schouts, who thought of the thousand crowns he had lost, when they seemed so certain, his anger blazed out at the Churchman's insults, and, lifting his great fist, he would have struck him down but for a remnant of superstition still lingering in his godless heart.

"But for the fact that you are a priest, I would have you chained where that Englishman lay!' he cried.

"He caught the lamp from Sprenkel's hand, and went to the wall where the iron ring had been torn away. He was almost speechless with astonishment, and the more so because he had marked, when he ordered Tyndale to be carried to the dungeon, how frail he was.

"Sprenkel told me that Cochlaeus raged and stormed, and vowed every curse on Schouts and his retainers that the Church could heap upon them, until, in his anger, Schouts gripped him at the back of his neck, hurried the Churchman up the steps and along the corridors, then to the gate, which the warden opened in amazement at his call. There, without a word, he hurled him from him, and Cochlaeus, staggering half-way across the draw-bridge, fell in a helpless heap, while the portcullis fell, and the gate closed with a clang."

The forester's face seemed aglow with delight, as he stood with folded arms and his back against the cavern wall.

"I've something more to tell you," he said, after a pause. "I was walking through the forest soon after I left you here, and, hearing the sounds of voices, the stamp of horses'

175

hoofs, and the jingle of harness and steel, I moved about as I usually do when I am out on duty.

"Hi, fellow!' someone cried, and, turning, I saw Cochlaeus and the City Guard. The Churchman, now on horseback, and greatly ruffled, demanded my name.

"I'm Otto Engel, your reverence,' I answered, 'and I am ranger of the forest.'

"In the pay of that robber lord in the castle?' he asked me.

"Nay; I do not work for him, but for a master whom I love.'

"Hast seen anyone in the forest—an English-man— that heretic fellow whom they call William Tyndale? He was a prisoner in the castle, but has got away, and must be hiding somewhere.'

"When was that?' I asked, as simply as I knew how, and with such an air of surprise that he never thought to ask me again if I had seen the man.

"Any time during the night,' the answer came, and at once lie made an offer which set my blood dancing. See, ranger, if thou canst find him for us, that limb of Satan, there are a hundred golden crowns for you, and the blessing of the Church.'

"Wilt come with me and I will show you places where a man might think to hide,' I said. But if I fail to find him I get nothing, and I lose the hundred crowns.'

"Nay. Thou shalt have ten, but it will be my joy if I have to pay thee the full hundred,' Cochlaeus cried.

"They followed me, the whole of the City Guard and Cochlaeus—the Churchman eager, the other horsemen in ill-humor, for they were hungry after a long night's fast, and worn out with their long waiting at the Castle gate, for the coming of the Deacon. How he had come out I had not heard then, for it was later when I met Sprenkel.

"We searched everywhere, in places likely and unlikely, once in the lair of a bear who made her onslaught on us, and had to be dealt with by cold steel, and once again I sent them down an alley in the forest where a couple of wolves leapt out, and there were snarls and snaps, and then unearthly yells, as the wild creatures fell before the deadly sword thrusts.

"We'll go to the city ! ' cried Cochlaeus, who rode swiftly back to where I was awaiting them, with my hunting knife in readiness in case any of those yelping, slouching beasts should get away and turn on me. Here are the ten crowns I promised,' he added, handing me the golden pieces with a trembling hand. But see, fellow, I spoke of a hundred crowns. Find me this William Tyndale and I will give you a hundred and fifty; but he must be alive, so that we may deal with him for his heresy and his pestilential work.'

"I took the gold, and watched them ride away. Some of the horsemen were wiping the blood from their swords, and most of them were sitting in their saddles in discontent, and gazing after the Churchman with a contempt one rarely has the chance of seeing. I stood looking after them till they had gone out of sight, when someone slapped me on the shoulder. Whoever it was, he had come on me unawares, and I swung round to find myself face to face with Sprenkel. I told him what I knew, and then I heard of what had passed in the castle. But here are the crowns, Master Tyndale, and shall I tell thee what I think it best to do with them?"

Tyndale looked at him curiously.

"I cannot say."

"I thought that you should have them, and use them for the work you have in hand. They would go some little distance towards printing that Word of God, and it would be safe to do so, since it would be but spoiling the Egyptians."

Tyndale hesitated; but at last, when the forester protested that he would not touch the money, he put out his hand, took the coins, and dropped them in his wallet.

"'Twas not God's money when you had it," he said simply, " but I will take it as His money now, and use it for the glory of God."

****

Far on into the night, while Tyndale was telling of his hopes, a night bird's cry came, and the eyes of those who were in the cavern turned towards the tree which formed the entrance to their hiding place.

"I believe that's Engel," said Herman, springing to his feet. Before many moments had passed the ranger came in, shaking his shirt into place as he stepped forward quickly.

"Come at once!" he exclaimed, before he reached them. "And take up your master's wallet, Roye. I have a boat down by the river which will carry you across to the other bank. I know of a hiding place in the forest where I cannot think that rascal of a Cochlaeus can ever find you, Master Tyndale, and when it is safe to do so, later on, we may get you to the place you want to reach."

There was a strange look on the man's face as he drew out of his bosom a heavy purse.

"If this be not God's way, I wot not what to call it!" he exclaimed, his voice tremulous with deep feeling. "I have heard my mother tell how, when the Israelites went up out of Egypt to go to the Land of Promise—I think she called it that—they spoiled the Egyptians, and got much from them for their desert journey. What shall we say of this, Master Tyndale? Your enemies have sought to hinder your work, and worse, they mean to kill you if they can. Yet I watched that man Cochlaeus fingering a purse and he took out the ten crowns which I brought here. I thought no more about it, but when I passed that way to make things ready for your escape, Master

Tyndale, my foot kicked against something, and it was that same purse. Here it is! It must have dropped while he rose to mount into his saddle. 'Tis God's gift. I'm sure of it! 'Twill pay the charges for a comfortable journey, and leave much over for your future wants."

The forester opened the purse, which was very heavy, and there was the gleam of gold. It was money in abundance, and Tyndale, taking it from Engel's hands, went on his knees.

# THE FLIGHT FROM THE HOLY HOUSE

FOR the whole of that long day which followed Margaret's next awaking, no one came to see her. They who kept the prison thought that the jar of water and the loaf would keep her from starvation, and it was evidently no part of their plan to make her comfortable. But the bird who had been before came to her, peeped into the cell between the window bars, twisted his little head inquiringly, and waited almost expectantly.

Margaret watched him, and wondered whether he had been fed by the prisoner who last lodged in this dismal place. Breaking off some of the soft part of her loaf, and having crumbled it in her hands, she approached the window. The bird was cautious, and drew back to the other side of the bars, where he was free to fly away if Margaret meditated any treachery. There he watched warily, twisting his head all ways, while she spread the crumbs on the stone sill.

She hoped he would come while she stood near, but he contented himself with peering and chirping impatiently, as if to ask her to drop back, and she understood. She stepped away to the middle of the cell, and when she did so he came forward to peck at the food until the last crumb had gone. By way of thanks he sang a song to the lonely prisoner, and flew away.

The loneliness that followed was unutterable. The hours dragged on, intolerable in their slowness. They must have been leaden-footed—the slowest hours that Time ever dealt out!

Night came again, and still there was no visit from the men who were so silent and forbidding when they were with her. There was no fresh supply of food because of their absence, but the loaf was not gone, nor was the water-jar quite empty. But these facts did not go far to lessen her anxiety about the future, for the question came to her as to whether this was the only food she was to have. The stories afloat in the city were that that was often the practice with the Inquisitors; they brought food at the start, just once, and no more, and then the victims were left to slow starvation, or so weakened by hunger and thirst that, when torture came, they collapsed.

But why was she here? Who could have suspected her of heresy by anything she had ever said or done outside her own pretty room at home? These Familiars were like bloodhounds. They could scent out heresy as surely as the hounds could smell a hunted man; and possibly they had discovered that she had befriended William Tyndale—had even been one of the two to bring him into the city.

She sat and wept at the thought. She wept as well to think that when her wedding day came she would not be at her father's house as bride. Her heart went out in yearning for Herman, whom she so dearly loved. She thought of his consternation and his grief when he found that she had not returned. It was more for him than for herself, and her misery at being lodged in this dreary place with no prospect but death.

Morning came with her silver light again, and the crucifix came slowly into view; and the face of the Savior was full of sorrow. It matched her own unhappiness. The light of the dawn showed her how small her supply of food was. She was intensely thirsty, but she felt she must ration both bread and water. She was afraid to do more than moisten her lips and swallow a mouthful to take the dryness from her parched throat. The bread had woefully dwindled, for the rats had been at it, and one or two scrambled across the floor when she flung out her hands to drive them away. The bird came for his meal, and she could not deny him; and in payment for it he sang a song which brought the tears; for it set her thinking of freedom, and made her yearn for it more than words could ever tell.

The loneliness, with nothing to do but think and pray, was intolerable. She was realizing that it is never good for one to feel the sense of being absolutely alone, for one would grow morbid, and distort the realities, and become fearful or bitter, as she feared she would do.

Perhaps that was a part of her torture. It was possible that the Inquisitors knew from their experience with other prisoners that loneliness was as much of pain in its way as the use of the thumb-screw or the hot pincers. Whether they did so or not, she felt that to the lonely one, robbed of liberty and companionship, the choicest and most entrancing spot on earth, "the valley of flowers and the hills of glory," becomes a desert which in time is peopled with horror and a deadly fear. How much more this dungeon in which she was lying!

When evening drew on, the shadows grew deeper in the cell. The crucifix was presently barely visible, and Margaret shuddered; for it seemed to her that the noisome creatures of the place were coming out of their hiding now that the light was going. Her heart leapt at a sound she heard, but she knew not whether to hope or fear. There was the noise of a key in the lock as she had heard it before, followed by the dropping of the bars and chains and the drawing of bolts. Then, with a slowness that was trying to her nerves, the door began to open.

Two Familiars entered, one blocking up the doorway, in case the prisoner should try to rush through in the wild hope of finding liberty.

The other approached the straw on which Margaret sat, looking up at the cowled creature wistfully, with her hands folded, the once rosy cheeks no longer colored, but white and wan. If this man who came disguised in that ugly cowl had known that tomorrow was her bridal day, he must have thought that there was nothing here suggestive of a happy bride as she crouched at his feet. His black robe rustled on the straw, sweeping across it when he bent to set another loaf and a jar of water on the floor.

Not one word passed. Of what avail was it to ask these men why she was here? They would not deign an answer, of that she was sure.

When this one who brought the food was once more at the door, he turned to speak.

"Tomorrow you are to appear in the Audience Chamber to answer certain questions concerning that Englishman, William Tyndale. If you do not answer satisfactorily, so I am told to say, you will be put to the torture."

"To the torture?" she cried.

She shivered at the word, and buried her face in her hands, while the Familiars passed away, taking no notice of her cry.

"Torture!" she moaned again, when she was alone.

She needed not to be told what was embodied in that word which thrilled the hearts of the most hardened with horror, and none ever asked what form it would take, since all had heard of the rack, and red-hot irons, and the pulley.

She was determined on one thing through those long night hours, when she was too distressed to eat and drink, although she was so hungry and thirsty. Whatever came, she would not betray William Tyndale.

She sat and rocked herself in the extremity of her dread, but after a time she rose from her seat and, kneeling, prayed. She felt that she could pray better in that posture, but the time which followed made the cell like a Gethsemane to her. She prayed as He did who hung upon the cross. She wanted the cup to pass from her, if it were possible. Those were her "hours of amazement"—hours of darkest, deepest midnight, when her heart recoiled from the promised suffering.

She was kneeling thus when she heard a sound, and she looked up quickly, wondering whether the Familiars were returning to tell her something more. She had not noticed it, but the moon was shining through the window, and as she turned to look, the shaft of light seemed broken, and something moved, a dark shadow like a man's fingers closing round the bars; then something like a man's head appeared, and a voice followed immediately.

"Margaret Byrckmann, are you there?"

The voice was familiar, and she sprang to her feet, overturning the jar of water as she moved.

"Who are you?" she asked, not seeing the face, which was in shadow.

"Heinrich. You know poor Heinrich, do you not? I know you are Margaret Byrckmann, now that you have spoken. I know your voice, for it has always spoken so kindly to poor Heinrich."

The voice was a man's, and yet there was so much of the child in it.

"Why are you here, Heinrich?" Margaret asked, going close to the window for the sake of the companionship after that long spell of loneliness. It was something to have this man, or this boy—this boy in a man's strong frame—near to her. She waited for his answer, wondering whether he had brought any message from her father or Herman.

"I was in the cavern and saw them take you away. They carried you because you were senseless, so I heard one of the Familiars say. I tried to stop them, thinking I might get you out of their hands, and I lay in their way across the dark path. Not seeing me, they stumbled over me and fell. Oh, how they cursed me!

"I did not do that again, for I thought that another fall would hurt you, lame you, perhaps; but I followed to see where they put you, but when once they carried you through their private door I could discover no more, for they locked me out. But I meant to find out. I have been trying to do so all these days and nights. I have gone from window to window, and now, God be praised! I have found you!

"Why have you come, Heinrich? Have you brought me a message from anyone?" Margaret asked, hoping that he would mention Herman's name.

"No. I have not left this accursed house, save to run home for something to eat and drink, and I have brought this."

He drew something out of his bosom, and laid its rough surface on Margaret's soft hand.

"A file!" she exclaimed, thrilled with a hope that came when she realized what it meant.

"Yes; I am going to file away these bars and get you out of that den. I will take you where they will never find you. Move your hand, lest I may hurt you."

Heinrich began to work at the bars like one possessed, and Margaret, standing near, could hear how the file bit into the iron. In the stillness of the night the sound was alarmingly loud to her, and she was afraid that someone would hear and come to ask the meaning of it. Now and again

Heinrich paused to look around, to know whether he was seen, or anyone approached.

Suddenly he set the file on the sill.

"The City Guard! Go on filing quietly. I'll come back." He dropped away from the window, and Margaret was alone again.

Using the file, she worked at the bar until her arms ached; but what mattered that? Was not liberty to come in payment for the toil? But Heinrich was so long away that she was afraid he had gone for good, and perhaps she would not escape at all. He returned, however, when the lane was clear and silent again, and, after working at each bar in succession, he exclaimed in exultation when his strong hand tore away the last one, and the space was open.

"Can you climb up on your side?" he asked, thrusting his head and shoulders through the opening and looking down into the darkness.

"I think so," Margaret said doubtfully, for the window was high from the floor. "But you must give me your hand." Her hands came up to him out of the darkness.

"Wait," the man whispered. "I will come down and give you a lift up. When you are where I am, you can drop down into the lane."

Telling Margaret to stand aside, he glanced up and down the lane to see that the way was clear; then he drew himself up, crawled through the opening, and dropped into the cell. Before she knew what he meant to do, he placed her on the sill, where the bird's meal had been served.

"How deep is it down to the lane?" she asked, for the moon had gone behind the cloud, and she was looking into blackness. "I'm afraid to drop."

"Then don't. Make as much room for me as you can," Heinrich whispered up to her. "I'll climb up and let you down easily."

Before many seconds had passed he had scrambled up, chuckling at his success. But he stopped, and almost roughly he pushed past Margaret and dropped into the lane.

She understood, and her hair seemed to lift and her heart to stand still, for from the cell from whence she had just been lifted came the sounds of dropping bars and the turning of a lock.

"Quick!" Heinrich called to her in a whisper. She moved on the instant and dropped to the ground.

"Come with me," he panted, out of breath; and, he ran with her, on and on, now down the lane, and always keeping in the dark, now through a gateway and across a garden belonging to one of the city merchants, down a narrow alley where, if they had gone side by side, Margaret would have scraped her arms against the wall, then across a broad street, deserted save by the City Guard, whose measured step sounded and whose gleaming halberds could be seen as they passed a huge bonfire which blazed in the marketplace to allay infection, since the Burgomaster and City Fathers feared the coming of the plague.

Heinrich did not pause, and Margaret, longing to escape the clutches of the Inquisitors, never asked him where he was taking her. The thought which absorbed her was liberty; and that remembrance of the sound of the shooting bolts and the fear that the Familiars, when they found that she was gone, would pursue her, using the window as she had done, made her feel that she would go anywhere, yes, anywhere, rather than fall into their cruel hands.

"On, Heinrich, on! I hear them coming!" she exclaimed, when her companion slackened his pace a little. "Oh, do not lag behind!" she added, panting.

"The danger is gone now," the other said, detaining her. "They do not see us, and they have no notion as to the way we took. I am taking you to a place where they will never find you."

Heinrich turned down a dark lane. His quiet confidence restored her confidence, and she was content to go his pace.

At last he came to a ramshackle building. It might have been an old cart house, or a place where cows were lodged, or a stable. At another time she would have hesitated to be drawn into such a darkness, especially as she could not discern what the place was like; but the instinct of flight disposed her to disregard everything in the way of doubt. She thought of nothing but that one purpose, to get away from those minions who had threatened her with the torture chamber. Going slowly, lest Margaret should stumble, he lead her round obstacles which he knew of and which she could not see, Heinrich stopped suddenly. Then he tapped sharply three or four times.

"Who is it?" came a woman's voice.

"Mother, I am here. Open the door."

# THE MILL IN THE FOREST

WHEN Tyndale and his companions stood on the river bank, after having quitted the cavern, there was no sign of any boat such as the forester had spoken of.

"I've come wide of the mark," said Engel, after looking up and down the stream as if to get his bearings. "Yes; but I see now. We must go a bit to the left and then we shall find Brunow, who said he would wait until we came."

The others started when they saw a black form rise as if coming out of the water.

"Who goes there?" came a quiet but manly toned challenge.

"Otto Engel. Is anybody about?" the forester asked.

"Not that I can see. The pirate lord up yonder has found enough booty to last two or three nights, and there is not so much as a sentinel at the landing stage. Still, don't linger. I'd like to get away. One never knows who may be about. Which is the Englishman?"

"I am," said Tyndale, going closer to the boatman, and before long he was seated in the flat bottomed boat, and, the others having stepped into it, the forester was helping to pull to the other bank.

"Now 'tis easy going, please God," said Engel, when they stepped out on the meadow and the boatman made his craft fast.

"I'd not be too sure of it!" he exclaimed, "and it were best to be alert when such an one as Cochlaeus is on the quest for anybody tainted with heresy."

The boatman stood in his boat and looked about him, and they could barely see his movements in the darkness.

"It's well that there was no moon while we were crossing, but I think she's coming. If you hurry over the meadow you may reach the forest yonder before she comes away from those clouds which look like breaking up. And we are not likely presently to have a very dark night."

"We'll go at once," said Engel, and, bidding Tyndale take his arm since it would help him, and telling Roye to carry the wallet, he bade the boatman "goodnight," and moved across the meadow.

They had barely entered the forest when the moon swept out into a sky where broken clouds began to drift, and the meadow they had crossed, as likewise the river, and again beyond it the forest where the castle stood, were in the full flood of silver light, only obscured for a few moments as a cloud veiled the moon. They paused to watch the scene, and then they exclaimed almost with one voice:

"Only just in time!"

Out of the forest they had quitted some horsemen rode into the open, close by where they had stepped into the boat. Steel glanced at every movement, and so plainly did everything come into view that they saw one of the horsemen looking around from beneath the hand which shaded his eyes.

"The City Guard!" cried Herman.

"And Cochlaeus, so I think!" exclaimed the forester, who was bending forward, watching every movement. "But what is that?"

Three or four great flat-bottomed boats were floating down the stream, and the horseman who was scanning the landscape beckoned to the men who were in them. What was said it was impossible to tell, but what followed thrilled them with a deadly fear.

"I didn't expect anything like that," muttered the forester, after watching keenly. "Do you see what they are doing? They must have seen or heard us, for they mean to come to this side of the river. See! The boats are drawn up at the bank, which slopes in such a way that the horses can be got into them!"

Tyndale and his companions seemed rooted to the spot. They knew that it was dangerous to linger, yet they found it impossible to get away until they saw in which direction the horsemen would travel when once they touched the other bank.

The great boats, filled with horses and men, came slowly over the water, watched by the unseen fugitives, who were fascinated with their movements.

"Shall we not do well to be moving?" said Tyndale presently, when the first boat ran up to the bank and the riders, leaping out, began to land their horses.

"Best to wait now, I think," said the forester quietly. "If we watch the direction they take we can go in another, and so avoid them."

"Very well," Tyndale responded, and they waited in such silence that every night sound in the forest could be heard—the roar of some prowling beast breaking the silence, and the weird and startling cry of a night bird. But even that went by unnoticed in the anxiety of those minutes of watching.

The last horse came on the bank, and before long, while the boats drifted back again into the current, the horsemen mounted into their saddles, and, gathering up their reins, waited for the next command. It came, for before long every horse was on the move, and steel helmets and steel trappings glanced in the moonlight as the cavalcade moved onward.

"They are moving away from us, thank God!" exclaimed the forester in a tone of intense relief. "They think, if they are after us, and they must be! that we should make for the beaten pathway, and they mean to take it themselves. This way, then!"

The forester took Tyndale's hand, and pulled it through his arm.

"Lean hard on me, Master Tyndale. God willing, we shall give Cochlaeus and his men the slip. I think I know this forest better than any of them, and I can take you by paths they have never seen. So I say, 'Thank God for the moonlight.' Now, art ready?"

The forest was a dangerous place to travel by night, when the wild creatures, the bears, the wolves, the boars, and wild dogs, were out for food. But they would scarcely face four men, each with some weapon, and moving in a compact little body, and alert for every sound and chance encounter. But even then, since this was a matter of life and death, there could be no thought of hesitation.

The last of the horsemen entered the broad forest path when Engel began to move in the other direction, away from them, and away, as he knew, from the place to which he had meant to lead William Tyndale. They went on and on, not going too swiftly, lest they should tire too soon, and always listening for the sound of horses' hoofs and anything like the jingle of steel, in case Cochlaeus had changed his course. Engel led them into the dense shadows, among the bushes, where, when the foliage screened the moonlight, the darkness was blackness. More than once something rushed past them with a snarl or a yelp, and sometimes they heard the jaws of a wolf, or other creature, snap again and again. Once, as the forester led Tyndale away to the left, a wild boar sprang up at their feet, and the glint of the moon through the break in the forest showed them his flashing eyes and his foaming mouth as he sprang away among the undergrowth.

"We are safe, Master Tyndale, since you prayed before we started that God would have us in His keeping," said Engel quietly; and Tyndale's answer told him of his quiet assurance.

"I know it, Engel. We shall yet praise God for His protecting mercies."

They had travelled a good distance, and more than once they had had to rest because Tyndale felt the strain. Yet so far there was no sign of Cochlaeus and his soldiers. Neither had anything human crossed their path. But at last they came to the open country, and across the meadow was a great windmill, now standing still, with no light within to show that anyone was moving.

"'Tis my father's mill!" the forester exclaimed; "and we may safely awake him, since you are tired, Master Tyndale. Some food and a rest will do you good, for I am sure you can have but little strength left."

"But what of those men who are on our track?" said Tyndale anxiously.

"My father will set someone to keep watch, and the country is open, so that no soldiers can come on us unawares.'

"But if they did?" Tyndale asked doubtfully.

"A word the moment they appeared anywhere out of the forest and we could get into the marshes, and no horsemen, unless they knew the way, could follow."

Tyndale assented, and gladly, for by this time he was almost exhausted. In a little while they had crossed the meadow and stood at the mill door.

"Who's there?" came the call from an upper window, when Engel had beaten loudly on the door.

"Otto, father, and some friends. Be quick, for we are in no small danger."

The head was drawn away from the window in an instant, and before long the miller was standing in the open doorway.

"Come in!" he exclaimed. "You're welcome since my son brings you here, although I do not know you!"

He had a candle in his hand, and he led the way into a kitchen, the forester staying to bar the door; but he was not long away.

"Father, this is that Englishman, William Tyndale, you may have heard of, whom Cochlaeus is after, meaning to burn him if he can lay hands on him."

"Ha! then thou'rt thrice welcome, Master Tyndale. I'd do ought to frustrate that Deacon of the Church of the Blessed Virgin. I shall never forget the inroad he and his made in our homes."

The man's voice trembled, and he brushed his great hand across his eyes.

"You want food?" he asked, mastering his emotion. "I'll get it;" and ere long the travelers were eating of the best he had to offer them.

"Lie down there, Master Tyndale, and you other men over there. I'll keep watch, and if any come this way I'll awake you in good time, and my son will take you to the marsh."

They slept in confidence with that assurance, but scarcely two hours had gone when the miller awoke them noisily.

"The horsemen have just come out of the forest, and they are crossing the meadow. Otto, take them away, and bide on the island there. 'Tis safe enough, if you're content to stay there till the danger is past."

By this time all were ready.

"My wallet!" exclaimed Tyndale anxiously, for even in this stress of pursuit it was too precious to be forgotten.

"I have it," Roye answered, and he threw it across his shoulder and stood waiting to be gone.

Going out of the mill by a back door, they saw the mere showing plainly in the moonlight. The sedges and reeds almost touched the wall, and Otto Engel hesitated, for he knew the danger. Even for him or his father, who knew the paths in the marsh, it was perilous; but by going cautiously he knew they could pass safely if the others would do exactly as he said. Otherwise it was death, and he told them so.

"If the soldiers should see us they could not overtake us, so be calm, and take your time. Look well to your footing, and we shall be safe."

He spoke with more confidence than he felt, for it was a long time since he had gone into the heart of the mere.

They moved on slowly, the forester telling them what to do from time to time, and they traversed the mere for fully fifty yards in safety, but hearing the sounds of galloping hoofs and jingling steel.

"We're safe now, unless they fire after us," said Engel, speaking thus to reassure them, and pausing for a moment to look behind. "Even if they see us you need have no fear, for they could not follow."

He was turning to move on again, when a cry escaped him involuntarily.

"They have seen us! But what of that?" he added. "They cannot follow."

"They are going to try!" exclaimed Herman, pointing to the horsemen who had come round to the back of the mill.

"We'll put as much distance between ourselves and them as possible," cried Engel, catching at Tyndale's hand. "Mark every word I say, and each one repeat it as he does it to the one behind, so that there will be no mistake."

They went on as swiftly as they dared along the winding path, sometimes hidden by the sedges, which in places rose high enough to shut off the view, while they could not see the horsemen, neither could they be seen until they stepped out again into a clearer space.

"Halt!" came the cry on the night air, and the voice belonged to Cochlaeus.

"On!" exclaimed Engel, moving forward; but a shot rang out, and then another, and yet a third, and they could hear the hissing as the balls flew past them.

"They have struck none of us, thank God!" said Tyndale, moving on again with Engel, after an involuntary pause.

The horsemen were in a group at the opening of the path, helpless and baffled, while the little company still moved on.

"We shall soon be safe," cried the forester. "Another hundred yards and we can be at ease."

"But they may follow," said Herman.

"They will be mad if they do," was the answer; but he had scarcely said as much when Engel's lips parted with wonder. "'Tis madness, surely. 'Tis death to some of them!"

He spoke because three of the soldiers had the audacity to try the path. One led the way on his horse, and another followed, with a third close on his heels. But the feet of the first horse slipped and threw his rider into the midst of the bog.

The scene which followed thrilled those who were watching with horror; not Tyndale and his companions only, but those who were grouped about Cochlaeus. The horse scrambled to his feet and reached the solid ground, but the soldier of the City Guard, throwing out his hands, implored the others to come to his aid. His voice travelled over the marsh, and they heard his hands beat on the slush in his frantic efforts to regain the meadow. It was only possible to watch in helplessness, and the marsh was swallowing him up. The soldier was ere long up to the armpits in the mire, but at last, with a heartrending cry, he disappeared, and the mud and water of the mere closed over him.

Tyndale and his companions watched in solemn silence; then, when Otto Engel spoke, they turned and followed him. They moved along the tortuous path, but halted behind 'a bank of rushes to see what was being done. They saw the horsemen turn away, and slowly ride out of sight, not even staying to speak to the miller.

The path ended at an open space of solid ground hemmed in by thick bushes and heavily foliaged willow trees, and to their amazement those who followed Engel's leading saw a strongly built timber hut, completely hidden from the view of any who were in the country on the fringe of the marsh.

"You are safe here, Master Tyndale," said the forester, as he flung the hut door open and bade his companions enter. "Neither Cochlaeus nor all the Familiars going can ever find you here. My father will feed you, and if you will, Master Tyndale, you may pursue your God made task, working and resting when you please."

# HERMAN'S RETURN

HERMAN satisfied himself that Tyndale was safe, and that everything was provided for his comfort, before he started on his journey home. Once on the way, he travelled in haste, but careful when he reached the city not to show any signs of trepidation. He passed through the gateway just before the gloaming fell, and the wardens gave him a friendly nod.

"How has your business prospered?" the chief warden, with whom he was a favorite, asked, as he so often did.

"Excellently well," was Herman's answer "How go things in the city?"

"Doubtful," the warden said almost impatiently, as if it annoyed him to recall something. "That Deacon, Cochlaeus, has worried the Council for days past, and the Burgomaster has had a troublesome time because, forsooth, the Churchman declared that the Englishman, Tyndale, has been hiding within the walls, but had, in some unaccountable manner, got away. And he must needs declare that we were not alert, else he would never have passed the gate. Then he came down on those who have to keep an eye to the ships, and he blames them and us alike, thinking to hit the right one with his random methods."

The man stamped out his annoyance on the hard stones, and Herman felt that if the chief warden could have his way Cochlaeus would have no gentle treatment.

"Didst say William Tyndale, here, in the city?" Herman asked, in simulated surprise. "You mean that English fellow who, they say, is come to this country to get his Bible printed?"

The men stared at him in equal surprise.

"Dost mean to say, Herman, that you do not know that it has been common talk in the city that he was hiding somewhere here? Cochlaeus was so sure about it, that every printer's shop has been searched, although he declared his conviction that the real culprit was Master Byrckmann, who is to be your father-in-law someday, so they say."

The wardens laughed, but Herman put on a look of supreme contempt for such an absurd charge against Margaret's father.

"I have been away so much of late," he explained. "And so many things happen in a short time. Have they found Tyndale?"

"That's just where the fun comes in," said the chief warden, his face, like his underlings', all smiles.

Before he said more, he looked about him in all directions; then he dropped his voice so low that the others could scarcely hear him.

"The Englishman was here without a doubt. I saw him. So did each of these. But not one of us would tell of him, although there was a price on his head; for who would sell a man to those tormentors? The poor man lodged somewhere, nobody knows where, and when night fell he used to come into the streets for an airing. But let that pass. I can tell you something more."

The warden paused to look about him again.

"Cochlaeus came back a few hours since, more like a madman than a reverend father of the Church, and his face was not pleasant to see. He had not passed the gate long before it got to be known that he had found that Tyndale really was in the city, and went away in a ship. He, and the City Guard, tracked him into Schouts' castle, up the river, and that saintly minded robber lord was ready to sell the Englishman for a thousand golden crowns. And how do you think the matter was settled?" said the chief warden, with a chuckle. "When the bargain was struck, and they went into the dungeon for Cochlaeus to claim his purchase, William Tyndale was gone!"

"Gone?"

Herman's face was the picture of astonishment.

"Do you mean to tell me that Tyndale managed to dupe Schouts, of all men in the world?" he cried.

"I do. And since I have no love either for the robber lord, who is a rascal, or the Deacon," said the chief warden, whispering behind his hand, "I'm glad the poor man got away. I hope he'll get clear out of the country and spoil the plans of the Inquisitor."

Herman looked at the man to judge how far he seemed sincere, but it was impossible to doubt him. So had he seen others look when Cochlaeus was spoken of—a man hated of all men for his work's sake, to say nothing of his well known mercilessness.

Herman moved on. He did not know, as he passed away from the gate, that the chief warden looked after him commiseratingly, and shrugged his shoulders.

"There's trouble in store for that poor fellow," he said to the men around.

At heart Herman was relieved to find that no whisper had got abroad that his home had given shelter to the man whom Cochlaeus was searching for. At first he walked along the street with a free step and a light heart, for he would soon see Margaret, and explain to her why he had been away so long. And tomorrow was the day of their wedding! He was home in time! He whistled gaily at the thought.

But for some unaccountable reason a sense of dread came to him. The gaiety passed, and the dread grew with every step onward, before he had gone far. The thought came that Margaret would blame him for neglect, leaving her for so many days without a word, and her wedding day so near! And yet he had sent her a message by a man named Jermyn, who knew the circumstances, since he worked at the windmill, telling her he would be home in good time for their marriage, but he must make sure that William Tyndale was safe in hiding, and beyond discovery. But his content, while on the road, had been rudely shaken, for when he came to a lonely spot on the way, he saw a man lying, beaten, and bruised, and bleeding by the wayside, and it was Jermyn, his messenger, scarce able to speak.

When he had lodged the poor fellow at an inn, and left money to cover his nursing, he had come on swiftly, anxious to set the misfortune right.

A sense of brooding calamity grew on him while he walked the familiar streets, but what form it could take he could not conceive. It was not that Margaret would resent his laggard arrival, and display unreasonable temper—he knew her too well to have that thought. It was a brooding fear of something infinitely worse than that. It might be that ruin had overtaken her father because Cochlaeus had discovered the part he had played in printing off the Scripture sheets. It might be— God forbid!

He stopped, and drops of sweat like great beads rolled down his face. Margaret might be dead!

He had turned down the street which led to his own home, thinking to see his mother first, and change his travel stained clothes for something better; but this possibility sent him down a byway which would take him by shortcuts to Margaret's home.

He went at first at a swift walk, but this unnamable horror grew on him so much that he broke into a run, so that when he came out of the alley almost opposite Margaret's home he was so spent and breathless that he had to stand a few minutes before he could enter the house and was able to speak.

When he entered the shop Margaret's father was standing behind the counter. The gloom on the printer's face forced a question from his lips.

"What is wrong? Where is she? Is she dead?"

He stood at the counter, his hands shaking as they rested on it, his face flushed with the heat of his run, his lips trembling, and his breath coming almost in sobs.

"I know not," was the slow and sad reply. "God knows, Herman, but we do not. And tomorrow was to be her marriage day. Come in, my son, where we can talk."

The printer led the way into the quiet parlor behind the shop, where Margaret and Herman had spent so many happy hours. There Byrckmann sank into a chair, and, resting his elbows on the table, buried his careworn face in his hands, and wept. And to see a strong man weep is like watching a strong swimmer in his agony in a sea that claims him, and is seeking to drag him down.

"My darling! My child! My child! Would God I had died for thee!" he sobbed.

Herman sat and gazed at him with hungry eyes. His soul was in a tumult. He wanted to ask what this meant, but he dared not, while this storm of grief was shaking Byrckmann. But bit by bit, in a little while the story came, so meagre since Margaret's father knew so little. Margaret had never returned home. He had gone to Herman's home, and neither had he come, and his mother could tell the printer nothing. She could only express the wonder whether the girl had sought to find her way through the cavern, while Herman had gone forward with Tyndale to see him out of danger, and she had lost herself in that great, wandering place, which had once lodged the larger part of an army.

Herman's mother and Byrckmann had gone down to the cavern, and had searched it through and through, not once, but twice, and even thrice, thinking that some corner had been left unexplored. Strange to say, they found a passage Herman's mother knew nothing of, but it seemed to end in a cul-de-sac. They found a lantern on the floor, broken and smoked, and a scarf. The lantern belonged to Herman, and the scarf was Margaret's; but that was all.

The printer had gone everywhere he could think of in the city to look for his daughter, and John Gropper had gone as well. He was out now, looking for her. So, too, had the workmen left the printing presses, which now stood idle, to search, in their love for her, even down to the boys who served the men; but it would be the same as before—the same story of failure.

Herman sat, stupefied. This was calamity. It might mean so much! It could scarcely mean less than death.

While he walked slowly home he was reeling as a drunken man, and people, in the darkest part of the gloaming, looked at him askance. But they understood when they saw who it was, since it had become widely known that the beautiful girl whose marriage was fixed for tomorrow had disappeared. Some had whispered the dread words—"The Inquisition!" Byrckmann had it in mind, but did not say the words. Nor had the wardens at the gate spoken of it, although they knew that Margaret was missing, and feared for the possible explanation—the Familiars!

"Mother, she's gone!" he cried, as he entered his home, and, staggering along the passage, stood, white-faced and shaken, in the doorway, where she sat, trying to do her usual work.

"I know, my son!" she exclaimed, coming to throw her arms about him to comfort him. But how could she do that when the uncertainty was beginning to vanish, and the thought was crystallizing in her mind that her boy's bride was somewhere in the Familiars' power? It had once been said that over the gate of Hell the inscription was cut deep in the imperishable granite:

"All hope abandon, ye who enter here."

Was the haunt of the Inquisition a place where Hope could come any more than in that Hell of which the poet wrote? And what was it to them that Margaret was tender and beautiful and young? That was no shield to ward off their torture strokes.

Herman's mother felt that it was useless to whisper any words of comfort, for she was borne down by anxiety, and fearful of the worst.

When he had had some food, and had washed away his travel stains, Herman went through the cavern, but the quest was an unsuccessful one. His exhaustive search brought him to the passage of which the printer had spoken. He halted in the cul-de-sac, with the rock in front of him, and examined it closely. All these underground ways and caverns which were common in that part of the country might have their arms or, as they seemed to him, their tentacles; and yet he was convinced that this was no dead end.

Standing in the dim light which his horn lantern threw on the walls, he tried to think the whole thing out, and form some plan of action; for if Margaret was alive he would find her, whether the search covered days or weeks.

He stood with folded arms, the lantern at his feet; but he bent down for it presently, and scanned the rock which closed up the end of the passage. He had thought of the cul-de-sac in the forest cavern, which the forester had shown him, and which proved to be an entrance to the castle of the robber lord.

Might not this be like that, and leading into some place where Margaret might be?

The thought began to frame itself into something like a certainty, for when he set the lantern on the floor again, he noticed that the earth which had drifted on the rock was beaten in, as though it had been trampled on by many feet. He went on his knees and saw some footprints—those of men who were not shod as he was. His boots were nailed, but these marks were not from them.

Presently his eyes, in that keen search, caught the gleam of something like gold, and when he took it into his hand and held it to the lantern light he exclaimed in wonder. This was the golden plaque; which he had given her on the day of their betrothal, and he wondered how it came here. Thrusting it safely into his pocket, he sat back on his heels and thought. Was this not a cul-de-sac after all, but the entrance to some house?

He endeavored to locate the spot. Hard by, just over the cavern, was the city wall. He knew of the houses that were there, but this passage, which was long and narrow, running inwards beneath the city—where did it lie? It ran level with the city wall at first, but then it took a turn, and at right angles it stretched along for many yards.

For a time he merely groped, as it were, in his mind. It was difficult to get his bearings as to streets and houses, but after a while the thing assumed such shape that a cry came from his lips, and his heart so throbbed with pain that his hand went to it to still it.

"The Holy House!" he exclaimed. "Margaret is there!"

He went over it all in his mind again, and knew it must be so, and then he saw what had happened. The picture was vividly portrayed, and his imagination served him so well that he could see men's faces, their doings, and his darling's horror. Margaret had gone into the cavern when he left her, and had fallen into the hands of the Familiars, who had walked down this passage and in some way through this place which was blocked by an apparently impassable wall of rock. And she was taken into that place of terror—that den of infamy. It must be so, for there were those dull footprints, such as Familiars would leave, and her plaque to show that she had been there. And every footprint pointed to the rock. None turned away from it, to suggest that they had found her here and carried her away.

He sprang to his feet, caught up the lantern, and tested the rock as he and Engel had done when they entered the castle in the forest to search for William Tyndale. He scanned it thoroughly, but for a long time saw no trace of any opening. At last he observed what looked like a crack, and drawing the dagger from his belt again he thrust the point at it. The thin, keen-edged blade went in some little distance, and he moved it upwards. It ran up and up, till it would go no farther. He turned the blade, and ran it from right to left for the space of a couple of feet. Then down the left side the dagger moved. At the bottom the blade travelled easily towards the right.

That was proof that there was an opening in the rock, and he believed that the rock would move. But how? Was there a spring anywhere that must be touched before it would shift inwards and towards him? He began to search for it. With the lantern's aid he scanned the surface, inch after inch, intent on finding this spring, for he meant to get in,

209

taking the tremendous risks, to look for Margaret and bring her away, if he could find her, whatever the cost.

Nearly an hour went, and although he began to despair he could not bring himself to give up the attempt. Margaret must have been carried through that space which was nearly four feet high, and he, too, would go and bring her from the Holy House. What could frustrate him when his dear one was there?

When the quest for the secret spring appeared so hopeless that he began to think the discovery was impossible, his finger, which travelled over the face of the rock nearby this door very delicately, marked something unlike what was near it. He pressed the spot, and to his wonder and relief, and yet almost to his alarm, because of what might follow, the door moved slowly back to the left, and there was an open space before him.

# IN THE LION'S MOUTH

FOR a little while Herman's courage failed him. To ascend those steps which he could see would probably mean such fearful experiences that the bravest of the brave might shrink back and leave his task undone.

Yet now that he had such unquestionable proof that Margaret had been at this door, and as certainly had entered it in the company of the black-robed ones of the Inquisition, how could he think other than that she was lying in one of the cells, if not already enduring torture? Loving her as he did, he could not be so craven as to turn away and leave her in the hands of the tormentors!

The bare suggestion in his mind that she might possibly have been done to death made his soul stand up in arms, and his hesitation was gone in an instant. He ascended the steps without halting until he came to the topmost one and found himself looking along a passage with doors on either side.

Were they the doors of cells, such as he had heard spoken of so often in the city, when men and women talked with bated breath of the horrors of the Holy House? And if they were, was Margaret in one of them?

The nearest door, when he ventured so far, opened as he pressed his hand against it. Looking in, he found the cell empty. It was the same with the next, the third, and the fourth, for he tried each door on either side. All were empty, but the straw lay on the floors, and the rats scrambled away when he entered. They had come to these dismal places to root among the straw for any crusts that might have been left by the prisoners who last occupied the cells.

Every place in the passage was unoccupied, and Herman ventured up twenty more steps to find himself in some open ground — a great garden bounded by some very high walls. He was so near to one of them that by the aid of the moon he could see the iron spikes which rendered escape impossible if any poor prisoner made the attempt.

He was in the greatest quandary now, for, looking along the garden, the immensity of the place set him wondering how he could possibly find Margaret. Some sixty yards away, beyond the grass and bushes, was the main building, and his darling must be there; but in which part? And how was he to enter unseen? If he passed along the passage at the top of this last flight of steps, what could he do? The cells that were occupied would be bolted and barred, and there was nothing to indicate the name of the victim on the other side of those strong, iron-sheeted doors.

He was dismayed with the thought of the hopelessness of it all.

Standing beneath a tree whose heavy branches hung round him like a tent, with an opening here and there, he watched the scene, trying to solve the problem of finding Margaret. The first thing was to make a bolder endeavor yet—going into the very heart of the danger—to see where the Familiars had placed her. When that was done he must get into touch with her; and once with Margaret, none of those who kept that fearful house should hinder him from taking her away. And surely God would help him!

The moon was brilliant. She was sailing at her full across a cloudless sky, throwing deep shadows everywhere, but lighting up the open spaces like day. If anyone crossed the green expanse of grass he would know who it was if he ventured with uncovered face in the fine silvery light.

"'Tis no use standing here," he muttered. "I must take the risks. She must be found."

He went forward while he spoke, and, entering by the doorway through which he had come a few minutes before, he moved on down the passage, trying the doors. Like all the others, they were empty, and the bitter thought came that those who had last lodged there had paid the death penalty for their heresy, and the Familiars were in the city on the quest for others to take their places. Otherwise, would it be likely that he could come so far and find no one who could challenge his presence?

He came to a door like all the others — iron-sheeted, with bolts and bars on the outside and a key in the lock. He pressed against the door with his hand, but while the bars were leaning against the stonework, and the bolts were not thrust into their sockets, the door did not move.

"She may be here," he muttered, and his heart beat more quickly at the thought. He twisted the key, and the door opened and he passed in.

He was not sure, but he thought he heard a sound, but that might be the prisoner moving on the straw. As he stood within the dark cell, he spoke.

"Is anyone here?"

There was no answer to the question, and he went farther in, holding out his lantern to scan the place with its aid. The straw was there, but no one on it. His foot kicked against a water jar, and he heard the splash of the water, and saw it gleam as it scattered on the horrid floor. A rat was not far away, trying to carry with him in his flight a piece of black bread; but, look where he would, there was no other sign of life. Certainly nothing human was there.

He turned away, in disappointment, but, looking up, he started, and the lantern almost fell from his hand in the extremity of his alarm. Two Familiars were between him and the door, one carrying a lantern, the other closing the door as though to shut themselves and this intruder in.

"Who are you? and what are you doing here?" the nearer one asked, in a sharp and angry tone. "How dare you intrude like this?"

Herman made no answer, and the instinct of caution made him use his free hand to draw his cap low down to his eyebrows, to hide himself as much as possible. He had a thought of what might follow if he got away, and these men should recognize him. And while doing this, and staring at these men, he was wondering what he should do next—how he should get away.

"Answer my questions!" came the demand imperatively.

"I'll answer no questions!" cried Herman, his courage rising; and he was resolute to stand at nothing rather than be held a prisoner, to be at the mercy of these creatures who were facing him. He thought, and quickly, that he would make a sudden rush.

He dashed his lantern into their lantern, casting the cell into sudden darkness. He bounded past them and into the hallway.

He closed the door swiftly, but softly. He twisted the key in the lock, and drew it away; and, carrying it in his hand, he strode to the door where, not long before, he had entered from the garden.

Out in the open he would be safer than within the house itself, and, hidden somewhere in the shadows among the dense bushes, he might think of some plan to scale the walls and get away. With the key still in his hand, he went to the tree where he had stood before to make his observations;

and while he was trying to solve the problem of his next course he was startled. A bush, like laurels or rhododendrons, towards which he began to move to be in safer hiding, parted, and a face appeared, and then Herman saw the rough hair and straggling beard of a man.

The moon fell full on the face, and Herman knew it; but he kept still and silent for a few moments, listening for some possible alarm in the Holy House; but everything was silent. There was no clamor of voices to break the stillness of the night, no sound of men beating on the locked door to arouse attention.

Precious though the moments were, he watched the bearded face. The man's eyes were turned to the building, and his hands held back the bush on either side of him, so that his view should not be obscured. In a little while he came part way out into the open, and Herman saw, by the man's full body, that he was not mistaken as to his identity.

"Heinrich!" he exclaimed, just so loud that his voice travelled over the intervening space.

The man was alarmed, dropped back into the shadow of the bush, and was lost sight of completely.

Silence followed, and Herman listened as intently as before for any sound of alarm in the cell; but none came. He broke the silence, for here was someone who might be of service.

"Heinrich, don't you know my voice?"

The face reappeared, and Herman saw how it turned towards the tree where he was standing unseen. He was struck partly with its terror, partly with its cunning.

"Is it Herman Bengel?" came the question.

"Yes. I will come to you, for I want your help."

Herman was still speaking, when the man crossed to the tree with swift strides.

"Speak, so that I may know where you are," Heinrich whispered. "Nay, come here, where the moonlight is, and I may see your face; or how shall I know that you are not one of those murderous hounds of that house yonder, trying to get your sharp fangs into me?"

Herman stepped out into the moonlight, and the other, who watched him, caught at Herman's hand and kissed it.

"God has sent you!" he exclaimed, below his breath, lest anyone might hear beyond themselves. "Come with me, and I will show you what will do your heart good! Ay, and it will gladden your eyes."

Herman wondered what his meaning was, but he told him why he was here in the garden, and how anxious he was to get away because of that struggle in the cell.

"Give me the key," Heinrich implored. "The day may come when I may use it and set some poor prisoner free." He put forth his hand for it, and Herman, having no need for it, gave it to him.

"But she is there, I feel assured, Heinrich, in that horrible place," said Herman anxiously. "And now I am helpless. I dare not go back for her."

"You need not!" Heinrich broke in on his words impulsively. "You need not. Go on your knees and thank God! Say what I heard Mistress Margaret say, 'Bless the Lord, O my soul!' Say it, for she is not there, in that accursed house. She was, but she is not now. She is safe. I got her away from the tormentors. Listen to me."

Heinrich dropped his voice to a whisper, and had put his arm about Herman's neck, to speak in his, ear.

"I have her in safe keeping, hidden where none of those Familiars can find her," he said exultingly.

"Do you mean it?" whispered Herman, trembling at what he heard. "Is she not in that house yonder?"

"No. She was there. She was to be taken to the torture chamber, but I took her away, and I have her now in safe keeping, thank God! Listen again. She mourned, in spite of her gladness at being free, because she had lost a plaque which you gave her on her betrothal day. I have come to find it. I am going to the cell from whence I brought her to look for it, and when I have found it I will take you to her."

Herman was elate with gladness, and his lips were quietly muttering his grateful thanks for God's deliverance of Margaret.

"There is no need to seek for it, Heinrich. I have found it. It was that which made me confident that she had been taken to the Holy House. See, it is here!"

Holding back one of the drooping branches, Herman held it where the gold gleamed in the moonlight.

"That is it, Heinrich. Will you take it and me to her?"

"I will!" the simple one exclaimed." Let me carry it. She will then know that I redeemed my promise."

Herman listened for any possible sound in the cell, but everything was silent. Even the night birds made no sound tonight, and the trees scarcely moved, so that there was but little rustling among the leaves. He was relieved, for there was no alarm as yet, and they might get away.

"Time is precious, Heinrich," he said. "Those men may call for help."

"I do not hear them," said Heinrich simply. "But let us go. How glad she will be to have this—and you!" He moved away while he was speaking.

"Where are we going?" Herman asked, when they stepped into the shelter of a bush after crossing a wide and moonlit lawn.

"To the wall. Can you climb it?"

A daring thought, since the silence was unbroken, came to Herman. It was next door to madness, but he yielded to it.

"I will take you by the way I came, Heinrich, and then you shall see how I came to feel so certain that Mistress Margaret had been taken to the Holy House."

"My way is best," said Heinrich doubtfully. "And it is safest."

"But 'tis worth trying. Come!" They went carefully, to avoid being seen, in case any who dwelt in the place should be moving about the garden, or any eyes should be searching the moonlit grounds from the windows. He went forward to the door, alert and ready if anyone strove to bar the way.

They stepped in at the doorway and listened, but all was silent; not even a groan from that cell where Herman had left the Familiars. He saw what he had not seen before—a lighted lantern on the floor at one of the doors. It was not there when he had first gone to the cell, so that his thought was that one of the Familiars had left it there before entering the place where they found him.

"We'll take that with us, Heinrich," he whispered. "Mine is locked up in the cell."

Going swiftly down the steps, and past the open cells, they came to the opening in the rock Heinrich's eyes moving in all directions to miss nothing. Herman watched him, and the thought came that he was projecting his mind to future days when he might use this passage and come to set some poor captive free, since it was his boasted delight to spoil the plans of the masters of the Holy House.

Heinrich watched with growing wonder how the rock door swung back noiselessly into its place after they had passed into the cavern, leaving no token of any opening.

"Show me how you opened it!" he exclaimed. "I may find my way in some day, and get someone out of this."

"You shall see," Herman answered, falling in with his desire. "Look at that spot there, where the rock by the door has scaled off ever so slightly."

"Here?" asked Heinrich, touching it with his finger.

Herman nodded. "Press hard."

Heinrich tried it again and again, watching with eager interest how the door moved back and forth at his will. Then the bearded face lit up with childish glee.

"I have been here before!" he exclaimed, looking round the place. "It was here that I saw them with Mistress Margaret. Yes, it was here. I shall often come here, and won't I spoil the Egyptians!"

He hugged himself at the thought, and was exultant while Herman led him to the cave's ,entrance, where they saw the great river rolling by in solemn silence, but shining under the moon's still rays. Heinrich gazed in all directions, and, rubbing his hands, he whispered, as though the bush had listeners in it:

"I know! I came into the cavern by this entrance. Yonder I shall find the gate. Away in that direction is the Burgomaster's house. Oh yes, I know! But let me be sure. There is this bush and that gleaming bit of rock, like a dog's head. Yes, 'tis the same. And to think of the dismay of the black Familiars when they come from time to time and find one of the cells empty this one today, and that one tomorrow!"

He stopped, with a puzzled look on his face.

"I want to take you to Mistress Margaret, but I cannot. We are outside the city walls, and we may not go in again till dawn of day, when the gates are opened. Let us go back to that accursed house, and into the garden, and climb the wall."

Herman smiled as he watched Heinrich's anxiety.

219

"There is no need. I am going to take you by a private way if you will give me your solemn promise never to betray it to anyone."

The other looked at him reproachfully.

"How could you think I would do so base a thing?" he cried. "I, who love so much those who have been kind to me? How could you even think of it?"

Taking Herman's hand, Heinrich gazed into his eyes still more, and presently a tear fell down the poor fellow's face, and yet another, and many more.

"How could you think it?" he exclaimed again, protestingly.

"Dry up your tears, Heinrich!" Herman exclaimed hastily. "I never doubted you. I only wanted you to know the consequences of a careless word, for it might mean death to one or many of your friends."

"And you can trust me?"

"As much as I can trust myself," Herman answered.

"Then I am content. Come! Let us be going, for Mistress Margaret will be anxious since I have been so long away."

Before many minutes had gone they had passed through the doorway of rock which the eagle eyes of the keenest of the Familiars would never have suspected as an entrance, then through Tyndale's room and up the secret stairs into Herman's home. His mother heard him coming, and then the story, was told.

"I shall go and tell Margaret's father!" Herman's mother exclaimed, her eyes gleaming with gladness; and although it was night, and the streets were dangerous for a woman to venture out, the thought of a father's and a sick mother's inexpressible anxiety, more painful because of her sense of helplessness, induced her to undertake the errand.

They kept each other company up to the point where they were compelled to part.

"Where is Mistress Margaret?" Herman asked, when he and Heinrich, watching his mother disappear at the bend of a street, turned into an alley.

"That's my secret," came the laughing answer. "Come and see."

They took all the byways, until Herman was completely lost, and then, unexpectedly, he was pulled up in front of a stable door, which Heinrich opened.

"Go in!" the simple one exclaimed, standing aside; "but wait," he added, when Herman stood within, not knowing where to move in the darkness. After some trouble, Heinrich lit his lantern and led the way up some rickety steps into a hayloft.

Standing on the top step, Herman saw a humble room where the furniture was scarce and poor. A table stood in the middle of the floor, and by it sat an elderly woman, working at a man's much worn garment by the candlelight, although the hour was so late. She looked up when she heard Heinrich's voice.

"Mother," he whispered, looking in through the half-opened door almost stealthily.

"Yes, my son."

"Is she asleep?"

"No. She was talking to me, anxious about you, until she heard you down below, and then she went to her room to be out of the way. But I heard someone else. Who is it?"

"Go and tell her, mother, to come and see Herman, the man she should have wedded tomorrow. Tell her that, mother."

Herman gazed around the bare and desolate place when he had stepped within. A few moments only had gone when a cry sprang to his lips. For through the open doorway which Heinrich's mother had passed, someone came. It was Margaret, her hands outstretched, her beautiful face wan and pale, transformed now from the consuming anxiety before the woman entered. Her eyes were gleaming.

"Herman!" she cried.

# THE GREAT ALTERNATIVE

MARGARET was still in jeopardy, and before many hours had gone it was known that she stood in danger of again being lodged in the place from whence she had just been rescued. What should have been her bridal day was spent in hiding, and her father did not dare to come to see her in the broad daylight lest someone belonging to the Holy House should be watching, in readiness to track him, on the supposition that he would be going to see his daughter.

It was dark when he came, but after he had gone home again, Margaret pleaded to be taken home, if only for an hour, to see her mother.

"No!" cried Heinrich, who had come back to the stable, pale and disheveled, the water dripping from him as he stood within the room. "No! Something will happen. You will run into the arms of those fiends who are seeking for you, and I have been told that they have sworn to find you, and break you on the rack, and after that to burn you in the Holy House garden, into which all who are confined there are to be brought to witness your sufferings."

Margaret shuddered, and hid her face in her hands.

"Who told you all that?" Herman asked, pale and trembling at the threat, but realizing, from what was common knowledge, that what the simpleminded man said was more than likely to be true. It was the thing one could have expected.

"I will not tell you," Heinrich answered, almost curtly. "Why should I? And yet, why not?" he added quickly, wiping his face with his kerchief, for it was streaming with the rain which could be heard pattering heavily on the roof. Before he said more, he looked round the room, and, uncertain about the door, went to it, and, standing on the top, called down softly to his mother, who was below:

"Is the outer door locked?"

The whispered question was answered softly, when, from the sounds that followed, they who listened knew that she had gone to the door to try it.

"Yes, my son."

"You are sure?"

"Certain."

Heinrich turned to the others with a look of relief.

"Now I will tell you. This afternoon I stood at the ferry, keeping well out of sight to see what the Burgomaster was doing there. Something had gone wrong, and he was directing some men who were working at the posts which take the chains that stretch across the watergate. Some of the men, who were standing waist-deep in the water, crossed themselves, and it was easy to see that they shrank from something. I bent forward to see what they were looking at, and there I saw them—two of those hungry vultures—walking noiselessly, side by side. When they had looked around, as if to mark whether they were observed, they disappeared among the bushes which hide the entrance to the cavern."

"What then?" Margaret half whispered, leaning forward in her chair, her lips white and parted, and her fingers on them, trembling.

"I followed them, and stole along until I, too, came to the bushes. They were gone into the cavern then, but I went also, and followed until I saw them, by the light of their lantern, going to the passage which leads into the Holy House.

224

They thought themselves alone, and talked freely to two others who had just come out of the Holy House, going, no doubt, on some nefarious errand.

"It was then, as I stood back in hiding, but craning forward not to miss a word or any movement, that I heard all. Those who were returning said that they had scoured the city, but found no trace of the missing girl. What next they said made me shiver in my boots. It was hard to keep my teeth from chattering, which I feared they would have heard. The two who came through the doorway said their orders were, at eleven o'clock tonight, when the people of the city would be asleep, to go to Master Byrckmann's house and search it, high and low, and if they found you not, to bring your father and your mother.

"So now, you know!" the simple one exclaimed, sitting on the floor in his soddened clothes.

A low cry came from the girl's lips, and she stood facing the door, with her hands clenched tightly, watching with startled eyes as though she expected to see those somber and relentless hunters in the doorway.

"Herman, I must go and warn my father. They will kill him, and my mother!" she exclaimed, in a broken voice. "And rather than that, oh, I would die!"

"No, Margaret, that must not be," said Herman, trying to soothe her. "I must take you away from the city at once. We must get you to my mother's house, and away through the cavern to the river; and after that God will tell us what to do," he said, in quiet confidence.

"Herman, I could not do that. They would take my father and mother away because I was not to be found. Rather than that, I would give myself up."

"Nay, that you shall never do!" Herman cried. "Listen. We shall think out some way of escape for us all, and while he is doing that I will go to your father and bid him and your mother come here, and we can all go to some safe place out of the reach of those who want to find you."

"You are safe for a time!" exclaimed Heinrich, who had risen to his feet and was standing before Margaret.

"Safe, Heinrich?" Margaret asked. "But not for long," raising her startled eyes to his, as though she would read in them the extent of her security. "'Tis my father I am thinking of, and my mother." she cried, in a broken voice.

"Let me think!" exclaimed Heinrich, throwing out his hand. "I am bewildered. Give me time, for it is a long while yet till the cathedral bell strikes out the hour of eleven."

Wet though he was, his soaking clothes clinging to him, and the water still trickling down his face from his soddened cap, he sat on the hearth in a huddled heap, and the others stood by and watched him in silence. They thought he had fallen asleep, he sat so still, and Margaret softly sank into her chair to wait.

He seemed to awake unexpectedly, and, springing to his feet, went to Herman and laid a hand on his arm.

"Go and tell Master Byrckmann what I have told you. Make him believe it, for every word I have spoken is true; otherwise he may bar his door tonight and refuse to hear the summons. Tell him more; to come here with his wife and whatever money he may have, for it is time to be gone. Tell him it is his last chance, and it is death to remain. It is as ill for him to remain as it was for those who remained in Sodom when the angels said to Lot, 'Up, get you out of this place.' Tell him I know how to get you all out of the city, and you can go into safety, away from those creatures who are bent on your destruction."

They looked at him in wonder. It seemed to them as though he was no longer the simple one of the city, but some inspired one with a message; and Herman, when Heinrich had ended, and had sunk down again to the hearth, worn and tired, took him at his word. Wrapping his cloak about him, went down the stairs and out into the driving wind and rain. He knew the way, dark though it was, and after traversing the empty streets, stepped abruptly into the parlor where Margaret's father was sitting.

"What news, Herman?" he asked, when he saw the young man's face; and while the story came, of the peril which threatened him and his house, the printer listened with his head bowed low and his hands tightly clasped.

"'Tis what I suspected, Herman," he said quietly, when all was told, "and Gropper and I have been talking of the possibilities. He may have passed you in the street, for he has been gone only a few minutes. Didst meet him?" Herman shook his head, and his own question came:

"What is your plan?"

"To get out of the city. I have lodged much of my money in the bank, and the banker, who is as a brother to me, will contrive to send it on to me, when I let him know where I am gone. And as for Gropper, he takes up the business. He has the contract hidden away in his bosom at this moment, and he will pay as God prospers him. We thought of starting in the morning."

"That will be too late," Herman urged.

"I know it now, and since I have told my wife what lies before us, she was willing, and is like me, like you, my son, and like our darling—we are all in God's hands. We will start tonight. I will go upstairs and bid my dear one get ready."

When he came back, Herman watched, and saw that he had brushed away some tears from his face. He did not speak, but, taking two strong leathern wallets from the wall, he went to the strong box in the corner of the room, and, unlocking it, drew forth a heavy bag and set it on the table. The chink of gold sounded as it touched the board.

"Herman," he said quietly, "this was set apart for Margaret—her bridal gift. I give it over to you for her. Use that wallet, for its safe keeping."

He returned to the box and brought two more bags, bulky and heavy like that at which Herman was staring in speechless wonder. Bringing them to the table, he placed them in the capacious wallet, which bulged with its burden, and then, while Herman followed his example, he flung it over his shoulder, and drew over it and himself his heavy cloak.

"God has been very good, my son," he said softly. "He is not sending us forth scripless and moneyless. Here is ample for our needs, even if it should prove our all, and I am thankful."

He fell on his knees at the table, and bent his head between his hands in prayer, and while he knelt someone stole into the room, ready cloaked, but pale, and went down by his side and put her arm about him.

"Let us go forth, dear heart," she said. "I long to see my child, and wherever God sends us, it is well."

The moments were very few before they stood in the doorway looking into the dark street. Almost like thieves in the night, when they had pulled the door after them and heard the latch fall quietly, they stole across the street into the dark alley, the mother with a man on either side of her.

# THE COMING OF THE FORESTER

"HEINRICH, take Master and Mistress Byrckmann to their daughter, and wait till I return," said Herman, when he stood at the stable door with Margaret's father and mother. "I am going to tell my mother what we think of doing, unless your plan will let you come with me to my mother's house, where we can use that secret way."

"Nay, 'twill not do," said Heinrich hastily. "We might walk straight into the arms of those whom we want to avoid. No, my way is best."

He spoke so certainly that Herman had no doubt, since he had often proved the simple one's resourcefulness.

"You will wait for me?" he asked.

"I will. We cannot start for an hour or two," was the ready answer; and Herman turned away, and ran along the streets swiftly, not to lose time.

He found his mother waiting in great anxiety, wondering where he was and what had detained him so long, and he told her in the fewest words of the plan for flight.

While he was busy, putting on fresh clothing and making ready for his journey, a loud knock or the street door startled them both. Herman's mother answered the summons, and, opening the door, stared at a man who stood at the bottom step with the rain streaming from his clothes.

"Your business—what is it?" she asked, with what courage she could muster, for this stranger's appearance at such a juncture shook her nerve, and she imagined that he had come to spy out something.

"I want your son, if you be his mother" the man exclaimed, loudly enough for any who might be passing; but he added in a whisper, "Tell him I am Otto Engel, and I have news for him."

"Come in," she answered carelessly, for the benefit of a man who was passing, and who, for aught she knew, might be a spy. She drew back to make room for the big man to enter the narrow passage.

Closing the door the moment he had gone past her, she led him to the room, and then called up the stairs warily, as though the walls had ears:

"My son, 'tis the forest ranger."

Herman had already heard the strong voice, and he was at the bottom step while his mother was speaking.

"What news?" he asked, when the two men had clasped hands warmly.

"All's well, Herman. The Englishman is still in the hut in the mere, and busy with Roye on that great task of his; but he is restless, and his appetite is whetted because Roye has discovered that the printed sheets that were on board the Marburg are waiting in the hold of the ship that lies at the quay in Worms, and the captain wants to know what to do with them. I'll tell you more. They say that the powers that be have at last plucked up their courage, and declare that this scandal shall be ended, so that Schouts' castle is to be stormed, and the robber noble is to be hanged over his own gate."

"If they can get at him!" exclaimed Herman, with a laugh of incredulity.

"That's how things stand," said the forester, shrugging his shoulders.

"What has all this to do with me?" Herman asked after a pause.

"Everything. Raymart, whom my father allowed to stay in the house where Master Tyndale is staying, has been prowling about in the forest, and a bear has mauled him so badly that he is ill; so that he cannot take the good man on to Worms. And I do not know the way. That's why I'm here—to get you to go, since you know every inch when once I put you in the forest."

Herman's heart leapt. It seemed now that the way for William Tyndale was marked out; and was it not safety for Margaret also? Once in Worms, where the lord of the place was one who would have no Inquisitors prowling in his streets, and, Pope or none at all, would hang them with short shrift if he laid hands on them—was not that the place to which Margaret and her dear ones might go?

"Sit down, Otto, while I am putting some things together, and I will tell you something," Herman said, and in the bedroom, after the two men had tramped up the stairs, Otto listened to the story of the contemplated flight from the city.

"God's hand is in this," the forester said, when Herman had told him all. "If that simple lad will let me join you, I can get you all to a place where I can hire horses, and we will ride to my father's mill, and on to William Tyndale. Then we can make our other plans; but this is the pressing thing just now—to get that dear girl and her loved ones away from the city. Shall I come?"

Herman looked at the ranger's giant frame, and his heart leapt at the thought of his help.

"It will be splendid," he cried. "Shall we go to Heinrich's stable now? I am ready, if mother has some warm wrappings for Margaret."

"They are here, my son," the woman said, pointing to a heap of things on the couch downstairs when they were all standing in the room which seemed small with two such men in it. "I will wrap them in a bundle, and you must be gone."

She told Herman how she would spend the night in prayer for their good speeding.

"Wilt come to me some early day, Otto Engel, and tell me how they fared?" she asked, standing with her hand on the lock before she opened the street door.

"With all my heart," the forester answered, and then the two men went into the street, where, as they faced the sweeping rain and wind, they staggered and fought hard to keep their feet.

# THE PURCHASE OF THE VAULT

"WHO is this?" Heinrich asked suspiciously, and pointing to Engel, who stepped into the stable after Herman, and stood nearby, waiting for the door to be closed.

"'Tis the forester who showed us how William Tyndale could be brought away from the dungeon in Schouts' castle," Herman explained. "You remember what I told you of him?"

"I do, and since 'tis he, he is welcome for what he did. Let me look at him," Heinrich went on, as soon as he had driven the bolt into the door, and, taking up the lantern, he held it so that the light fell full on Engel's weather-beaten face.

"I can trust you," he said, after a full scrutiny. "But how late you are," he added half peevishly. "'Tis time we started. Hark!"

The great bell of the cathedral boomed out the hour of ten, and Heinrich counted the strokes half audibly before he moved.

"Stay where you are. I'll bring the others down, for 'twill be waste of time to go up the steps only to come down again," he said peremptorily, and he turned to mount the flight to bring the others to them.

"But wait," cried Herman," Mistress Margaret must not go through the storm in all this rain and wind without something warm on; and here are things my mother sent for her."

Heinrich shrugged his shoulders impatiently. He knew how precious the moments were, and this meant delay.

"Give them to me, and hold this lantern!" he exclaimed. "I'll take them to her, and her mother and mine will make her fit to travel."

He caught up the bundle and moved two steps at a time, while Herman and Engel watched him amusedly.

"He must have his own way. Otherwise we may confuse him," said Herman, as the simple one entered the door at the top of the steps.

"'Tis Herman and the forester who helped to bring the Englishman out of the dungeon," they heard him say in quick, sharp tones. "And Herman's mother has sent these warm, dry clothes for Mistress Margaret. But she must be quick. The moments are precious. The cathedral bell has already struck ten, and what I have to do must be done before eleven, or we are lost."

Herman saw him drop on his knees and unfasten the bundle on the floor.

"Why, the wind may blow how it will, and the rain may come down in a flood, and you will be both warm and dry!" he exclaimed, changing his tone to ecstasy because of what he saw. "But be quick. I want you to have ample time, and avoid those creatures who are seeking for you."

He stood at the top of the steps, his foot tapping impatiently, and again and again, although the moments were but few, praying that Margaret would speed her preparations.

"At last!" he cried; and then, beckoning to them to come, he descended the steps, where again he waited for the others.

"Take this lantern, forester!" he exclaimed, having hurriedly lighted one which hung on a nail.

When the last one had come away from the steps, and all were expecting him to open the door, which rattled with the storm, he surprised them by dropping on his knees nearby where Margaret was standing.

"What are you doing?" she asked, wondering why he did not open the stable door, and yet, like the others, perplexed that he should have these lights for the streets, and invite attention.

Heinrich's hands moved swiftly, and they watched him with breathless interest. His fingers were sliding along the edges of some of the stones, and he pulled them up one by one until he pointed to a flat stone about two feet square. His fingers were soon busy with this, and he raised the stone, leaning it back against the wall beneath the manger.

They looked into cold and forbidding blackness, and felt a chill air come up which made them shiver. Heinrich caught up his lantern, and held it far down in the dark opening, showing them some wooden steps which rested on a stone floor.

"We are going down there," he said decisively, putting one foot on the top step. "Mother," he said quietly, "when we are all gone, drop the stone down and make all tidy. I'll give you the sign when I come back. But perhaps I shall come along the streets. It all depends."

He was looking serious, but a smile came to his face, and with his free hand he threw a kiss to his mother, who was standing a little way back, listening, as if to know whether anyone approached the stable door, which was rattling violently with the wind.

Heinrich went down the steps swiftly, and stood on the floor below, waiting.

"Come quickly!" he cried, standing back from the steps to make room, but throwing a light on the steps for the others to know where to put their feet.

"I will go first. Come close after me, my dear," Herman said to Margaret, who turned and kissed the woman who had sheltered her.

Carefully placing her foot on the blackened step, she descended slowly, clinging timidly to the frame-work, but gathering courage as she went, until she stood at Herman's side, waiting for the others.

"Mother," said Heinrich, when the others were standing in a group about him, "shut up the hole at once. We will wait until 'tis done;" and the woman, going on her knees, looked down to bid them all God-speed, and a safe deliverance, before she dropped the stone into its place. They waited a little longer, and heard her replacing the smaller stones one by one, Heinrich counting each little thud.

"That's the last," he said contentedly. "Now we can start."

He led the way across the empty chamber to a door, bolted and barred; but Heinrich moved the bolts and bars, ready to open the door.

"If I say put out the light, do it instantly, or else cover it over with something. Your cloak, forester, is the very thing, and 'twill save the trouble of lighting again. And, mark this, whenever we come to any door, let me always go in first to see that all is clear, lest someone may be about. Forester, cover that light."

He hid his own lantern under the cloak he had flung over his shoulders, and the whole company stood in darkness, not knowing what Heinrich was doing, nor where he went. They heard no sound which would tell them that he had opened the door; but before long, and through the open doorway, they saw a light. Heinrich was there, waving the lantern, and a low call came to them to come.

The forester brought his lantern from beneath his cloak, and the little company moved forward in wonder. They found themselves in a great vault, full of stores such as would be brought into the city by the ships that came up or down the river. There were casks and boxes, coils of rope, chests of all shapes and sizes, anchors and chains for the shipping, barrels of biscuits and meat for sailors, a medley of things brought down for storage, to be carried away as the owner of the place had customers for them.

These were set down in such a way that there was no clear path towards the spot where Heinrich was standing, waiting for them. At times Engel was able to find a way, and threw the light of the lantern on the floor, but many a time they had to climb over the stores, stepping from one cask to another.

It was easy enough for the men, but for Margaret, even with her spirit, and for her mother, who was weakened by sickness, it was a task that made the others anxious. At last, however, they came to the spot where Heinrich was awaiting them with the greatest serenity.

"Do you know this place, Master Byrckmann?" he asked, as if, now that they were really on the move, he was enjoying the venture.

"I was never here," the printer answered, looking about the great cellar, and seeking to recognize it, if possible, with the aid of the two lanterns.

"Then I'll show you something," said Heinrich gleefully. "Read that;" and he pointed to a huge bale on which Byrckmann's name was printed in rough characters. "There's that, and that, and that," said Heinrich, in quick succession, "and they all have your name on it. Can you guess now where you are?"

"Is it in Bremner's warehouse?" the printer asked, in some amazement.

"That is the very thing," cried Heinrich; but he stopped and stared behind him, listening intently.

"Come after me. Oh, come quickly!" and he led the way, showing the others where he went by flashing his lantern in such a manner that they saw all that he did. "Now in here! quickly! and bend low. Crawl in among the bales," he whispered. "Bear away to the left, forester, and you will find a hiding place among those planks. Then when I say it, cover up the lantern. Don't let a chink of light come through, or we may be lost."

The forester dropped on his hands and knees, and already Heinrich had covered his own light under his cloak. Squeezing his great form in between some heavy bales of cloth, Engel crawled along, while the others followed him, all save Herman, who remained with Heinrich to see what this threatening danger was.

"Art safely inside?" came Heinrich's whisper.

"Yes," was the answer. "Although 'tis a tight fit for so many," said Engel, with an assumption of ease he did not feel. Better, he thought, that they had taken the risk of the streets and gone to Herman's house to take that underground passage to the river. The same thought was in Herman's mind, but it was too late now. They were in God's hands, and they must abide by the issue of this venture, which might well mean life or death.

"A tight fit, didst say, forester?" Heinrich whispered. "I spent many a night there and found it large enough; but, hush! Cover the light. You are safe there, and only need patience."

Herman, watching with him, felt his heart almost freeze at what he saw. Away through the door which Herman had already opened, he could see a great chamber like this in which they were hiding, choked as this one was, with stores. But what he centered his attention on was a company of men, six of them in all, each carrying a lantern, and finding their way among the merchandise, and at the same time

238

approaching this cellar in which Margaret and he and the others were hiding.

He went sick with dread when the men came through the doorway, where they halted in a group.

"Is this the last?" asked one, and Herman not only knew the voice, but saw the face of the speaker as the lanterns threw their light on it.

It was Cochlaeus! The Captain of the City Guard was there, and a third was one whom Herman knew, Bremner, the owner of the great warehouses on the quay, and the wealthiest man in the city. The others were ecclesiastics whom Herman had seen, either in the streets, or taking part in the cathedral services.

"This is the last," said Bremner, standing apart for a moment, and staring about him with an air of proprietorship. "And as for strength, you have nothing stronger in the Holy House, and nothing better suited for your purpose, since you may make as many cells here as you please. And every outer wall is three feet thick in stone and cement. The very place for new quarters, which you seem anxious to add to the place you already have."

"'Tis true," said Cochlaeus. "But I like not your price," he added, as he moved in and out among the goods that were stored so thickly in the place. "'Tis two thousand golden crowns too much, and even at that lower price you make it far too dear."

He spoke petulantly.

"'Tis for our Mother Church, and you should bear that in mind!" he exclaimed, when he moved still nearer to where Herman and Heinrich were standing.

"I bear it in mind," Bremner's answer came. "I have again and again refused the price I asked you at the first, but because it is for the glory of God, I named this low figure."

239

"Two thousand crowns too much!" reiterated Cochlaeus. "You forget how many crowns we shall have to spend to make it fit for our purpose."

"Nay. But I do not want to sell," cried Bremner half impatiently, restraining himself because of his knowledge of the temper of this man with whom, by this chance, he was dealing. "I shall have to spend five thousand crowns more than you will give me to buy another storage place, so that I stand to lose a great deal."

"And you get the Church's blessing. Fall in with the price I name, and I will secure you favors rarely granted to any like yourself!" exclaimed Cochlaeus, stopping abruptly, not many feet away from where Herman and Heinrich were crouching, and in readiness to go into that hiding place where the others were sheltering. He faced Bremner, and said peremptorily, "Your last word in this matter."

There was something almost menacing in the tone, and Herman saw Bremner's face. It became white with fear, and he saw, as well, how the man's hand trembled as his fingers rested on his lips.

"The Church must have it," he said falteringly.

Cochlaeus answered back exultantly.

"'Tis noble of you, Bremner. I knew you would fall in with my wishes, and you shall not be a loser."

There was silence for a time, and then, anxious though Herman was, his fear was almost more than he could endure, because of the possible consequences to Margaret and those others nearby in hiding. Cochlaeus broke the silence and pointed to the wall against which Herman's back was resting.

"I'll go yonder just to be assured that the walls are as firm as these others;" and because he could not pass on the floor, he stepped on some bales, and stepped from one to another, each step bringing him closer to the spot.

"Get inside," said Heinrich, whose teeth were chattering, and they had barely joined the others when Cochlaeus sprang from one of the bales to the floor, so close to Herman that, had he stretched out his hand, he could have gripped the Churchman by the ankles.

"Yes; they seem as good," said Cochlaeus; and then he paused to look around again.

"I would that there were time to look all round, but I must be gone. There are three at least who must be in our hands tonight, and be safely lodged in the dungeons of the Holy House. One is that Byrckmann whose bales of paper I have seen yonder. There is his wife, as well; and there is, besides, his daughter, who has contrived to escape from the Holy House, and must be even now in her father's house."

Bremner spoke quietly, and his voice was tremulous.

"I have known Byrckmann all my lifetime, and I believe him a faithful son of the Church," he ventured. "I can't believe him capable of heresy."

"A man may deceive his best friends," said Cochlaeus shortly. "At all events, he is to be waited on. I must go."

And, standing again on one of the bales, he moved away, as he had come, and before long the vault was in darkness again.

# THE HOUSE ON THE WALL

HERMAN and Heinrich came out swiftly from their hiding place, whispering back to the forester to stay near the others and protect them. When Engel gave his assent, they ventured stealthily through the vaults, using one of the lanterns when necessary.

They were bent on assuring themselves that Cochlaeus and those who were with him were really gone, and as they dogged their steps nearly all the time in darkness, Heinrich whispering to Herman when to turn to right or left among the storage, they scarcely lost sight of those whom they were following.

Not one among them all, so far as they could tell, turned to look back, and at last they mounted some broad stone steps into the warehouse on a level with the wharf. Listening intently, Herman and his companion heard the jingle of keys, the creaking of great hinges, the sound of heavy boots on some stones, and the noisy clang of the door as it was closed. The key turned in the lock again, and all was silent.

"Gone!" exclaimed Heinrich, in a tone of relief. "I was fearful lest we should be found when Cochlaeus came so near to our hiding place. If he had discovered us, with all those armed men near, what would it have availed to fight?"

He shuddered.

"Didst hear my teeth chatter, Herman? It was from real fright," he confessed openly. "But come. The way is clear, and since they have locked the door the place must be empty of any men who could challenge us. Come at once. We'll get out of the city before that Churchman finds that his birds have flown, and there are not many minutes left before he will be at the printer's door."

He turned away, and hurried back, winding in and out among the merchandise, using his lantern freely for Herman to see the way; and as soon as he was within the doorway of the cellar in which Margaret and the others were in hiding, he threw all caution to the winds.

"Come at once. The way is clear," he cried. "Forester, help Mistress Byrckmann. Take her in your strong arms if needs be, and Mistress Margaret and her father can carry the lantern and show you where to step."

He had scarcely ended before Margaret had come away, and Herman could see her holding up the lantern. Then her father came, handing out his wife, and last of all was Otto Engel, who did as Heinrich suggested when he saw that already Margaret's mother was overwrought and unequal to the call upon her strength.

"Lead on!" he exclaimed, as he bent low and gathered up the sick woman in his strong arms.

Heinrich led them up the stone steps and past the great double gates, on through the great warehouses, which were windowless, through the stables where the horses looked round at them sleepily, until they stopped at a door which opened outwards. As they paused there they could hear the wind screaming past the door outside, and the rain patter against the woodwork, as well as bubble in at the doorstep, blown there by the gale which was sweeping across the city.

"We must hide our lights the moment I open the door," said Heinrich; "but don't put them out, for we shall want them presently. Art ready, Herman?"

"Yes," came the answer, for Herman had taken the lantern from Margaret and had led her by the hand through these dark places, always alert for any danger that might menace her.

They could hear the stealthy slipping of the bolts, and then the scarcely stifled creaking of the hinges as the wind drove in the door the moment the latch was lifted.

"Pass out, one by one," said Heinrich. "Bend your head, forester, for the door is only a low one. Ah! I thought as much. Hast hurt thyself?" he asked, in some concern, when Engel caught his forehead against the lintel.

"Not much," whispered the forester, although the blow had staggered him. "Fortunately I was going slowly." But with that he stood in the open with the wind playing about his face.

"What next?" asked Herman.

"I'll shut this door to save suspicion, if the wind will let me do as much," said Heinrich, struggling to pull the door together, but failing till Herman caught it, and closed it on the latch after putting both hands to the task.

"The street is empty. Now follow me."

Heinrich crossed the road, his form dimly showing in the darkness, and the others followed, swaying and staggering with the wind, the forester more than once beating against the wall while carrying Margaret's sick mother.

Heinrich moved down an alley, going slowly, each holding out a hand to either side to keep in touch with the wall, and feeling with their feet, not to trip over any projecting doorstep. No harm came, and then the alley was left behind.

Where they were none knew, save Heinrich, for the darkness was dense, and the street into which they emerged was like so many others, narrow and tortuous, with the wind screeching along and causing the swinging signs to creak and scream as they moved before the blast.

"As straight across the street as you can go," said Heinrich aloud, and even then they barely heard him in the roar of the wind and the pelting rain. He moved forward, but staggered, and, his frail form unable to withstand the rush of wind, he fell heavily on the stones.

"Art hurt?" Byrckmann asked anxiously, stretching out a hand to help the poor fellow to his feet.

"Not much. Only bruised a bit. But that won't count," he added cheerfully. "Come along."

They reached the other side of the street, but, going past the door of an empty house, Heinrich led them down a side passage and halted in comparative calm at a doorway.

"We are here," he said, when they had again grouped about him. "And here, please God, we shall find respite from the wind and rain, and, better still, confound that monster, Cochlaeus."

He chuckled as he pulled a key from his bosom, and, telling them to go carefully and turn a little to the right when they were once inside, he waited for them to file in, standing like one on guard at the doorstep to keep out any intruders.

"Feel your way!" he exclaimed, when he had closed and bolted the door on the inside. "We dare not show a light on this side of the house. Put out your hands, and that will help you. Ready? I'll count the steps I take. One, two, three."

He counted up to fourteen and halted, and again the others, groping in the darkness, were about him. There was no sound while they stood in stillness, save the howling wind outside and the scramble near them of a startled rat who was taken by surprise at the intrusion.

"We are going up a stone staircase, which tends to the right the whole way. I have counted the steps scores of times, for I have often been here, and there are twenty-eight of them. Now come after me. I'll throw you a light as soon as we take the first bend, for there are no windows this side of the house, and no one can see us; not even the City Guard if 'tis bold enough to come out on such a night."

He hurried up the stairs in the darkness without any hesitation, because every step was familiar, and after he had mounted a dozen he threw some light on the stone staircase to show the others where to go. From this point they mounted the remaining steps, both lanterns showing light, and those who followed him watched in wonder. The staircase had its way in solid masonry. Here and there were slits in the walls, just wide enough for a man's head to fit in, but too narrow even for a child to enter, and each slit was eight or ten feet deep, perhaps more.

"Where are we?" asked Herman, looking about him.

"You shall see presently," was the lightly spoken answer. Heinrich was exuberant. Whether danger had passed or not, the others could not say, but his gay spirits, in contrast to his previous care, gave them confidence, and they followed him without hesitation. At the top of the steps he turned into a room, so small that a tall man could hardly lie full length upon the floor, while the place itself was hemmed in by, or formed a part of, some solid masonry.

In one side of the room was a window, broad enough even for a man of Otto Engel's proportions to crawl through, but to pass through it was impossible, for there were bars from top to bottom, and bars crossed these from right to left.

"What's next?" asked the forester, who had gently placed Margaret's mother on the stone floor, and now stood panting with his struggle against the storm when so heavily burdened.

"We're going through that window," said Heinrich, with quiet assurance and a contented smile on his face.

"Art mad?" cried Engel, staring at the bars and then at their guide. "Who could get through that window with those irons crossed like that?" he asked almost angrily, half disposed to think that this poor madman had duped them and had brought them here to no purpose, unless to hide and starve, unless he could bring them food.

Heinrich laughed outright, and rubbed his hands.

"I thought you would say as much," he answered gleefully. "But wait. Have patience, and ere many minutes have gone you shall be outside the city."

He was serious now, and they watched him wonderingly, still thinking him mad. He went out of the room, and they heard his boots beating on the stone steps as he clattered down them in the darkness. A suspicion came that he had served them treacherously and had gone away, leaving them in this empty house, which might, for aught they knew, be some part of the Holy House, and this one of the dens in which some poor prisoner would sigh out his hours, by day and night, until the tormentors chose to deal with him. Even Herman and Engel felt their faces blench as this thought thrilled them, and Margaret, was feared as much as they.

"Has he tricked us, think you?" asked the forester, going to the door to stare down into the darkness of the stone staircase. But when he had stood there a moment or two he heard returning footsteps, and Heinrich came up, two steps at a time, carrying a coil of strong rope.

"Didst think I'd gone and left you all?" he asked half roguishly. This gay side of him had rendered him oblivious of their anxiety, and he was gloating over their surprise when he let them into his secret.

"I did," said the forester, completely puzzled.

248

"You might have trusted me," Heinrich exclaimed half reproachfully as he uncoiled the rope, making them wonder all the more. As he threw down the last coil, he crawled along the stone recess to where the bars were, and then they were amazed. One by one he took a bar in his hands as he knelt before them. Lifting one, as if it fitted into a socket, he drew it away and laid it by his side. He did the same with another, and yet with more, until every bar was lying on the great stone windowsill, and there was a clear and open space as soon as he threw the glass window back on its hinges, broad enough even for the forester to pass.

While they watched him in silence, he leant out and gazed about in all directions; now to right, to left, and downwards, and, satisfied with what he saw, he came back to them in happy complacence.

"Go and look for yourselves!" he exclaimed, as his feet touched the floor; and the forester, nearest to the window, climbed up and moved on his hands and knees to the opening. The others heard him exclaim in wonder, and presently he came backwards, and was once more with the others.

"Heinrich!" he exclaimed, catching at the simple one's hands, "I wronged thee, and from the bottom of my heart I crave pardon. You have brought us to deliverance."

"'Tis true," said Herman, who had gone into the embrasure and, having gazed for a few moments, turned round to speak back to the others. "We are on the outside of the city. This is part of the city wall; yonder is the river, and the harbor too, and away here to our right, close by, is the forest which leads to Engel's hut. Margaret, we are safe if we can manage to let ourselves down by that rope, and if you and your mother have courage enough to be lowered so far. And yet," he added doubtfully," I know not how the last one can come, for it will want a stronger man than Heinrich, even with the most willing heart, to lower the lightest of us."

Heinrich laughed and skipped about in childish glee.

"Come back and I will show you!" he exclaimed. "Besides, 'tis well not to waste time," he added, changing suddenly to seriousness.

Herman crawled back, and was near to the edge to drop on the floor when Heinrich stopped him.

"See!" he said, taking one of the bars ; and, scraping away some of the mortar which was powdered only, but carefully catching every grain in his cap so that none should be wasted and fall to the floor, he drove the bar far into a hitherto unseen hole so that it stayed firm in the wall. He took the rope, and, making a strong loop at one end, he passed it over this, and they understood.

The last that came could lower himself by sliding down the rope, whereas the others could be let down safely with a loop and a sliding knot about their body.

"Who will go first?" asked Heinrich.

"Someone who can help the women when their turn comes," suggested the forester.  "Suppose you go first, Herman. Then Mistress Margaret, and then her mother, and her father to follow. After that, either Heinrich or myself."

The noose went round Herman's body, under his arms, and, not to lay any strain on the others, he threw out the whole of the rope that was at liberty, and suffered himself to go down, hand under hand, until his feet touched the ground below. He loosened the rope, and when it was drawn back, Margaret came to the window, and he dimly saw her sitting in the loop and clinging to the rope while they were lowering her gently, but swaying in the furious wind. Before many moments she was with him.

"God is going to send us into safety," she answered, waiting with him in the darkness until it was time to render service to her mother, whose turn was next.

The last to come was Heinrich, who had gone down that rope so many times, and they gathered about him to bless and thank him for what he had done.

"Heinrich," said Margaret, "in God's dear mercy you have been our deliverer. We owe so much to you—our lives, I doubt not, and our liberty."

He stood and gazed at her in happy laughter.

"'Twas God who made me your helper," he said, his voice thrilling with gladness. "But you must be gone. Yonder is the forest, and the forester knows it well. He can lead you there ten times better than I. Now I am going back to my mother, for if Cochlaeus has bought those vaults he will not fail to find his way into our home. We must find another. Perhaps they will suffer us to live in this house we have just left."

"God speed you!" he exclaimed, careless of the wind and rain, and holding out his hand to each of them in turn.

"Good-bye, Heinrich," she said, almost weeping. "I shall never forget. Oh, never! I shall never fail to remember how you were ready to give your life for mine."

She made him glad almost to delirium. He hurried away to the wall with happy laughter, and when he had climbed up the rope and they knew that he was safe within the house, Engel took Margaret's mother in his arms, and the little company walked on into the dark forest.

# THE NIGHT RIDE IN THE FOREST

ONCE within the shelter of the forest, Engel placed Margaret's mother carefully at the root of one of the giant oaks and on the sheltered side, so that neither wind nor rain could harm her.

"We will wait here a little while," he said quietly, "and that will give you time to recover a bit from all the exertion and pain to which our adventures have put you, Mistress Byrckmann."

"No, let us not stay!" she exclaimed, taking her husband's hand, and by an effort which surprised him drawing herself on to her feet, where she stood with her hands on his arm. "Let us go forward. They will find that we have left our home, and they will say that we must have left the city; then they will come here to search for us."

Shuddering at the thought, and weak though she was, she drew her husband forward.

"Then you shall take my arm; or, better still, since I am fresh and Engel is not, I will carry you!" exclaimed Herman; and before she could say a word by way of protest, he had her frail body in his arms.

"Go ahead," he said, when Engel protested that he was equal to three or four miles more. "Show the way, since no one knows the forest as you do."

More than once, when the wind howled among the trees and made the going dangerous because great branches sometimes broke away and crashed to the ground, the travelers thought they heard the cries of men, and they paused to know whether they were being pursued. When an hour had gone, and Margaret's mother had twice changed bearers, the forester said they were nearing a farm where he thought he could hire some horses. He was going to point to a clearing where the house was standing when the sound of a horse's hoofs was heard, in spite of the swish of the forest leaves in the storm.

"They are after us!" said Margaret, in awestricken tones, and she looked around, dark though it was, to know if any place offered for their hiding.

"Come this way!" the forester exclaimed, and, having just given up his burden to Herman, he caught at Margaret's hand. He drew her, and the others followed, among the bushes, away from the road, and waited in hiding to know what the sounds meant.

The horse came on, regardless of the road, and in the darkness he was making for the bush behind which they waited. The creature came close to them, not seeing where he went in his evident terror, or else spurred on by his rider, but he stumbled at a hidden root, made doubly treacherous by the rain, and fell heavily. His rider crashed against a tree, and fell without a groan and lay still, while the horse, scrambling to his feet, dashed away into the darkness and was no more seen.

The forester ran to the rider, and, bending over him, lifted him in his arms; but he laid him down again.

"He is dead," he said quietly. "His neck is broken."

Horrorstricken at the tragedy, they moved on, leaving the dead man where he lay, and did not stop until they reached a spot where the bushes were so dense that even in broad daylight they would scarcely be seen.

"I'll leave you here while I go to a farm nearby and wake up the master. He has horses he can lend me if I pay the price." He paused. "I doubt whether he will let me have them without the money down," he added hesitatingly. "I haven't enough with me."

"'Tis my charge, Engel," said Byrckmann. "Take my purse, and use it as you deem best."

"Ah, now I can get them easily!" the forester exclaimed, with elation. "Keep well in the shelter here, and neither Cochlaeus nor all the City Guard will see you if they bring a hundred lanterns to light up the forest."

He went away, and for a long hour they waited for his coming, hearing all the sounds of the forest, the moaning wind, the cracking of roots like the rattle of musketry as some great tree was torn up and fell with a crash. Even the animals who had their home there were too startled to trouble themselves about those who were coming by night into their domain, and the fugitives could hear them whimpering in their terror.

The hour seemed never ending. The moments were leaden footed, and more than once Margaret's mother expressed her fear that Engel had left them to get through the forest how they could.

"Don't say that—don't even think it—of Otto Engel," Herman protested. "He is the soul of honor. The farmer must be a heavy sleeper, hard to awake; or there may be some difficulty in getting as many horses as we need all ready for the journey. And Engel would insist on their having a good meal of corn. All takes time."

Half an hour more went by, with longer moments still in it, it seemed to the anxious watchers, but then they heard some neighing horses, and the tramp of hoofs, sounding more plainly because the fierceness of the storm had passed.

"Where are you?" came the sonorous cry of the forester, and Herman called back; so that he was soon with them, leading a string of five horses, saddled and ready for hard travelling. One of them had a pannier, so arranged that Margaret's mother, when the forester lifted her into it, was able to ride in comfort.

"It was that which took up the time," Engel explained. "It took an amount of contriving, but the farmer was willing enough."

Herman lifted Margaret into her saddle, and, helping her father into his, he sprang into his own seat, and the company rode on through the forest.

"We must go in single file," said the forester, when they came to a path made faintly visible because the rain had ceased, and although the clouds were spread along the sky, the moon had begun to make herself felt. "Herman, bring up the rear. I want to get first of all to my hut, and then I'll tell you what is working in my mind."

They were moving now among the trees, and the forester from time to time spoke back a word of warning, when to bend and avoid the trees.

"Trust to me!" he exclaimed once, when all seemed wrong. "I am like a cat in the dark, and I am going the way I want to go, and a way I know."

His sturdy confidence robbed his companions of their fears. Grown accustomed to the darkness, they could see his thick frame, the well set head on the broad, square shoulders. At times, as the darkness grew less dense, they could see his body bend, and they, too, without his words, though he sent them back to them, lowered their heads to pass the branches. But even thus Margaret more than once, when an occasional gust of wind came, felt the branches whip her face, making it smart with pain.

Unexpectedly the forester dropped out of his saddle.

"This is my house," he said, coming to Margaret's side to help her dismount. He lifted her mother out of her pannier as though she was little more than a child, while the printer, unused to the saddle, felt himself standing on his feet almost before he knew.

"Tie up the horses, Herman, over there, where 'tis in the dark. Then come to the hut. We must have something to eat, and I want, as well, to take my dog with me. I may be away a few days, and the dear fellow would starve if I left him here."

Half an hour later they were in the saddle again, the horses, as well as themselves, the better for a meal. Before he moved on he explained his purpose.

"I want to work our way round Schouts' castle, where the path is little more than a sheep walk; but we can do it. I can't conceive that anyone would be out on such a night as we have had, so that we need have no fear that the robber lord's retainers will bar our way."

A thrill of fear passed through the others, but they had confidence in him, and followed his lead without demur; but when they had gone some distance the forester called a halt, and the company grouped about him, wondering what was wrong.

"We're too near the robber's den," said Engel quietly. "I can see the castle lights. And would you believe it? There are torches moving on the slope, and Schouts and his men are out for their savage work," he muttered. "Follow me. I'm going farther into the forest before we ride direct to our destination. I had no idea that there would be piracy on such a night, and at this mad hour!"

Turning his back on the castle and the river, he rode on into the darkest part of the forest, frightening some of the creatures who had already feared the storm. When he had gone a mile or more, he turned sharply round, and presently they came to an open glade, which they could clearly see, in contrast with the dense wood through which they had been riding.

"We must cross that bit of grass, and from that moment you may all dismiss your fears," said the forester, in a lighter tone than he had used that night. "I have gone through the forest a hundred times and never saw anything human in it yet in these parts. And what is more, there is no path, so that I must pick my way, and you must follow."

The forester went forward like a man with an easy mind. Any fears which the others had, dropped away from them when they heard him talking to his horse, or whistling a song which the Protestants sang in their secret forest meetings. Margaret rode at Herman's side, so much at ease with this new confidence that she could talk with him.

They rode on for a couple of hours, and then the dawn came. Almost insensibly they halted to watch the beauty of the morning after such a night of storm. The sun came up in silvery splendor above a wooded hill, and a radiance seemed to rest as on a cushion of the mist. Trees and undergrowth, forest path and fallen branches, were all hidden until the daylight conquered, and the great orb of day, riding above the wooded depths, sent forth his light, so that there was no more night, and no more mist.

But with the glory of the new day, and the songs of the birds, there came a thrill of fear. A forest clearing was before them, and beyond it they saw the great river rolling by. In the midst of the clearing was a hut, and already some blue smoke was curling from its solitary chimney.

Margaret's eyes fastened on the place, and her eyes betrayed her fear.

"Is it not dangerous to be so near that house?" she asked, turning her anxious face to the forester.

He laughed at her words.

"Fritz Schiller is as true a Protestant as any man in the land. Ask him for a Lutheran Testament, and he will show you one. Let anyone ask him for you if you are sheltering in his home, and if he has promised to hide you he would die rather than betray you. I had thought at one time of bringing William Tyndale here, but took him instead to the mere near my father's house, but not because I did not trust this man."

"Fritz!" the forester shouted, his stentorian voice startling the birds that were near, as soon as he had dropped out of his saddle.

Crossing the clearing, he shouted again, and banged at the door of the hut. It opened presently, and a man stood in the doorway whom Margaret and her father had seen in the streets of the city, but did not know.

"What art doing here, Engel?" asked the grey-bearded man, who held a hatchet in one hand and a block of wood in the other.

They heard so much, but what followed they did not know, until the forester called on them to come forward and bring his own horse with them.

"We're to stay here till it is safe to go forward," said Engel. "The river is too wild to cross, and we may wait here for a day or two, but there is nothing now to fear. You can rest in sweet content, Mistress Byrckmann, and as soon as we can manage it, you will be safely over the river, and out of danger."

# THE NIGHT RIDER'S CALL

THEY were away at day-dawn, and long before the sun had risen they had crossed the river in the great ferry boat, which carried them and their horses safely to the other side.

They rode direct for the forest there, and Engel, who knew every yard of the path, was making for his father's mill. Unexpectedly the miller himself was in the path when they were but three miles from what they thought would be that day's journey end.

"Is all right?" Engel asked anxiously, reining in his horse.

"Yes, thank God. But I came on the chance of meeting you and saving you a useless journey. As the good man seemed anxious to get a little nearer to their goal, and because the way was clear, I sent him across to Raymart's hut, and there he is safe, and the more content because he is a few miles nearer to his destination."

"Then we'll ride on at once, father," said Engel, who swung round into another forest path, with the others following.

It was nearly evening when they halted outside a charcoal burner's hut, and when they entered the humble home they saw William Tyndale seated at a table with a Lutheran Testament on one knee and two other books open before him. Opposite to him sat William Roye, a pile of papers on either hand, writing, while in low and thoughtful, and sometimes hesitating tones, weighing in his mind the value of one word against another, his master dictated to him.

They were so absorbed in their work that neither of the men had heard the tramp of horses, nor the voices of the riders. Not until Margaret had spoken, as she stood in the open doorway of the room, did they look up.

Tyndale spent the whole of the night in preparation for his journey to the town which he looked upon as "a desired haven." He anticipated that when he got there he would have advice on many a point which perplexed him, scholar though he was.

Those who lay in the charcoal burner's hut, or in his stable, wherever room could be found for so many, could hear him moving about in the tiny inner room, going lovingly over the sheets in the pile of manuscript which he had dictated to Roye. Sometimes he came to a line on which his forefinger rested, and his face betrayed his anxiety as to whether it was the best phrase possible. Time was precious to him, since the journey was to begin at dawn, and he would have but little space for sleep; but he sat down presently, and, taking up his pen, scored out a word and put another in its place.

He sat on thus, forgetful of everything until Herman, who came in from the stream which ran dancing in the morning sun, fresh after bathing his head and face in its cool waters, saw him sitting at the table, lost in thought. "Master Tyndale!" he cried. "Have you forgotten? It is dawn, and we start at once. The horses are saddled and at the door."

Tyndale looked up, as one forgetful of everything. It was only slowly that he realized the meaning of the young man's words, and he sprang to his feet, his face displaying his concern.

"I quite forgot, Herman!" he exclaimed. "That passage in Romans had been on my mind ever since you left me in the marsh, and when I came across it in the manuscript, it occurred to me how it ought to run, so I sat to put it right. Fasten these in the wallet while I get ready, my son. I will break my fast while we ride through the forest."

When Herman had packed the wallet, and had carried it out to bestow it in the saddle, Tyndale shut the door softly and dropped on his knees at the table. The birds were in full song outside, and the horses snorted and moved about restlessly, but Tyndale neither heard them nor thought of the glories of the newborn day. The all absorbing thought was the well-doing of his work. He was working as "under the Great Taskmaster's eye"; and now that he was kneeling, he asked for a safe journey for the work's sake, for strength and quietness until the task was ended. And then—ah! then the ending could come in what form it would.

He came into the sunlight with a face full of thought; but the gay greeting from Margaret roused him to note his surroundings. He smiled pleasantly when he saw her, beautiful in the fresh morning air, with the sun sparkling in her dark eyes and her lips parted as they gave the morning salutation.

"I am late, and I crave your pardon, friends. Herman, give me a lift into that high saddle, for I am not as active as I was a score of years ago."

The little company rode down the forest glade. Blithe though the morning was, they went in silence, for they were beginning a dangerous journey. At first the path was fairly well marked, for Raymart's cart had gone that way three or four times a week for many a year, carrying charcoal to the town; but when they scanned the narrowing track farther on into the forest, they thought to take the beaten road.

They halted sharply, just as the forester's horse had stepped away from the trees. Glancing along the road, he saw some horsemen, and by the glancing steel in the sunshine, he knew them to be soldiers. He reined his horse back on the instant, and, saying what he had seen, he led the way more deeply into the forest and took a more unfrequented path. It was the only thing he could do when it was possible that the horsemen were under the command of Cochlaeus, again in pursuit of Tyndale.

The path which Engel took through the forest was at first tolerable, but in time it was nothing more than a mere track, very narrow, winding among thorny creepers, and over beds of decaying leaves, but that did not deter them. At odd times they saw a village and two or three times, approaching with care, they ventured into a quiet inn to get food. But they were compelled in the end to take the public road.

The sun was low down, and sent his golden, slanting beams among the fir trees when they left the forest, in which they had travelled for so many hours. There was an inn on the roadside, and, taking the risks because their horses, like themselves, were tired, they rode up to the door as carelessly as though there had been no need for care. The open space in front of the inn was clear. None were sitting at the tables under the trees on the opposite side of the road, and the house bore the aspect of quietude, almost of desertion.

Engel stayed outside to look to the comfort of the horses, but the others moved along the passage, thinking to go to the general room, but before they got as far as the door a woman came.

"'Tis full, lady," she said, turning to Mistress Byrckmann. "But I can find you room elsewhere, if you do not mind it being small," she added pleasantly, looking at the sick one and marking how worn out she was.

264

"Anywhere, so long as we may rest, and these two ladies may presently lie somewhere in quiet and comfort," interposed Herman. "They are both very tired, for we have had a long journey."

"Come this way," the woman answered, turning away to the stairs. She took them up to a large room which opened into one on either side. "There is a sleeping room there, for the ladies!" she exclaimed, moving towards the door, which she flung wide open, and waited for Margaret and her mother to enter. The room was small, but clean, and Margaret smiled her thanks in a way which won the woman's heart.

"The others must do as they can," she said, going back to them. "There is that little inner room, but this room will do to sleep in if you will let me send a man up with some clean straw. I am sorry I can't do more. Will it do?"

"Excellently well," said Byrckmann, glad like the others that for that night they would sleep under a roof, whereas they had expected to lie down beneath the stars.

Before long the mistress of the inn had brought them up a meal which was appetizing to hungry travelers. She bade them eat and be at ease, and left them; but Herman and the forester saw with much disquiet how she looked at Margaret and then at Tyndale.

"What did that mean, think you?" Engel asked in little more than a whisper when they presently stood at the window, looking out on the long, white road which lost itself in the growing darkness of the evening.

"And yet it was not an unkind look," said Herman. "It seemed to me that she was concerned—that there was some kind solicitude, and when she glanced away from Tyndale to Margaret it was as though she felt a womanly tenderness for her."

"I pray God you may be right," the forester answered.

When it was dark and the blind was drawn, and the little company—all save Margaret's mother, who had gone to bed—drew round the fire to talk awhile before they separated for the night, the door opened softly and the mistress of the inn appeared. Every eye was turned her way, and each heart beat quickly when they saw the anxiety on the woman's face.

"What is your will, mistress?" Engel asked, in little more than a whisper when he marked her stealth and seriousness, and saw how she closed the door softly behind her and came towards them before she said a word.

What she said was barely audible, and she glanced at the door in a way which betrayed her fears.

"If this be Master William Tyndale," she exclaimed, pointing to him with her forefinger, "and this sweet young lady Mistress Margaret Byrckmann, I have news for you that is disturbing."

"What is it?" asked Margaret, bending forward in her chair, her rosy cheeks gone pale, while her startled eyes were fixed on the woman's face.

"Are ye whom I think?" the woman asked. "Tell me truly, for it is no idle curiosity on my part. It may be a matter of life or death for two among you, perhaps for all."

"What if we say they are?" asked Master Byrckmann who was near.

"Then you must be gone."

"Gone. But why?" asked Tyndale, who, so far, had not spoken.

"I brought you all up here, Master Tyndale, because when I saw you enter the inn—you and this sweet girl—I feared that you were those who are being sought for by Cochlaeus, who is hoping to carry you back and lodge you in the Inquisition dungeon from which this pretty one escaped."

She paused, but none spoke, for the consternation in every breast robbed them of speech. Had they come so far to be captured when so near to safety! Each longed to know what the danger was which made it necessary, worn out though they were to go out into the night.

"You wonder at me, I am sure," the woman whispered, her eyes on the door while she was speaking. "I am one of yourselves, though some tell me I am one who worships like Naaman in the house of Rimmon. But that is not what I came to say. I want you to be gone—to find safety if it be possible."

She went to the door, opened it, and went outside; then, having glanced down the passage and the stairs, she came back again.

"I'll say more!" she exclaimed, still with her eyes on the closed door. "There came to the inn this afternoon a Churchman, who said that he was Doctor Cochlaeus, a Deacon of the Church of the Blessed Virgin. We all know him for a notorious heresy hunter. With him were half a score of horse soldiers, every one of whom is lodged in this house, while their horses are in the stables.

"While I was serving him he told me he was looking for an Englishman named Tyndale, who was busy, translating the Scriptures, but had escaped just when it was thought that he would be captured and burnt. He suspected that a young man was with him, but he was not sure, and perhaps a young maiden named Margaret Byrckmann, who had escaped from the House of the Inquisition. Had I seen them? He asked me that, and I answered truly that I had not.

"Now you know!" the woman exclaimed. "And you must be gone; but you need not start till midnight. I will bid my stableman feed your horses 'well, and when the house is quiet he can muffle their feet in straw and get them away to a copse just off the road."

267

She left them softly, and presently, from time to time those who sat about the fire, wondering how the night would end, heard her voice as she gave her orders to her maids and serving men. During that long, anxious evening they heard the soldiers singing their drinking songs.

The hours went slowly, and none of them were able to rest, although Tyndale and Margaret went to their rooms in the hope of getting some sleep. Their thoughts were on the perils of the night journey, and they wondered whether they could cover the fifteen miles that lay between this inn and Worms. Was it possible that they would after all fall into the hands of the tormentors? What if, before they could get away, Cochlaeus should discover that they were in this house? All they could do was to pray in silence, and leave themselves in the hands of God.

"An hour longer, and then it will be midnight," said Herman, who, with Margaret, had been looking out of the window, waiting in the hope that the moon would rise, to make their going easier.

He had scarcely spoken when there came the sound of a galloping horse, but it pulled up at the door of the inn, just below the window.

"Is Doctor Cochlaeus here?" the horseman cried, still in his saddle.

"Yes," came a woman's voice. "What is your will?"

"I want him this instant. Go and call him. Bid him come down from his bed, if he be in it! Tell him I have news for him."

"Come in and see him for yourself," said the mistress of the inn sharply, not caring for the man's peremptory orders. "Why should I obey the orders of any night rider who chooses to pull up at my inn door?"

"I cannot waste my time. I want to ride elsewhere," the man cried irritably. "Tell him it will be necessary to come at once. And look you, mistress, if you stand idling there, and things should go awry, Doctor Cochlaeus will make it bad for you."

The woman turned away and went into the house, and the watchers at the window heard the rider call loudly for a stableman to bring his horse some water. The light over the inn door showed them a man in the saddle of a foam covered horse that breathed heavily with his hard journey. They could hear the burst of his breath, and still the man sat on, turning an eager face towards the door.

Someone came out, and Herman and Margaret knew him.

"Cochlaeus," the girl whispered, shivering with fear.

"What is this news you bring, fellow?" cried the Churchman, with some asperity at being called out of his warm bed.

The rider did not waste an instant.

"My lord of Hautcoeur has a man in his dungeon who, he says, is that English heretic, William Tyndale. He passed the castle gate a few hours after you had gone, and he bade me ride hard after you and bring you back at once, that he may get his troublesome prisoner off his hands, lest he may escape as he did from the castle of the lord of Schouts. Will you come at once?"

The rider's strident voice rang through the night, but the answer was decisive.

"Ho, there! Adam Kraft, call your soldiers to their saddles. That fellow, Tyndale, is in the dungeon at Hautcoeur, and we ride thither at once. Mistress, tell your stableman to get my horse ready. I must start at once."

There was an instant bustle. One by one the soldiers came round with their horses, grouping in the open space before the inn, and their helmets glanced in the light which streamed from the passage. Then came the horse which

Cochlaeus was to ride, and before many minutes, with a soldier's aid, he was in the saddle.

"Are you ready?" he asked, looking round when he had gathered up the reins. The answering cry assured him, and, bidding the mistress of the inn a curt farewell, he spurred his horse and galloped away into the darkness, followed by his men. At every bound he was leaving the man he sought for farther behind him.

The night settled down into silence when the last of the horsemen had disappeared.

"They are gone," said Herman, meeting the woman on the stairs.

"Yes. Now get you gone also, in God's dear name. Was ever anything so good? To think that my lord of Hautcoeur should think he hath Master Tyndale in his dungeon! "The woman clapped her hands in ecstasy.

"'Tis God's doing, mistress," said Herman, and she looked up at him with glistening eyes.

Half an hour later, with all the lights of the inn put out, so that nothing should betray their going, Master Tyndale and the others were on the road.

"This is the Lord's doing!" he exclaimed, lifting his cap reverently; and he had barely spoken before the horses were on the move.

# THE ELEVENTH HOUR

ALTHOUGH Cochlaeus and his riders had galloped away, leaving the road apparently clear towards Worms, the forester was doubtful as to its safety. He was afraid to travel on it lest the Churchman, in his eagerness to capture Tyndale, had already sent some armed horsemen forward to intercept him.

"The longest way is the quickest and the safest, Master Tyndale," said the forester, who had been the first to mount into the saddle, and had, indeed, gone forward at a canter to look along the road beyond the bend.

"I think so, too!" exclaimed Byrckmann; but he looked anxiously at his wife, and wondered as she sat in her rough-and-ready pillion how long her strength would last after a day of hard travelling and many dangers, and the sleepless night. It was the only way, however; for with Cochlaeus or his minions riding in the country, it was best to take the smaller risk, go as gently as they dared, and keep well out of the beaten paths.

"Just as you think," said Tyndale quietly. "I am in your hands—and God's," he added, a moment later. "But I fear me Mistress Byrckmann will find the longer way too much for her little store of strength."

"I can go as far as need calls," the sick woman answered bravely. "I am so comfortable here that a few miles more or less cannot harm me," she said; but there was a tremulousness in her voice which made Margaret watch her mother anxiously, and she drew closer to her side, leaning in her saddle to lay her own on the thin, transparent hand.

"It will be all rest, mother, when we get to our journey's end, and we will not travel fast to shake you," she said tenderly. "Will you bear that in mind, Master Engel?"

"I will," came the good natured answer from the man who had become the natural leader of the little cavalcade. "We're going to leave this dusty and too open road and make for the river, and then for miles we shall be in forestland. Isn't it so, Herman? You know as well, perhaps better than I do."

"It is so," said Herman, who was going to ride in the rear, alert for every sound, lest by any ill chance the Churchman and his riders had changed their course, and had not ridden on to Hautcoeur.

"How long, think you, will it take Cochlaeus to get to the Castle of Hautcoeur?" Margaret asked, after they had been riding nearly an hour at little more than a leisurely jaunt because of her mother.

"Three hours at the least," said the forester.

"And if he discovers that he has been duped, and decides to ride back to the inn, three hours more!" Byrckmann exclaimed. "He will know as soon as he goes down into the castle dungeon that he has either been fooled or the lord of Hautcoeur has been misled. Then he may come back in hot haste. That means, he will be at the inn again in six hours—nay, five by now."

"By that time we shall be in Worms!" Engel exclaimed, with apparent carelessness, but by no means easy in his own mind. He was disposed to avoid Worms, and move round the city, or travel wide of it altogether, rather than run the risks of any horsemen lying in wait, ruining all their plans at the eleventh hour. But, whatever his own anxiety was, he would not suffer any of those who were with him to know, unless he took Herman into his confidence.

They rode on at that easy trot, in and out among the forest, where he seemed so thoroughly at home, although he did not know it at all, and presently; turning in his saddle and laying his hand on his horse's flank, he called to Herman carelessly to come forward, to talk over the possibilities of the forest paths.

Asking Byrckmann to keep a look out behind, lest any robber or prowling beast might make a spring, Herman rode to Engel's side.

"You're going all right!" he exclaimed, quite easy in his mind, knowing nothing of the forester's misgivings. "We cannot go wrong if we keep the river in view most of the time."

"I know all that," said Engel speaking low; "but my trouble is a twofold one. First of all, Cochlaeus may have some of his riders with him, but not all. He's out for capturing Master Tyndale, on whose head there's a very big price, and I've been thinking that, guessing that he may be making for Worms, he has sent forward some men to bar the way, and snatch the poor man out of our hands."

Herman felt himself shiver coldly; then heat swept over his face, and he brushed away the dampness from it with his sleeve; for he thought that if Engel's fear proved true it would not be Tyndale only who would be in the toils, but them all.

"I never thought of that!" he exclaimed quietly, that the others should not hear; but his voice was unsteady. "When I saw that Churchman ride off at a gallop I was exultant, and with only fifteen miles to go, I thought we were as good as safe."

Engel shrugged his shoulders, and as they were riding at the moment in a bit of open, moonlit glade, Herman saw the movement, and saw as well the forester's grave face.

"What's the other anxiety?" Herman asked, remembering that Engel had said that his trouble was twofold.

"When Cochlaeus gets to Hautcoeur, and the master of the castle takes him down to the dungeon, he will see at a glance that the prisoner is not the man he wants. He will not stay an instant longer, and I can imagine his chagrin. I can seem to see him coming up the steps out of the dungeon in a whirlwind of anger, and after some maledictions on the lord of Hautcoeur, he will get his men and horses out, and they will come back in haste as hot as when he left the inn."

"We have six hours' start," said Herman, easy on this point.

"I know; but mark the pace we're going, and must go, because of that poor woman in the pillion behind us. We can't go faster than she can travel. It would nearly kill her if we mended the pace. Given a free hand, we'd be at the gates of Worms in two hours; but with our going at this pace Cochlaeus will be there, waiting for us."

"Then it is sheer madness to make for Worms!" exclaimed Herman. "We must go somewhere else, and take Worms later."

They were in the forest depths again, and although they were talking they were keeping a keen look out. Both riders halted suddenly, and the others behind, brought up unexpectedly, were in a bunch, the horses beating against each other.

There was no necessity for speech. Each clutched the horse's reins on which he rode convulsively, and a thrill of fear passed through them.

274

"Let us get out of this path," whispered the forester, swinging his horse aside. "Follow me, but quietly. I'm going over there, where it's dark, and we shall not be seen." He said it easily, but he was afraid.

As the others drew up with him among some bushes, so high and dense that no passer-by on the forest path could see their horses, they watched, their consternation none the less; for who could tell what might happen!

"Keep perfectly quiet," Engel whispered. "I pray the horses may neither neigh nor jingle their harness."

Away on the forest path they saw some horsemen, they knew not how many. Some of them carried flaming torches, the light of which fell on themselves and their comrades, on their own armor, which glanced as the light played on it, and on the weapons and metal trappings of their chargers. They were soldiers, moving on with a steady going easiness, in no great haste, and careless as to whether they were seen and heard.

At first there seemed to be a score of horsemen, but, as these came on, others emerged from the forest darkness in their wake, and others after those. On and on they came, and presently the foremost rode past, easily and carelessly, talking, and at odd times snaps of a soldier's song came. The cavalcade moved on, and it seemed to those who watched, bending low in their saddles and peering through the bushes that hid them, that there were more than scores. They seemed to be hundreds, each man fully armed. Then after them came the rolling wheels of heavy guns drawn by horses who sometimes strained at the weight when the wheels sank into the soft moss-grown path.

It was a little army, the rear being brought up by more horsemen, whose faces were lit up by the flaring torches.

The watchers looked anxiously, unconsciously, indeed, to know whether Cochlaeus was amongst them, and there was the feeling of intense relief when they found that he was not.

"Where can they be going to?" each asked, as the last of the horsemen rode out of sight, and no more light from the torches lit up the forest trees ; but the cavalcade had gone, and the road was free.

They started on their way again, Herman and, Engel discussing the alternatives.

"Let us take Worms later," said Herman again, just as he had been saying when the soldiers came into view.

It was one thing to say so much; another thing to tell where the other place might be; but the suggestion set the forester thinking.

"I know!" he exclaimed, slapping his thigh with his great hand, and the smart crack made his horse start. "I know a man—and he has a daughter—and I love her, Herman, just as you love that sweet girl behind us. And she loves me."

He said all this in little more than a whisper, but Herman marked the thrill in the forester's voice.

"She lives two miles from here, in a mill like my father's, and just now she's all alone, for her father's away, and will not be back for another month. She can hide us all, and the horses can go out to graze, and no questions asked, because the man deals in horseflesh freely, making a mint o' money. I'll only have to say, Mary, we're in trouble—every one of us, and in danger, too, and it means the rack for some of us, or worse, if you can't hide us somewhere.' And she'll do it. I know she will, if only for her love for me; but add to that her love for what Cochlaeus would call heresy, and we shall win her care. Shall we try it?"

"Why ask me?" exclaimed Herman, whose heart was beating high with hope, and who was thinking of the safety it promised for Margaret. "Turn that way at once, if you know how to get there."

"I've never got there from this side, but always from across the river, where I know every inch of the way. If we get a bit nearer the water I can, perhaps, get my bearings."

They turned away to the right, and soon they saw the great flood of the noble river rolling steadily on towards the sea. Vessels were moving slowly down the stream, picturesque in the fleeting moonlight, and a great raft, such as had passed the cavern when Tyndale was waiting for the coming of the Marburg, was floating after them. On the other side was a ruined castle, scorched and blackened by fire, and Engel knew it instantly.

"A mile and a half higher up the river and we are there!" he exclaimed; and with low laughter he added, "And then I shall see my Mary!"

He hugged himself in his delight.

" You know, Herman, I'd have married her a year ago, but her father wouldn't hear of my taking her to that poverty stricken hut, and I've been saving for years to get enough to buy a mill. A hundred golden crowns more, and the thing's done."

He stopped at that, and the exultation passed.

"A hundred golden crowns want a lot of getting," he said gloomily, a few moments later. "We shall be older than we are, and older than I like to think, by the time I've got them, at the rate I'm going."

"They'll come all right, Otto," said Herman confidently. "Your ship will come home unexpectedly. See if she doesn't." The forester flung aside his gloom, and every yard they travelled lifted his spirits. He was thinking of the girl he loved, and he was soon to see her.

The forest came to an abrupt ending. Before them was a broad sweep of open country, at least two hundred acres of fine grazing land, dotted with trees and sleeping horses and cattle, and in the center of all, standing on a high mound, a fine old mill, whose arms were motionless.

"That's the place!" exclaimed Engel, pulling up his horse. Turning in his saddle, he spoke to those who were behind him.

"We must halt here, while I go to the mill and ask my Mary to give us shelter for a little while."

"Why not go on to Worms?" asked Tyndale, in surprise. "I thought we only had a few miles to travel in order to get there."

"I did not dare to take you there tonight, Master Tyndale, lest Cochlaeus should have sent some horsemen forward to intercept us. We must travel slowly to go more safely, and there is secure hiding in his mill. You and Master Roye can sit somewhere in quietness, and at your ease you can go on with your work—as well here as anywhere. Mary can hide you as securely as though you were already at Worms."

"Then I am content, if the others are," said Tyndale. "What say you, Master Byrckmann?"

"More than content, since it will give my wife the rest she needs," the printer answered, looking anxiously at his wife, as the light of the moon played on her face.

"Then let us go forward!" exclaimed Tyndale, shaking the reins to urge his horse on.

"Nay, I must go to the mill first," said the forester, catching at the bridle to prevent Tyndale from riding into the open. "Herman, keep a sharp watch. Get back, each one of you, into the shadows, where you can see and not be seen."

The forester moved onward while he spoke, and put his horse to the canter. They saw him drop out of the saddle and knock at the door of the mill. The sound of his loud tapping reached those who were watching; then a woman's head and her white linen-covered shoulders appeared at one of the windows. They heard an exclamation of pleasure, and the head and shoulders disappeared, and before long Engel entered by the open door. Before many minutes had passed he came away from the mill, his heavy boots brushing among the dewy grass.

"Come," he cried, before he reached them, beckoning with his hand. Before long the whole company were in the mill; the horses were at the door, munching oats hungrily, after which they turned to the meadow to sleep out the remainder of the night; but as for the others, Mary, when she had set food before them, went to prepare for their comfort in the safe hiding place of which the forester had spoken.

****

Two days went by, and none but Engel ventured out of the mill. The others stayed within doors, always ready to go into hiding if the warning came. They were content, because they realized the absolute safety they enjoyed in the great cap of the mill, into which, when they entered it, they could draw the ladder, and shut down the heavy trap door, leaving the place unsuspected. From a small window here and there they could see the country for miles. In the far distance was the city that had been their home. In the other direction lay the city they were eager to reach so soon as it was safe to venture; and between rolled the winding, stately river, with its rich forest beauty, and hiding among the trees lay castles that won for themselves a doubtful reputation.

William Tyndale was absorbed in his work, but the others often watched what was going on outside.

"Did you hear the sound of firing?" Margaret asked, one fine evening, before she would say "Goodnight," and go to bed. She was gazing out of the window while she spoke.

279

"Yes, I heard it!" Herman exclaimed, coming to her side, and taking his place at the tiny window. "There it is again. And again. 'Tis like the discharge of cannon."

The cannonading lasted for some time, and they listened in wonder, but thought of those soldiers and the cannon that had passed them in the forest.

"Does it mean war, Herman?" Margaret asked.

"I can't think it does," he answered.

At last the sounds were gone, and the night silence settled over the country which was now in darkness. They were about to kiss each other and say "Goodnight," when Margaret pointed to a distant spot towards her old home. A dense cloud of smoke was rising, and flames were leaping up amongst it, like forked and fiery tongues, and lighting up the broken clouds.

"'Tis a fire!" she exclaimed, and the others came to look through another of the windows from which the little wooden shutter had been flung back. "But what place can it be?"

"It must be Schouts' castle!" Herman cried. "I'm certain of it!" he added, when he had scanned the country and was able to judge the distance of the burning mass from the city.

As the hours passed the flames died down, and later still the clouds of smoke dwindled away, leaving nothing but a red light in the sky. But in time there came the sound of a terrific explosion which seemed to shake the mill. It came again; and after that there was a hush, and the countryside subsided into silence and dense darkness.

"I'm going to find out what it means," said the forester; "but while I'm away be careful. Do whatever Mary says."

He moved down the ladder swiftly, and before long he was riding through the forest with his faithful dog at his heels. He did not return until next day; the moon had risen, but none had gone to bed, all being eager to know what he had seen, if he should return that night.

"You can have easy minds!" he exclaimed, when he and Mary had mounted the ladder, he to tell the news, and she to hear it. "Sit down, every one of you," he said, with laughter in his face and eyes, and exultation in his voice. "'Tis fine news! Schouts has been so much a terror of late that the river became impassable, and men would stand it no longer. Even the Emperor, to whom appeal was made, outlawed him; but he tortured the messenger, and drowned him in his moat. That roused His Majesty, and he determined to deal with him as one would deal with a savage beast who is a menace to society. He took his steps accordingly.

"A ship went down the stream—an innocent looking craft, apparently full of merchandise, and the great bell of the castle rang out its loudest, and Schouts and his men went down the grass slope and boarded her. They found her empty of life, save for a man at the helm, and the moment the first of Schouts' soldiers clambered on board he dropped into the river and swam ashore. Then to Schouts' horror, as I suppose, cannon roared out at the ship from amid the forest on both sides of the stream and sank the boats that carried his soldiers to the vessel. Soon her deck became a shambles. The robber lord and his men were caught like rats in a trap. Schouts sprang overboard, to swim back and look to the safety of his castle, but a cannon shot caught him at the leap, and he fell dead in the stream, for he sank like a stone, and his heavy armor helped to drag him down. None who leapt into the water escaped, whichever bank they thought to reach.

"Cries and the sound of guns had all the time been coming from the castle. There, too, the soldiers who had been sent to deal with the building itself were busy. The sound of the first shot fired at the decoy vessel was the signal to hundreds of soldiers who were hiding in the forest, close up to the castle moat. They swept out of the dense shadows in silence, and rushed across the drawbridge before the amazed wardens could drop the portcullis. In a few minutes the soldiers were swarming through the robber's stronghold, killing wherever there was resistance. So many of Schouts' servitors and fighting men had gone to the river to take part in the attack on the ship that little more than a handful were left to guard the castle, and these were either slain, or threw up their hands in token of surrender.

"Then came the task of searching every corner, from roof to dungeon. Three or four men of note had lately been carried there, and were to be found, if they yet lived. In some of the horrible cells, like that into which they had thrust Master Tyndale, the Emperor's soldiers found some prisoners—poor creatures who had refused or could not pay the preposterous ransom, some of them nearly dead, and more than one demented with the horror and the loneliness. Such as could walk came out tottering, but others had to be carried, and were set down in the banqueting hall, where they were fed and tended by the soldiers.

"But, strangest thing of all," exclaimed the forester, and those who listened wondered at the look on his face—"I would that Master Tyndale were with us in this room to hear what next I have to say," Engel said, breaking off in his story; "but the good man is buried in that holy task of his, and I must tell him of it later on."

"Nay, friend Engel, he is here, and has heard the whole story!" someone exclaimed, and, looking round, those who were gathered about the forester saw William Tyndale standing in the doorway. "Go on, friend," he added, coming in and sitting on a stool. "You were saying, 'But, strangest thing of all.' "

"I was, Master Tyndale, and it was the strangest thing—the most unexpected. The soldiers were searching the castle to rifle it of its contents, thinking to carry its treasures away, and the booty the robber lord had taken from many an unfortunate ship, when they came across a body, lying in that room where you and I, Herman, had seen and heard Cochlaeus bargaining with the lord of the castle for Master Tyndale's ransom. He was lying face downwards on one of the costly rugs, and when they turned him over, marveling to find a Churchman of high rank in such a place, they saw that he was none other than the Deacon of the Church of the Blessed Virgin."

"What!" cried Tyndale, startled at the words, and rising to his feet. "Do you mean to say that it was Cochlaeus?"

"I do, Master Tyndale. How he came to the castle, and why, I cannot say. Whether he thought that after all Schouts had cheated him into believing that Master Tyndale had escaped, and that in reality he was in the castle after all, there is no telling. No one is left to tell the story. Some hard words must have been spoken on both sides, and Schouts, filled with mad anger at what the Churchman said, must have struck at him, for he lay there, dead, and a jeweled dagger was driven into his heart.

"When the castle had been thoroughly rifled, and all its valuables lay in great heaps on the grass outside, booty waiting to be divided among the Emperor's soldiery, the officer commanding fired the place. When the fire had nearly burnt itself out, and the soldiers were about to move round to see that the destruction was complete, there was an awful explosion. The fire had reached the powder magazine down in the dungeons. Another explosion followed; then a third; and after that, when the smoke had cleared away, there was nothing but a heap of ruins.

"And there was the last of Schouts, the robber lord, and the last of your tormentors, Master Tyndale," said Engel quietly, turning towards him. "The man who was so eager to carry you to the tormentors, and bring your work to naught, is dead."

There was silence. Everyone realized the meaning of that tragedy at the castle by the river. It meant much for law and order, since a brutal minded, godless, and tyrannical nobleman had come to the end of his infamous career. It meant that Master Tyndale was no longer a hunted fugitive. The man who had set himself to bring about his ruin was gone, and the simple souled and lowly minded scholar was free to go where he listed—to stay in the mill, or move on to Worms —and Cochlaeus would no more dog his steps.

"This is the Lord's doing," said Tyndale solemnly, and breaking the silence. "Let us kneel and thank Him for saving us in this eleventh hour."

He dropped on his knees, and when the others did the same, he poured out his soul in grateful thanks.

****

Two days later those who were with him rode into Worms—all save Mary, who remained in the mill. As the horses crossed the bridge at the city gate they turned to look back on the road they had travelled, and their faces were lit up with the glory of the evening sun.

"At evening time it shall be light," said Tyndale softly, and, shaking his horse's rein, he rode along the street after asking the warden of the gate where they would find housing.

It was early next morning Margaret and Herman were married.

Half an hour later the forester was in the saddle, ready to ride back to Mary, and his eyes were twinkling with mirth, and his face had never been broader with smiles.

He called Herman to him when he had said "Goodbye" to all the others. Bending in his saddle, while his dog was waiting, impatient to be gone, he put out his hand.

"Shake it, Herman, and in the dear Lord's name wish me joy!"

Herman gazed into his face, wondering at it.

"What for?"

"Because I am going to marry Mary tomorrow, please God, if she'll only say Yes '; and I believe she will. Master Byrckmann has forced two hundred golden crowns upon me for what he calls my splendid service. I didn't think of any payment, God knows! and I didn't want to take it, big though the temptation was to do so. But he gave me no alternative. See! It is here!"

He slapped his hand on the leathern pouch at his belt, and Herman heard the chink of gold.

"I wanted a hundred crowns, I told you, to buy a mill—and I know of one—but this leaves me with a hundred in reserve. Bid me joy, Herman! You said my ship would come home. It's come!"

"I do, with all my heart!" Herman cried.

And a moment later the forester was galloping along the street towards the city gate.

*** THE END ***

# AN AFTERWORD BY THE EDITORS

William Tyndale gave his life that the English common man might have the Scriptures available to him. While the Roman Catholic Church did everything in its power to prevent the dissemination of the Scriptures and to retain its power over the people, Tyndale and others knew the importance of all men having access to God's Word.

He stated: "I perceived how that it was impossible to establish the lay people in any truth except the Scripture were plainly laid before their eyes in their mother tongue." - Tyndale

The Scriptures are the key not only to releasing men from the bondage of sin and iniquity, but from the unrelenting chains of error, false religion and deceptive doctrines.

The Night Rider's Call was here presented for your enjoyment and edification, but I would like to speak to you now on a more sober note.

I would like to ask you about your perception of the Scriptures. Are they important enough to you, as they were to Tyndale, to die for? Do you take the possession of your Bible for granted or do you hold the very Word of God in high esteem?

In our day, because it no longer has the ubiquitous power it once wielded, it is not the Inquisition of the Roman Catholic Church burning "heretics" and deriding the printing of the Bible that is the issue. Rather in our day the battle is much more clandestine, and much more dangerous. It is not the printed word but the veracity of the Scriptures themselves that is under assault. Today, Satan does not care if people read the Bible, because, in this hour he has so manipulated the minds of the hearers that he has turned away adherents to sound doctrine and filled the earth with so many different concepts of "Jesus" that the resultant smorgasbord contains a flavor for every palate. In this way he has retched the Scriptures from the possession of the common man, while they cling to a very marred caricature of Biblical Christianity. In effect, creating a modern "dark ages" where access to Truth has been obstructed, not by the absence of Truth but by the pervading presence of error. And men starve in the midst of a feast; they wither away in the presence of provision.

In the Bible the prophet Amos declares:

Behold, the days come, saith the Lord GOD, that I will send a famine in the land, not a famine of bread, nor a thirst for water, but of hearing the words of the LORD: (Amos 8:11)

Because men have willingly turned their ears from the truth and embraced fables, God has sent a famine. But, even as in a natural famine, for those who are willing to glean the Truth, it is there for their nurturing. "They shall not be ashamed in the evil time: and in the days of famine they shall be satisfied," (Psalms 37:19) says the Psalmist. As for those who cultivate the grounds of deception, malnutrition and death. The Psalmist continues, "But the wicked shall perish, and the enemies of the LORD shall be as the fat of lambs: they shall consume; into smoke shall they consume away." (Psalms 37:20)

Are you, as Tyndale, jealous - yea, zealous for the Truth of God's Word? Do you contend for sound doctrine in the midst of adversity or wither under the hot sun of controversy?  Do you stand for the incontrovertible principle of objectivity or fall under the assailing mantra "truth is relative"?

There is of necessity only ONE Truth, and it can be known.  The Truth comports with the entirety of Scripture.  If your belief or denominational doctrines are at odds with ANY of the revealed word of the Lord contained in the Scriptures, i.e. the Old AND New Testaments, then it is your belief that is in error, not God, his character, his justice nor his word.  Your belief must comport with the entire corpus of Scripture, or your doctrine is fallacious, your belief counted as unbelief.

For what if some did not believe? shall their unbelief make the faith of God without effect? God forbid: yea, let God be true, but every man a liar; as it is written, That thou mightest be justified in thy sayings, and mightest overcome when thou art judged.  (Romans 3:3-4)

It is our position that the singular difficulty of sound Biblical presentation in this hour is the inordinate number of Jesus' available from which to choose.  There is a variety to fit every occasion and temper available.  The problem for mankind is that only one Jesus is the Right Jesus and only those who are striving to follow Him will be acceptable to the Father on that day.  The idiom, "The man hardest to convince of the Truth is he who thinks he already has it" is so relevant in this situation.  The devil has done such a masterful job of inoculating the professing church to sound doctrine, that when it is presented it is summarily rejected as heresy, regardless of the Biblical support for such doctrine, and the errors propagated are supported by dismal misappropriation of portions of holy writ divorced from the whole.  God does not take kindly to those who misrepresent Him and subvert his holy, and immutable Word.

Woe unto them that call evil good, and good evil; that put darkness for light, and light for darkness; that put bitter for sweet, and sweet for bitter! Woe unto them that are wise in their own eyes, and prudent in their own sight! Woe unto them that are mighty to drink wine, and men of strength to mingle strong drink: Which justify the wicked for reward, and take away the righteousness of the righteous from him! Therefore as the fire devoureth the stubble, and the flame consumeth the chaff, so their root shall be as rottenness, and their blossom shall go up as dust: because they have cast away the law of the LORD of hosts, and despised the word of the Holy One of Israel. Therefore is the anger of the LORD kindled against his people, and he hath stretched forth his hand against them, and hath smitten them: and the hills did tremble, and their carcases were torn in the midst of the streets. For all this his anger is not turned away, but his hand is stretched out still.  (Isaiah 5:20-25)


I ask you a question, is your Jesus biblical?  Are you sure?

As William Tyndale devoted his life for the preservation and propagation of the Scriptures, and eventually went to the stake for that devotion, are you willing to expose the pervasive false concepts and misapplications of the Bible, casting down imaginations and every high thing that exalteth itself against the knowledge of God?  Are you willing to stand, alone if necessary, on the hilltop testifying of the true grace of God, and sound Biblical doctrine unfettered by the cumbersome chains of denominational presupposition, apathy and compromise?  Are you willing to go to the pyre, all the while praying, "Oh Lord, open the church's eyes?"

If you would like more information on the importance of upholding a comprehensive Biblical Jesus in this Age of Deceit please visit:

therightjesus.com or apprehendingtruth.net.

This book is also available in Audio Format.